VANISHED !

Doug Evans

Dedicated to all those wonderful people in the aviation industry: the world's safest form of transport, Est: 1903

The relentless rush of the airstream over the plane's huge fuselage was not just numbing, but re-assuring; a permanent guarantee that yes, they were still moving through the endless black of night and that this motion should naturally continue forever.

With tired eyes, Ray Cardin fought his fatigue. Soon he would be due for a rostered break when his First Officer returned to the flight deck after her brief rest. As the captain of this Air Australia Boeing-747, Cardin had allowed her to take the first down-time and he would struggle on till about midnight local time - whenever that was. At such times he often felt lonely and introspective, even though some might wonder how anyone could feel lonely on an airborne ship with over 400 souls on board, but Cardin was stuck in a tiny room - the flight deck up the front. Often with just one soul to talk to and with scarcely anything to do, he was regularly paid serious money to endure tedious hours of nothing.

Once again he scanned the glowing instrument panels to gaze at flickering numbers and various data on the array of glass screens. But now, not even the radios spoke to him because they'd flown out of Australian VHF radio range and the static background noises of HF were eliminated because he had selected SELCAL watch. A gong would sound if any Air traffic control centre was calling him but tonight, however, he hadn't received any such gongs at all.

Usually there'd be en-route weather updates or other messages about operational matters from the company. Or requests from ATC about their position over the ocean with an ETA for their next waypoint and for the final destination which was Los Angeles. But they'd received nothing for several hours now, and surprisingly there'd been no acknowledgement of his last position report, even though he'd carefully transmitted it twice, then tried to raise the Sydney HF Centre at various times ever since. He'd also tried blind calling on several VHF channels in the expectation that other en-route aircraft within range would answer him. This communication outage was odd, but had occurred sporadically before. He wasn't unduly worried; they should regain contact sometime soon. Meanwhile, everything else continued to function perfectly on board the big Boeing.

When he first commenced flying international long-haul, Cardin couldn't believe how exciting it was. Now, after many years it was, he admitted, often quite boring. Sitting in a seat for endless hours of tedium, waiting for something to do, anything at all – especially descending and landing. Many flights seemed to last forever, and some trans-Pacific flights almost did – although, unknown to anyone on board, this routine flight would very soon transpire to be the very antithesis of boring.

Gazing out at twinkling stars that drifted slowly overhead, the captain thought about the early days of aviation when celestial navigation was of prime importance. In the middle of a vast ocean like this there were hardly any landmarks and no radio beacons to guide their path, so air crews needed star-reading skills along with bulky chart tables of latitude and longitude . . . plus a fair amount of good old fashioned luck in what was often called Ded Reckoning; the 'ded' being short for 'deduced'. In such hit-and-miss navigation back then, flights sometimes became hundreds or even thousands of miles off course, especially after forced diversions around storms or over featureless terrain or water.

Today, air navigators can safely ignore these majestic kaleidoscopes in the sky because modern technology has far outstripped the ancient skills of charting your course by the stars. The advent of inertial navigation, which ran from high-speed spinning gyros inside the plane, instantly made the old crew position of 'navigator' redundant forever. With INS, a small green screen between the pilots showed a constant readout of their current 'lat & long', and even displayed the actual outside winds with a precise groundspeed – an unheard-of dream to aviators of old. The INS guided all the world's jumbo jets since their inception in 1969 and no-one ever imagined that such wizardry could possibly be surpassed. Incredibly, a plane could fly from Australia to London and the INS would guide it - not just to England, but to its exact parking bay at Heathrow airport – give or take a few metres.

Then along came GPS and all its associated uses. The display of data from GPS was even more accurate than INS, with dozens of positioning satellites providing pinpoint trigonometrical navigation without the need for constant 'DME updating' – a necessity that over-water/over-desert flights once required - if available. GPS also improved precision approaches and landings, often in zero visibility.

Then the magic glass screens on some of the B747 series arrived and boasted six screens including moving map overlays. Pilots only need watch their toy aeroplane cursor moving slowly across the screen to see precisely where they were at all times. So Ray Cardin held no concerns for his navigation on this very dark night, while air traffic centres could locate him if they wished from their transponder 'handshakes' that beeped up to satellites and bounced back down to ground receivers. Thankfully, annoying radio silences like the current one were now rare indeed.

He glanced at the time – although time can be confusing in a fast-moving jet. The local time back in Sydney was simply irrelevant as they were well east of there now. Similarly, local time in Los Angeles was just too far away to matter: they wouldn't be near there for another twelve hours or so. So just what was the time? His screen said 16:17. This is called GMT, or Zulu. Greenwich Mean Time is the world-wide benchmark of time. Just now it was 16:17Z throughout the world of aviation and shipping - wherever your craft might happen to be. The local time below you, perhaps on a tropical Pacific Island, was of no significance unless you intended to land there. But overflying planes have no interest and operate on their own time zones (GMT).

Yawning, Cardin knew that his co-pilot/first officer Roslyn Steinhouse had asked to be woken at 16:30Z. She seemed to be a pleasant person and this was their first trip together today. Soon he would leave her in charge of his 'ship' - assisted by Second Officer Tom Tyson for a short while, as he napped. By that time they should have transited this rather odd 'zone of silence' and continued winging north-east towards the Hawaiian Islands.

Again he tested all the HF radio frequencies for this Pacific area and, though he repeatedly called out from the immense blackness of the night-time ocean, silence was his only answer. Soon he would inform his F/O and order her to continue calling until contact with ATC was re-established. Meantime, he sent satellite text messages to the company back in Sydney and forward to Los Angeles. This was an electronic system called CPDLC, a data transfer system between airlines, their airliners and ATC centres. It provided a comforting safeguard for lonely pilots calling from an oceanic wilderness. He tried them again, but for this lonely pilot they still did not reply. Slightly concerned, he transmitted blindly: 'No VHF or HF contacts tonight. Nice smooth air for anyone following us. We have a pleasant 47kt tailwind. Please ask ATC again if they are receiving us because we are receiving no-one just now. Thanks from Cardin.' He waited for replies but none were forthcoming.

Just then he was astonished to see the entire night sky illuminate with one enormous white flash! Wow, that's odd, he decided, because there were no thunderstorms forecast for out here tonight.

Then a cheery voice behind him spoke, 'Hi Captain! I woke a little early but had a nice rest. Do you sleep well on your breaks?'

He turned around to First Officer Roslyn Steinhouse, an attractive woman of about thirty with short brown hair. 'Oh, hi. Ah, yes, I sleep okay sometimes when everything is running well, but did you happen to see that? '

'Yes, there was a big lightning flash just as I left the rest bunk. Any cells on the radar?'

Cardin looked puzzled. 'No . . . strangely. And most importantly, I haven't had any comms since before we tried to call Departures at 150 DME Sydney. So I'm basically talking to myself here; a dry argument, you might say. There's still no VHF or HF and now the company back in Sydney won't answer the link . . . so maybe nobody likes me anymore. '

The first officer smiled as she settled into the right-hand seat. 'Well, we had a few hours without a data link last month on the way to Jo'Burg.'

Cardin replied that in this instance it was more than a few hours, but he fully expected to hear from someone – anyone – soon. 'Would you like me to stay here for a while, Roslyn?'

'No thanks,' she smiled. 'I like a challenge to keep me occupied. You take your break. See you in a while.'

But Cardin wasn't at all sure about leaving his post, even though for some odd reason he was feeling very fatigued and desperately needed to close his eyes for a while. In a quandary, he ventured aft to the tiny crew rest area behind the flight deck. Pulling the curtain across the narrow bunk bed and dousing the light, he relapsed into a restless sleep almost immediately. Although his F/O was just as qualified as he was, she had much less flying experience. But Cardin knew she was a fully qualified 747 pilot and he respected her grinning confidence and air of professionalism. Meanwhile, far below, the blackened waters of the vast Pacific Ocean with its 64 million square miles of area passed slowly beneath Cardin's plane, just as they had done so many times in the past.

While the tech crew onboard flight 200 were remaining cautious of their blackout status, aviation authorities back in Australia had already flagged Air Australia flight 200 because it had not been seen since controllers observed it depart from Sydney airport then bank out to sea and fade into cumulus cloud build-ups east of the coast. So, from the very start of the flight when the pilots of AA200 obviously thought they were, to use aviation parlance, "operations normal", some air traffic controllers were far less confident and soon became alarmed that this flight might in fact be anything *but* normal.

To confirm this view, fifteen minutes later at a compulsory reporting point 150 miles off the coast, they failed repeatedly to answer their radios or SATCOM systems to the extent that some Air Services personnel already feared that flight two-hundred may have simply vanished.

But had it?

2.

"What we have here is a failure to communicate."

These were the infamous words from that great old movie *Cool Hand Luke* starring Paul Newman. Newman was a prison camp escapee who taunted the authorities with his daring escapes, and when finally cornered by his masters he refused to surrender. Instead, he yelled back at them, mimicking the words of the prison governor who now stood down below his hide-out beside an expert marksman who was armed with a high-powered rifle.

Foolishly, Cool Hand Luke catcalled his famous last words out a window at them: "What we have here is a failure to communicate!" In reply, Luke was instantly shot dead.

Now, Captain Ray Cardin was asleep, thirty-nine thousand feet over the Pacific Ocean. He was dreaming these very same words from his favourite movie. 'There's no great problem here; we just have a failure to communicate.' He dreamed on, mumbling the same words over and over. But it was a restless sleep that gave him no respite from worry.

He rolled over, 'Come on Luke. You can do it! If not, then *she* can do it.' But who was 'she'? He couldn't remember her name or see her face, but he'd just handed over this entire ship of the air — *his* ship of the air — to her.

He jerked awake, shivering. How long had he slept? An hour? Three? The outside airstream still rushed past the fuselage, just as it always did. He cocked an ear but heard no desperate screams of 'Mayday! Mayday!' coming from the front of the flight deck. His first officer was definitely not in trouble and was competently handling *his* giant plane just as she was supposed to be doing. So, should he rush into the cockpit and flaunt his authority over this failure to communicate, or just leave her to it? Or perhaps he should casually saunter onto the deck, mumble some excuse as to why he was back so early - or simply not go back at all? A captain could mostly do what he pleased. It wasn't up to her.

He stumbled from his dark bunker and passed Second Officer Tom Tyson as he emerged from the flight deck for the toilet. Always grinning, Tyson was surprised to see the captain and smiled, 'Hi, Boss. Are you returning to duty already?'

Cardin cleared his foggy mind and replied, 'Ah, just wondering . . . how long have I been gone?'

'About one hour. But you still look tired. Are you sure you should be coming back?'

'Of course. I need to see how the First Officer is going with that comms problem.'

Tom looked disappointed. 'Well, we've had no success and there's been nothing heard, actually. We've really had no comms from anyone anywhere since ATD plus thirty.'

'Hell!' Cardin was annoyed. 'I hadn't envisaged that it would last quite this long. I was very tired. Ah, what about CPDLC datalink?'

'Nope. We couldn't get any answers. Seems dead.'

'No answers from our own company? Nothing?'

'No Boss.'

Annoyed, Cardin glared at him. 'Then why didn't you wake me?'

'Sorry, Boss.'

'And don't call me Boss.'

Cardin pushed angrily past the F/O and strode onto the flight deck where a worried-looking Roslyn Steinhouse was bent forward, talking loudly into her headset. But was she getting any replies?

'Nandi, Nandi, this is Australia two-zero-zero. Do you read? Oakland, this is Australia two-zero-zero, do you read?'

'What are you doing?' Cardin demanded. 'Haven't we had comms with anyone at all tonight? Why didn't you call Nandi on VHF when we were abeam them?' Cardin was still fatigued and also irritated at their helplessness to communicate because this was quickly becoming an acute embarrassment for a captain.

The F/O turned to face him. 'I couldn't raise Nandi. In the whole night I've only heard one brief broadcast on HF where someone stated that we had completely *disappeared* from Earth!'

Cardin was incredulous. 'What the . . . ? That's totally ridiculous, Roslyn! What a bloody stupid thing to say. Who told that station to broadcast such nonsense without any foundation? Disappeared from Earth? We've only been out of comms for a few hours. This isn't an historic occasion, as you know. It happened to you only recently; and it's also happened to me many times. In fact, it's happened to pilots everywhere. Communications aren't always perfect and HF is notoriously unreliable, while VHF is line-of-sight only and good for about thirty minute's coverage in a cruising jet. And sometimes the CPDLC can go down too; so nothing is faultless.'

As he wriggled into the captain's seat and buckled up, his co-pilot glanced across at him in alarm. 'Look Captain, now a PFD screen has gone blank, too! I've never seen one do that before. What does that mean?' Cardin cursed his failure to notice his own FMS screen. One screen still glowed, but mostly he faced a wall of black.

They were navigating along a Great Circle track over the ocean, from their departure point in Sydney to Los Angeles. This was a straight line over our curved Earth's surface 'as the crow flies' and not at all like a straight line drawn on a flat map. This track line resembled the way a tight string would connect two points around a school-room globe. Crows are canny and they don't waste time or energy flying erratically from A to B. Aircraft also need to fly the shortest distance, not in the least to avoid fuel wastage, but also to transport their passengers and freight on time. After all, it's normally 13½ hours from SYD to LAX as it is, and no-one wants to spend any longer than that en-route.

Recent years had welcomed bold innovations in oceanic long-haul flights where aerial navigators often chase the pressure patterns to pick up favourable tail winds. Here, pilots must remember, however, that the weather patterns are reversed in each hemisphere with the lows spiralling clockwise in the Southern Hemisphere and anti-clockwise in the North. So it's often a game of cat and mouse as every flight starts out on a

Great Circle track, but may deviate from it should reported tailwinds indicate that, strangely, a crooked path might be even quicker. And if a track-line map later revealed the actual flight paths taken, it might display a series of strange arcs, or snakes' trails, where the flight twisted this way then that, then this way again. North of the equator, the turns were in the opposite way.

To Ray Cardin, he knew that this twisting and deviating off the published track often resulted in them not seeing other aircraft lights going the other way, because those planes would be avoiding the very headwinds from which he was currently hitching a free ride, and so opposite direction traffic could be hundreds of nautical miles away and thus unseen to him. But on this moonless night it seemed that no-one else was out there at all. 'Seen any opposite direction traffic at all, Roslyn?'

'No sir. They're probably staying well to the north of us.'

The happy-go-lucky Tom Tyson returned to the deck just as Cardin felt more alarm. Now he faced another blank MFD screen. He rubbed his chin and decided to act quickly. 'Alright, I'd like you both to get out all the emergency manuals and go through absolutely everything to find out how a communications failure on all channels plus a loss of half our mapping data, could possibly be linked to no sightings of, or contact with, any other aircraft in the night sky.' Soon his mind was racing as he feared the answer to this dilemma might not exist because the manual writers may not have envisaged such an abnormal scenario.

Scrambling through heavy emergency manuals, his two co-workers delved into this maze of information while Cardin himself enabled standby mapping upon the centre EICAS screen. Here, the computerised displays usually held a wealth of emergency procedure commands if you selected from the items on the drop-down menus, but tackling this current dilemma of partial blackouts was a tricky undertaking. Normally, this screen would automatically notify the company of their predicament, but achieving this was part of the problem in the first place.

Tom Tyson found an obscure section about seeing few other passing planes passing. He read it out: "There are numerous reasons why nothing else may be seen; not the least being that it may be an unscheduled time of the day or night. In some countries, hardly any flights depart after midnight for community noise abatement or other civil restrictions. Also, bright starry nights might obscure other aircraft nav lights as they pass by."

But there was nothing really specific to this particular case, except to say, "Unless you are staring out a window at the precise moment in time when another plane goes by, you can easily miss it altogether."

They'd all drawn blanks. 'Okay people,' Cardin spoke. 'Let's just open the conversation to one and all. I'm willing to listen to any damn thing – no matter how crazy or irrelevant it may seem. Who wants to start?'

There were a few seconds of silence, then Roslyn spoke softly. 'Umm, it seems we must have suffered some kind of electrical event that we simply weren't made aware of at the time. Apart from that one big flash to our north-east, I didn't notice that we'd taken any lightning strikes since take-off. Or did one of you?' The other two shook their heads. 'Then something has certainly happened and our whole electrical system has just gone weird . . . I suppose.'

'Hmm, weird eh?' Cardin repeated. 'But not a very technical word, Roslyn.'

Tom said, 'I've checked all the fuses and circuit breakers, so I reckon it could be a generator failure that has maybe caused damage around the circuits and bus bars, giving us intermittent and spurious information with readout losses here and there.'

The captain said, 'Weird and spurious. But what about something specific? I can't act on ghost stories and I can't scramble out into the wings and trace all the wiring looms myself because there are hundreds of miles of the stuff. And anyway, even if we are suffering some major malfunctions we've been flying for nearly six hours now and still haven't sighted one other plane or heard anyone else on the radios. Why not?'

Roslyn said, 'Maybe there's just no-one else near our track. Or we might have simply missed them – like the manual says.'

'Then why can't they hear our radio calls on HF or 121.5?'

Just then the captain's main MFD screen blinked back on . . . for some unknowable reason. But a worrying glance at it now showed his little aircraft target located several hundred miles away from the one on his F/O's screen. 'Hey, look at that!' he yelped.

The F/O cross-checked then wrinkled her face, 'Gee, it's nothing like mine - which has been perfect. I wonder what's happening here.'

Tom was also puzzled. 'So which one is right, Boss?' They all stared hard at the now unreliable screens as consternation mounted.

Cardin recalled the major emergency that happened to Qantas flight 32 that took off from Singapore in 2010. Just on take-off an oil blow-pipe shattered in one engine and caused massive haemorrhaging to fuel lines, along with surging electronic data flow disruptions to the flight deck's main computers. This was an Airbus A380 where problem solving challenges are similar to most other aircraft types, but the A380 is very highly computerised. In this Airbus case, the pilots battled for over an hour with hundreds of warnings romping across their screens: some real and many false, while ruptured fuel tanks vented thousands of litres of Jet-A1 over the port wing and all around the sky; showering communities below them. Eventually the QF32 pilots became quite bewildered under the sensory overload of so much dire information glaring at them, while they still weren't being told the real cause of the incident nor what they should do about it. Instead of returning to land, they elected to keep the flying bomb aloft for an hour.

After that lesson, Ray Cardin resolved to never allow minor predicaments like his to overtake and confuse his overall judgement. After all, he'd only had one warning so far: the intermittent failure of his multi-function display (MFD) screen which had since restored itself - albeit with a crazy read-out of spurious data.

"Let's order coffee and some desserts,' Cardin announced. 'We'll keep discussing this all night if we have to, but let's get things straight right now: the outside world will be receiving our transponder beeps even if they don't hear our position reports. They'll be watching us carefully by now and have probably declared an emergency SAR phase on us. Eventually we'll get closer to Hawaiian airspace and obtain radio contact. There I will request a diversion into Honolulu. But even if we could talk to them right now they'd probably ask: "So what's your problem?" And what could I say except that my screens went down and were intermittent for a while and that we've seen no other air traffic tonight? So really, compared to QF32 we have hardly had any problems at all.'

'We must bear in mind that the US military has defence satellites, spy flights and God knows what else surrounding Hawaii. They're still acutely conscious of the Pearl Harbour attacks back in 1941 and they won't allow any repeat performances of that - I can assure you. So when our ETA for their FIR boundary approaches, they'll be looking damned hard at that spot on their super-snooper gear and will probably have some fighters already airborne aiming to visually identify us.'

'Will they?' asked Tom in fright. 'What could they do then?'

'Whatever they like, but they'll probably intercept us in close formation to see if we're polite enough to wave back. If we don't, then all hell might break loose.' The crew digested these uncomfortable thoughts as Cardin suggested they study the manual's instructions pertaining to "interception by military" just

16

as two pretty stewardesses brought refreshments onto the flight deck.

Cardin turned around and told them: 'Now listen-up, ladies; we've had some annoying radio and navigation problems for several hours now. It's no big deal but I don't want to announce it over the P.A. and alarm the sleeping masses unnecessarily. However, at this stage we might need to divert into Honolulu so the engineers can inspect the ship. We simply can't just barge into the busy L.A. airspace tomorrow morning without radios or flight data or anything. So I'm confident it will all come good before then and I'll keep the crew informed by intercom, but not with general announcements to all. Please tell Mr Zaresh the Purser, okay?'

The women exited the flight deck as one said to the other, 'Well, it actually suits me if we get a stay-over in Honolulu because on my last trip I found the absolute *best* fashion store right on Waikiki. And the prices are just so reasonable, too.' The other girl's eyes lit up and she said, 'I'll come with you!'

The flight known as AA200 droned on through the night sky as its young second officer wondered if he too might get another chance to meet up with a certain Hawaiian lady who had promised to wait for his next flying visit. In just over four more hours anything could happen, they supposed, but Roslyn the conscientious first officer wasn't dreaming of any shopping or romantic liaisons in downtown Waikiki because both glass PFD and MFD screens on her side had now gone blank!

3.

Someone cursed. 'Shite!' The three pilots jerked up and stared at this latest stark development as the first officer gasped in fright: 'Captain, now they've nearly all gone! I've never practiced this in the simulator – ah, have you?'

Cardin's eyes bulged wide as he answered truthfully, 'No.'

Nervously, Roslyn suggested, 'Maybe we should just turn back now . . . or divert somewhere?'

Cardin didn't answer, while Tom Tyson's mind raced forwards. 'So how will we navigate with just one PFD operating? And I suppose that if they can't identify us properly at the FIR boundary they might, ah . . . '

'Might what?' asked Roslyn.

'Well, you know, they might . . . Ah, I've just finished reading a book about that Korean Airlines Flight-007 back in the eighties. Well, the Russians claimed that it was spying by deliberately straying into Russian airspace and so they just shot it down and it plunged into the sea between Japan and the Kamchatka Peninsula.'

Cardin spun around in his seat. 'And us too? You're implying that they might shoot us down like KAL-007? Don't be bloody ridiculous, Tom. I won't tolerate any of this type of wild and unfounded speculation on my watch, thank you. I merely said that we could be subject to military interception. Now, even though all this gear will be back on line soon enough, you two

18

nervous Nellies have got us being shot down already! We will proceed on our planned course.'

But Roslyn wasn't listening to Cardin's lecture and interrupted, 'Yes, I remember that too, Tom. There was lots of world-wide conjecture that it *was* actually spying and because this was at the height of the Cold War then I suppose anything could have happened. But just imagine anyone shooting down a passenger plane full of innocent passengers.'

Cardin waved his hands. 'Hey! They weren't spying at all. And they weren't inside Russian airspace, but near it. The Russians just got trigger happy because they hated the Americans so . . .'

Tom differed, 'But it wasn't an American airline, Boss, it was Korean.'

'Jesus, Tom, it was an American-built Boeing-747, just like this thing. They're all the same to the Ruskies. Anyway, I thought I just ordered everyone to drop it, please? Yes, we've suffered some electronic outages but now we're delving into absurdities and speculation about what will never happen. I asked you two for sensible and professional rationalisation of some on-board issues that have already happened numerous times in the past to some other flights and flight crews . . . so *enough* thank you*!*'

Cardin wondered if he might be invisible because Tom continued to natter quietly to Roslyn. 'But the KAL plane was surrounded by Russian Migs while those Mig hotshots were calling the 747 on all frequencies. They could actually see each other because they were so close together: wingtip to wingtip. So why didn't the Korean pilots answer? Couldn't they at least have pleaded "Don't shoot!"

A new voice joined the fray. It was Haneed Zaresh the purser who Tom had admitted to the flight deck. Zaresh said, 'It was because the Russians didn't bother to call them on the 121.5 emergency frequency, but on their military UHF frequency. That's why KAL never heard them.'

Ray Cardin looked about to jump down Zaresh's throat because the last thing the captain needed right now was one more amateur speculator injecting fire into the frying pan.

But Zaresh spoke first. 'Captain, I must protest most strongly. The best interests of my passengers are always paramount, but I've been informed that we might be diverting into Honolulu while somehow I'm not allowed divulge this fact to our fare-paying passengers. Yet it remains my duty to do so, and to remind you that they all might have arrangements to change and many persons to notify if they will now be held overnight and thus delayed into L.A. Many will have business arrangements or social events like weddings to attend. Some might even have funerals, christenings or reunions . . .'

'Great screaming jet engines!' yelled the infuriated captain, wagging a warning finger at the purser. 'Funerals? Reunions? Give me a friggin' break! I've just had multiple electronic failures following total communication outages and we are almost like a blind goose flying through a snow storm. So let me make this clear to all of you right now: I actually do not give a flying duck about wetting some baby's head or champagne glasses clinking

20

together at some wedding ceremony because I've got a very big plane here that might have some *very* major troubles – especially in communication and navigation, so just now the passengers' trivial inconveniences can all go to hell! My job is to get us safely back on the ground *somewhere* and get these damn things fixed, and then will we proceed further if it is safe to do so. Get it, everyone?'

Tom Tyson interrupted urgently. "Boss, as you can see, Ros's whole NAV display has blanked out! So where the heck are we now? And remember that your last display showed us way off course and hers seemed right, but which one was correct?'

The dark-haired purser was craning his neck between the two pilots and glancing in fear at the blacked-out walls of the control consoles. 'So we actually *are* lost, aren't we captain? You don't know where you are but you told my crew earlier to expect a diversion and not to tell any passengers. This is totally unacceptable and I will report this to dispatch as soon as we land . . . whenever that is.'

Cardin was infuriated. 'Just shut the hell up, all of you! These damn failures are occurring as I speak. Now, I'm the captain here and I just want to cool down any panic while I grapple with this latest crappy onslaught from Hell! So, I especially don't need any fear on the faces of our purser or any cabin crew which will clearly inflame the passengers and cause escalating alarm. In about four hours we'll be on the ground in Hawaii and that's now a certainty because that's where I'm going and so are you. And no, we won't be shot down by the U.S. military just because some other plane was shot down more than thirty years ago in the entirely different circumstances of the Cold War. For everyone's info, we are *not* flying dangerously close to anyone's prohibited airspace like that Korean plane was doing so very long ago, and this is definitely *not* the Cold bloody War! Remember, we are allies with America, not their enemies. Australia holds decades-old treaties with the U.S. - both politically and also in aviation and other transportation arenas, and we fought the Battle of the Coral Sea together, remember?'

'Now, it's becoming possible that as a result of our long silences plus this latest development, ATC and the U.S. military might be considering our flight as either hijacked or crashed into the sea. And after September Eleven 2001, they will be quite jumpy about the spectre of any hijackings – to say the least. But they certainly won't be shooting us out of the sky before they have thoroughly investigated the whole issue.'

'How do you know?' interrupted Roslyn hotly. 'Yes, we are their allies, but only when we can communicate with them and obtain the appropriate airways clearances. If we don't or can't answer them by radio or electronic data, then just what are they supposed to think? I say we should turn back now.'

Cardin barked at her. 'And I say we don't because they have procedures in place, Roslyn . . . for Christ's sake!'

Tom interrupted again. 'Like the Russians? They had procedures in place, too. Their ground controllers radioed that Korean plane dozens of times and Japanese ATC were also calling them. Getting no replies, the Ruskies' angrily scrambled their interceptor jets. They followed all the procedures to the letter. In the end, the Russian generals became infuriated by the Koreans' continued silence and asked Moscow to order the shoot-down. Then it was all too late.'

Now Captain Ray was livid. 'That's enough everyone! *Enough!* Am I in charge here or not? Do I have four gold bars on my shoulders solely for decoration or for some other damn reason? Huh? And Haneed; you are just the purser, are you not? You expertly manage our cabin service, of course, which is mostly about serving food and beverages, and you also oversee our cabin attendants. But with all due respect, what the hell would you know about complex air navigation problems like this?'

'So we *do* have big problems, then? Or to be more precise and to quote you: complex problems in air navigation and communications.'

'I'm not really sure yet, Haneed! We just have to wait a while and it should all come back online again.'

Second Officer Roslyn whispered, 'And it might not . . . '

'Captain!' Tom squawked. 'Now they've all gone blank! We've lost the lot!'

Horrified, Roslyn Steinhouse's face turned white. 'My god! Now we haven't any clue where we are while the whole U.S. military might be waiting to pounce on us!'

Cardin glared at her. 'Well, what about utilising all your basic training, Ros? Use the damn standby instruments! Remember the old adage from your first flying lessons: "When the shit hits the fan, fly the plane first?" '

The outdated analogue air pressure instruments appeared to be still working okay, so they both gripped their control wheels while bouncing straight back to square one: seat-of-the-pants flying - just like the WW1 days of Tiger Moths. At the same time, the purser fled from the flight deck in mild terror but at great speed. It was almost time to wake his trusting fare-paying passengers with a familiar gong and an assuring cheery call announcing happy details of their arrival time for their various engagements in the United States of America. But now, what could he say?

In the right-hand seat, First Officer Steinhouse found herself trembling as she blurted: 'Oh no! It's crashed into the sea! Yes, that's what they'll most likely be assuming on the ground already.'

She was instantly struck by ghastly memories of the ill-fated Malaysian Airlines flight MH-370 in 2014. She had once shared a rented home unit in Melbourne with a friendly Asian uni student who was later on that flight. It mysteriously disappeared over the Indian Ocean and her good friend, along with all 239 souls on board, was now dead. She desperately hoped her Captain wasn't noticing the cold fear written across her face because she was controlling this 747 jet and all the people behind her had placed their trust - and their very lives, in their supposedly calm and fearless pilots.

'What's the matter, Roslyn?' the captain asked. 'You look ghostly white. We'll get through this but I need your solid support. I might be in charge but I'm not a damned one-man army, you know. I need your backing for the next few hours. Right now you're driving this thing, Tom will be manually plotting our course, and I'm supervising it all. Okay?'

She tried to smile but failed. "I, ah, was just thinking about that Malaysian plane a few years ago. MH-370 it was. I lost a nice friend on that flight when they took off from KL and just vanished over the Indian Ocean somewhere . . . '

'Oh for Heaven's sake, Ros! What is this? World's Greatest Air Crashes? You people can sit up and watch all that stupidly morbid plane crash stuff on TV back home. While I'm sorry about your friend, I have repeatedly demanded a positive attitude on this flight deck tonight because we certainly need it. And how can it possibly assist us by dwelling on big crashes from the past when we know for a fact that *we* haven't crashed and *we* know that *we* haven't been hijacked . . . don't *we*? It's just that the *world* doesn't yet know why or how we've disappeared. Eventually it will all be resolved, but in the meantime it's heads down and tails up for us.'

'And Tom, I'd like you to quickly head downstairs and look around. Do a survey of how many people still have their laptops and other electronic gadgets working. Since much of our gear isn't working just now, I wonder if the passengers' devices are still functioning through this strange interference. But please don't make it obvious that you are spying on them, just smile and ask how they are enjoying their flight. Also talk to the cabin crew in private and see if they appreciate our situation. Make sure you are not overheard. Tell them I am insisting there be no awkward looks on their faces when they attend to people. Imagine if we frightened the whole lot of them with nothing but half-truths and inconclusive guesswork. So I don't want a riot to erupt down there because there are only eighteen of us against nearly four hundred people and we don't have four hundred sets of handcuffs. Get the picture?'

'In the meantime, Ros, it's basically manual navigation with the old analogue dials for us. Just keep steering 027 degrees as we were before it all went haywire. And Tom, hurry back up then find a pencil and start plotting our course on that old HAC chart and work out our ETA's for each waypoint to come. A bit like the old days when you did your first navigation exercises. I'll keep manually calculating our flight fuel and our new destination of Honolulu, okay?'

Roslyn nervously gripped her control wheel. It had been fourteen years since she'd navigated an old Cessna across Victoria's Dandenong Ranges at night, tracking on one navigation beacon plus good old *ded-reckoning.* The twenty-year-old plane only had one engine and she'd been very afraid of it suddenly stopping as there was only a yawning blackness below her.

Now she was commanding four powerful Rolls Royce RB211 jet engines that were purring away - just as they were engineered to do, but there were no navigation aids way out here over a boundless ocean, and her ded-reckoning skills were mostly forgotten because no-one ever imagined that they'd be needing them again in this modern day and age. But now she forced herself to follow the aircraft's compass, just as mariners of old did to discover the New World and Australia. She also utilised the standby directional gyros (DG's) to assist, but they could easily lead you astray. A pilot needs to regularly re-align DG's to the magnetic compass - but how often? She'd forgotten. Was it every fifteen minutes, or was that just for slow moving Cessnas plodding along? No-one had ever taught her about performing all these rudimentary steering chores on big speedy jets.

Then she remembered: it was called *precession* of directional gyros. They move, or precess, but why? How? And will these ones do it now? At their cruising speed of nearly 500 knots, just the smallest heading mistake could rapidly carry them hundreds of miles off track, and they were already prone to be off track to start with. Gulp: this had become a nightmare.

On the headsets she overheard Ray Cardin listening to the static of multiple frequencies of HF radio. Without SELCAL selected, all the noises of the night skies crackled together from their headphones. Cardin looked very frustrated as he obviously heard no voices at all - just static.

He looked unhappy. 'Must be a solar flare, then.' Solar flares – sometimes called Sun spots, are gigantic magnetic storms that suddenly rage from the Sun's surface at irregular intervals. Taking eight minutes to reach Earth, some solar flares have the knock-out power to drown most communications on Earth by causing havoc with electronics. In 1989 large parts of Canada's electronic systems were crippled by an enormous geomagnetic solar storm.

Cardin lent over to his F/O. 'Yes, I'm betting that's what it is. It's a massive solar flare that must have hit just after we departed

Sydney. It's affected our primary NAV and SATCOM platforms - plus who-knows what else, but thankfully the engines are still purring like kittens.'

Tom Tyson interrupted. 'Or a meteor strike. Could be a huge meteor shower that knocked away everyone's antennas.'

Roslyn decided, 'Well, if that's the case they'll know all about it on the ground because other aircraft must have been similarly affected. And they'll know that we haven't plunged into the sea or been hijacked. They will realise that when the solar flare or meteor shower abates then we must reappear eventually.'

Tom said, 'And the US Airforce will be looking for lots of missing targets - not just us, when everything is restored to normal.'

Cardin was pleased with this supportive reasoning; it certainly made sense. 'But they'll still be very careful in case we *were* hijacked, although it would be a big co-incidence for hijackers to strike simultaneously with the occurrence of a major solar flare or other natural phenomena.'

Tom departed downstairs on his mission, then soon returned briskly to the deck. 'Boss, I looked around the whole business and economy cabins and some laptops are still going, but barely. It seems that many of them appeared to run out of battery power early, and most of the rest are fading out now. Most kids' toys are dying - but all this might be explainable. Our auxiliary power for recharging them could be upsetting them like it's crippling our instruments. But I can't make a definite conclusion, sorry.'

Hmm, laptops running low on power? Kids toys stopping one by one? The captain considered it all then discussed it amongst them. They tossed around many ideas but Cardin wouldn't talk about historical plane crashes, considering that subject to be not only negative, but highly unproductive. They eventually agreed that they would safely escape from this predicament one way or another; then, after a few hours of engineering inspections in Hawaii they'd be flying once again; winging their way due east towards Los Angeles and a well-earned two-day lay-over.

In the rear-most galley, two stewardesses were having a lively discussion. 23-year-old Ayli Gorshe was chatting to her friend Suzy Tayne as they prepared the late evening snacks.

'I've always been interested in science fiction,' said Ayli. 'My Mum got me into it when I was about twelve. So I reckon this problem must be from aliens in our atmosphere. They come here all the time, you know. Sometimes they land, sometimes not. But this time they've emitted some sort of powerful signal that causes planes like ours to lose our navigation and communications.'

Tayne asked, 'But why would they do that? Aren't they friendly?'

'Well, lots of them are friendly but we frighten them away by pointing cameras at them - or guns. Such people are just so stupid because it can only be in our interests to welcome aliens to our planet. Surely there must be lots to learn from them if they can fly right across the galaxy to get here. '

As Ayli Gorshe sliced Kiwi fruit into crystal bowls, a friendly voice interrupted. "Excuse me ladies. But who are we going to welcome to our planet?'

Gorshe turned and smiled at an elderly man. 'Sorry. We're just chatting about science fiction and aliens - my hobby. What can I get you, sir?'

'I've ordered a special snack for my wife who has diabetes. Did you get my order? Kennard is our name.'

'Ah, yes sir. We won't be long.'

The man smiled and turned to go. 'Just one other thing, if I may. Did I overhear you saying something about planes like ours losing our navigation and communications?'

'Oh no sir,' assured Suzy Tayne. 'It's just our sci-fi talk; something to chat about during these long hauls. Ayli loves all that stuff and reads it all the time, but I can't get into flying saucers and little green men myself, can you?'

The man shook his head and returned to his seat. After a while he turned to his wife and whispered, 'It's probably nothing, my dear, but I happened to hear two hosties whispering to each other about our plane being lost and its radios are dead. But don't tell anyone please because it's probably just silly gossip.'

Mrs Kennard was justifiably shocked and a short while later whispered to the woman beside her, 'Did you happen to hear about anything being wrong with this plane?'

'No, what?'

'Oh, when Keith went back to see the hosties he overheard them whispering about how our plane was about to crash . . . '

'Crash!' the woman squawked. 'Ah . . . is it really?'

'Sssh!' she was told. 'I think they're just silly young girls gossiping. They were also talking about little green men in flying saucers and how we should be nice to them.'

The woman twisted around to observe the two stewardesses still chatting while preparing meals. She felt assured that nothing was about to crash if the two girls were still making fruit bowls while chatting merrily. But what a strange thing to be told! It made her feel quite uneasy and she started to count down to their arrival time in Los Angeles while tapping on her fading laptop which soon died. Unfortunately, the big movie screen ahead of them on the cabin wall had also gone blank. Previously it had been showing a little red plane crawling across a map of the blue Pacific with numbers announcing their ground-speed, altitude and ETA for arrival. Now there was nothing. She made a note to complain to that friendly dark-haired purser the next time he passed.

4.

In Sydney, the Senior Operations Controller - designated the SOC, was on video link-up with his counterpart at the American FAA. The FAA was most concerned that this Air Australia plane had departed Sydney for Los Angeles and then simply vanished soon afterwards. While they believed that there was a high probability that the 747 had suffered some catastrophic failure and plunged into the ocean off eastern Australia, it was also possible that it had been commandeered soon after take-off and was now under the control of terrorists. And if those terrorists had forced the pilots to keep flying towards America, it could easily become a re-run of September eleven 2001 where not one but four planes were overtaken and flown to their doom.

The FAA senior controller asked his Aussie counterpart: 'Please confirm again: what was the very last contact they made?'

The Soc replied, 'They reported leaving VHF range and were instructed to call Oceanic HF on the applicable primary or secondary HF frequencies, but the HF controller has confirmed that they never contacted him - although he and Auckland HF continued to blind-call them for some hours. Nandi in Fiji also transmitted to them. And as you know, Oakland in California has also been alerted to call them.'

The FAA official replied, 'What about SATCOM back to ATC or their company? Has nothing at all been received? And their engine transponders: anything recorded from them? Also, any

Sarsat distress signals on 406 MHz? If there is any CPDLC data I want it all examined thoroughly. We can't have this plane just wandering into US airspace at will. We all know what happened before.'

The Sydney SOC answered all these questions then replied, 'This is why I don't think it's a hijacking at all. Their engine transponders have simply ceased sending any handshake beeps and no hijackers can simply turn them off from the flight deck - nor can any pilots. So unless someone crawled out into the wings to snip the wires . . . . '

'Sure; so is there any other way they could be disabled?'

'No. I just spoke to the Chief Engineer for Air Australia and he says that the plane must have definitely crashed somewhere because the engines have stopped functioning. Now, maybe just one of those beeper devices could have failed by itself, but for all four of them to stop simultaneously can only mean one thing . . . '

Surprisingly, the FAA official sounded somewhat gladdened at this prognosis; relieving the Americans of the worry of another terrorist attack on US soil. The bleak fact that a plane load of people had probably plummeted into the Pacific Ocean well clear of the good old USA was apparently a much more preferable outcome.

The SOC whispered to a colleague, 'Wow, this is a real "not in my backyard" case. They're happy so long as it's not headed their way.'

The assistant replied, 'But we'd be the same? We wouldn't want some American flying bomb barrelling down on us. It's the NIMBY syndrome.'

The FAA asked again to confirm if ATC comms with all other air traffic had been normal all night. The Sydney SOC related, 'Only the usual minor hassles. You know HF and its incredibly long range, but the reception and static can often make it difficult to read. However, most of our HF and data links have been routine tonight with only one other flight, Pacific Blue, losing contact with us for twenty minutes.

The FAA man said, 'Well, we've got our satellites switched to high alert just in case; and our AWACS are out there too. Apart from routine ops, they can't see anything unidentified to the south or south-west of the Honolulu FIR, so it sure looks like you Aussies have lost this one somewhere nearer to you. But good luck with it, guys . . . '

Yet the Americans weren't totally heartless. The US Navy had been conducting naval patrol exercises in undisclosed areas east of Australia's coast. Now with this Air Australia flight missing, they'd been diverted to work with the Australian Navy and were steaming towards the area of AA200's flight track. This was under orders from the Admiral of the US Pacific Fleet himself. While Sydney authorities were greatly pleased at this offer of assistance, the stark reality was that the Pacific is by far the world's largest ocean and any wreckage still in existence could be floating anywhere at all.

The SOC recalled the missing Malaysian Boeing-777 flight MH-370 which, despite numerous spurious finds, nothing of substance has been located in the several years since its disappearance. After all, when a jumbo jet hits the water, thousands of pieces and fragments, large and small, will most likely sink immediately, while no person would survive the impact.

'Our engines, thankfully, are still fine,' reiterated the Captain. But First Officer Roslyn was feeling an unpleasant tightening in her chest as she manually steered this enormous plane blindly and without faith through the black night. She'd heard almost enough of the captain's bold bravado and baseless optimism and decided to argue; challenging his authority. She would not let this man play with her life and the lives of all on board.

Eventually she took a deep breath then spoke up. 'I still maintain that we should have turned back to Sydney or Auckland long ago, captain. I am entitled to express this differing opinion.'

'Yes you are, but why?' Cardin asked, hands upraised as though beseeching her. 'We've all had HF outages before, as we've discussed several times. So, when we could not make contact I presumed that it would all come good again soon – as it always eventually does.'

She argued, 'I was resting then, but after such a handicap had persisted for any more than two hours I would have considered turning right around and heading for home. I would not have attempted to cross the whole Pacific Ocean with no outside contact or help from anyone in the world.'

Cardin tried to reply but his F/O spoke over him. 'I realise that you had no idea that all our SATCOM and data links would subsequently let us down as well, but you nevertheless just kept flying us into a sort-of . . . big black hole.'

'Oh, don't be so ridiculous, Roslyn! A big black hole? How amateurish does that sound coming from a professional airline pilot? Now, you're not going to throw some kind of female tantrum, are you? I asked you before for full support in this . . . dilemma, not a bucking of my authority.' More harsh words and ill feelings sparked between them while Tom Tyson sat behind them in the jump seat and listened with mounting alarm to the breaking down of coherent command at the very time that crew unity was critical.

A buzzer sounded behind Tom and he admitted the purser into the flight deck once again. This time Haneed Zaresh's usual smiling face was showing great concern. He barged past Tom and glared at the captain and the F/O. 'Captain Cardin, I must protest again about the current state of the cabin, its crew, and its passengers!'

'Why, what's wrong?'

'You asked me to cover up our current predicament - which you admitted could be serious, and not to tell the passengers anything just yet because of the risk of panic.'

'Yes?'

'Well, a woman stopped me and asked why have our movies and map screens stopped working, and are we about to crash?'

Cardin was irritated. 'You simply tell her that there's a fault in the movie software gizmo and we certainly won't be crashing just because one stupid movie screen has gone on the blink.'

'But it is a lie, isn't it Captain? She and I can both see that all the screens and all the seatbacks have blacked out in *every* cabin - not just one. And we have a major problem, don't we? I wondered why she asked me about crashing, so when I queried her she said that a man told her that he overheard some stewardesses whispering about it.'

'Oh, I see now. So *some* woman said that *some* man told her that *some* cabin personnel had said something about something. Haneed, please, I have ordered a lid kept tightly on this, not a general broadcasting of vague back-alley scuttlebutt.'

Zaresh argued, 'But Captain, isn't it your duty to keep the passengers informed of all eventualities? Anyway, many other passengers are now talking about it; it's only natural. They are frightened by your silence and especially by the gossip originating from our own AA crew. At the moment I foresee waves of alarm breaking out at any time. You must make an announcement!'

'Yes, but I can't.'

'And why on earth not?'

'Because I don't fully know what is happening myself, that's why.' The three of them gawked in fright at their captain and leader; their supposed saviour in times of dire straits. 'Haneed, just imagine if I made an announcement saying we are up the creek without a paddle but I don't know what we can do about it *yet* . . . if anything.'

Roslyn Steinhouse turned around angrily and revealed to Zaresh, 'I have already told him that we should have turned back towards Sydney ages ago. *That's* what we could do about it!'

Zaresh was genuinely shocked and thrust his face at Cardin. 'Is *that* right?'

The F/O persisted, 'Yes, and I still insist we turn back now. We've got tonnes of fuel at the moment – thank God – enough for the entire Sydney to L.A. flight, then back to Hawaii again. But if we had turned around much earlier . . . '

'And just when in Christ's name was much earlier?' asked the furious captain.

'When I first asked you. I'm not sitting in this seat while you insist we fly towards a massive and hostile military force that is armed to the teeth to defend the USA and the Hawaiian Islands. They are never going to permit another September Eleven or Pearl Harbour to happen. And if we don't or can't speak to them then they'll shoot us down - simple as that!'

'But our own Australian military could be just as hostile,' warned the ever-knowledgeable Tom Tyson.

Cardin argued, 'What rubbish! The U.S. would never dare shoot down an airliner called *Air Australia*. Neither would Australia. It's their sworn duty. But they could certainly force us to land and then surround us with more cops than you've ever seen.'

'Well I wish they would,' said Roslyn.

Cardin was totally exasperated. 'Now everybody please just give me a break here! This is not a magical mystery tour. There are age-old, laid-down procedures for communication failures which we've been following. That is: continue on current course. Hold assigned altitude. Continue to attempt radio contact. Squawk 7700 radio failure - and all the rest of it as you well know. But now you are proposing to discard all this and turn back to Australia, *only* seven thousand kilometres away? So just what might I tell our passengers about that, pray tell?'

The purser reminded him, 'Especially the lady in 47F.'

'To hell with the bloody woman in 47F! And any other rumour monger too!'

In the right-hand seat, the first officer was at breaking point. She'd been manually flying this 350-tonne Boeing-747 for over an hour and was mentally exhausted. Finally, she decided. 'Captain, I'm turning this plane back to the southwest. If you don't consent then curse your rotten soul. You've got a wife and a little baby back in Sydney. I don't have children but I still have a life and a family. Also, Mr Zaresh and all of us on board have families to think of. Even Tom must have someone who loves him . . . '

There were some half-grins as Tom rued, 'I did have a girlfriend, but only yesterday she texted me that it's all over.'

Roslyn continued, 'Hmm, so whatever our various circumstances we absolutely cannot barge into a hot spot of military might where it is possible they'll shoot first and not ask questions later. Eh, captain?'

Tyson agreed with her. 'Yeah Boss, why not turn back and head for home? You can announce honestly to everyone that we've had many hours of radio and electronic problems and now Honolulu won't give us an airways clearance into their airspace - which they surely wouldn't.'

Cardin replied, 'I see. And just how will we navigate at night over seven thousand featureless oceanic kilometres without any nav or radios operating?'

Tom stated, 'Australia is a very big target. We can't possibly miss it - even with DR.'

It was then that Cardin felt the plane commence a mild left turn away from track. 'Whoa! Did I say we turn back, anyone? I am still in friggin' charge here . . .'

Roslyn Steinhouse screamed at him, 'I'm not going to end my life because some hero captain forced me to fly into hostile and dangerous airspace, or to end up a piece of meat in the sea for the sharks to eat. You can have me tried for treason later because I just don't care! I say we take a vote to endorse my about-turn actions because we are the four persons most responsible for this aircraft and all those on board.' Tom Tyson shuddered. He had been convinced Ros would never do this, but now she actually had!

As three voting hands shot up, the startled captain glared at them. 'Well . . . this is nothing but a goddamned mutiny! So what's my name, Captain friggin' Bligh?'

Once again the purser snapped his heels and spun like a drill sergeant-major to quickstep from the flight deck. Before slamming the door, he barked, 'You have five minutes to make the announcement, captain - otherwise I will make it myself.'

In the upper business class area several people asked him, 'What's going on? What was all that yelling in the cockpit? Do we have a problem? Tell us!' But Zaresh strode past them, his face dark and thunderous.

On the flight deck Cardin cursed the other two. 'This is air piracy! You can't do any of this. Who bestowed upon either of you – or Zaresh – the arrogant gall that you know more about flying than me? I've got nearly twenty thousand hours' experience while how many have you got, Roslyn? Two thousand? Three? And Tom, how about you? Fifteen hundred - and mostly on little prop commuters, I suppose?'

But Cardin said no more and, quite amazingly, did not attempt to twist the VNAV/heading dial back to its original course, but simply allowed the plane to continue its gentle left turn then stop to lock on a magnetic heading of 241 degrees. Tom noticed with relief that they still had a functioning autopilot - albeit intermittently.

When the giant plane levelled it wings onto the new course heading which aimed back towards far-away Australia, Cardin seemed to have involuntarily agreed to the inevitable. Next to him, a frightened Roslyn waited for him to erupt, but, amazingly, his continued silence seemed to confirm acquiescence. More likely, Cardin could also envisage himself as a floating chunk of meat somewhere in the North Pacific . . . and he abhorred sharks. Soon Roslyn became hugely relieved that he seemed to have capitulated to her extremely daring decision for now, but how it would all pan out in a court of law much later could be a very different matter indeed. For her future, she could clearly see herself sitting in a jail cell one day; vilified as the world's first female hijacker. Behind them, Tom's eyes remained bulging wide. He simply couldn't believe any of this.

A gong soon sounded. It was the purser calling. 'Captain,' he demanded, 'what is your decision?'

A subdued Cardin answered, 'Ah, I have already turned around . . .' Steinhouse glared daggers towards him over his audacious use of the word "I" as he continued 'and we are now heading back towards Australia, Haneed. So I am about to make the announcement.'

Cardin swallowed hard then took a few deep breaths before pressing the P.A. button. 'Ah, Ladies and gentlemen, boys and girls, this is your captain. I must be perfectly frank and honest with you . . . ' Roslyn Steinhouse glared more hateful daggers at him as he continued. 'This flight is now headed back towards Sydney because it has some, ah, major problems, but I don't want anyone to be alarmed.'

Tom Tyson could clearly picture the explosive panic down below following those appalling words: "I don't want anyone to be alarmed."

Stuttering, Cardin pressed on, still slightly unsure of what he would say. 'So I, ah, have decided on this course of action because, ah, the problem is that we lost all our normal communications with Air traffic control and our airline company not long after we left Sydney. There are other ways apart from radios to contact them but unfortunately those methods also, ah, seem to have become unreliable . . . one after another. Now, I know that was over six hours ago but normally these things soon rectify themselves so I pushed on in that knowledge, confident that soon we might . . . '

His first officer was wagging an angry finger at him that clearly warned: 'Don't lie!'

Other intercom phones gonged repeatedly. Tyson answered the purser who asked: 'They want to know how many more hours till they're safe. They've already been flying six or seven hours and now they have to go all the way back again. What about their holidays? Their accommodation in L.A.? Business meetings? Their connecting flights? What about all that?'

On another phone, a stewardess pleaded to Ros Steinhouse. 'The captain told us cabin crew hours ago about navigation and communication problems. Why didn't we turn back then? Or head for Nandi or Auckland? Why?'

The Captain's voice was still droning over the loudspeakers everywhere, but it seemed no-one was listening. Instead, Ros could hear shrieking and crying in the background. This was the general panic that Cardin had feared might erupt - and it was exploding right now!

Cardin continued, 'So I can assure you all that we have sufficient fuel for this return journey, and on behalf of Air Australia I once again apologise for this most unfortunate and annoying event. I will keep you informed at all times. Thank you.'

Roslyn snapped at him. 'Annoying? Is all this just an annoyance to you, Ray?'

Cardin's bravado had returned. 'No, of course not. Anyway, Mrs Fletcher Christian the pirate mutineer, just exactly when did you tell me to turn back? Actually it was never. You merely suggested a few things while consenting to follow our flight plan and my directions, didn't you? Also you agreed with me that all this could be solar flares or meteorites, while you continued to believe that infantile assertion that we'd flown right off the planet - as that crazy nut proclaimed. So why didn't you speak up more clearly long ago? I will be testifying on absolutely everything when the appropriate enquiries take place and nothing will be omitted, I can assure you.'

She screeched venom back at him. 'Don't you dare talk down to me like I'm a child – or because I'm a woman! And I am not a pirate or a mutineer because I *did* speak up! I suggested that we divert several times but you just ignored me. Anyway, if it turns out that I eventually saved all our lives by turning for home against your strongest and most strident orders, then how exactly will you explain *that* to your fancy commissions of enquiry – let alone the media?'

Cardin slumped down in his seat. 'Oh well, at least I don't have to worry about terrorist hijackers taking over this flight because I already have one right here beside me, don't I?'

Tom Tyson interrupted urgently. 'Excuse me, you two. But we require mutual co-operation here so let's cool it, please. After all, we still have a long way to go and it will take three good pilots working hard together as a team to get us out of this, ah, whatever *this* is. Meantime, as we have many hours remaining, who would like to take a break? I'll hop in to relieve someone while we try to ease this tension. You both need a few hours apart to clear the air.'

'Excellent suggestion, Tom,' agreed the stony-faced captain. 'I'm desperate for a short break because it could be a very long night.'

'It already is!' cursed Roslyn the co-pilot, glaring at the blank screens in front of her.

5.

Towards the forward end of the 747, in row 8, first-class passengers were, understandably, conducting a lively debate about their imminent fate. Standing in the aisle, scientist Stuart Rhys was trying to joke: 'They send me first class and this is all I get: a lying pilot!'

'They lie about everything,' sighed fashion designer Maggie Silverstone. 'An engine catches fire and they say 'Oh, by the way ladies and gentlemen, we have a small defect but not to worry.' Or, 'that last fall of seven thousand feet was just minor air turbulence. We sincerely hope you didn't spill your coffee and ruin our seats.'

A professional stand-up comedian did just that: he stood up. "Hi boys 'n girls. Guess what? Our left wing just fell off. But not to worry because shit happens! And anyway, at least nothing worse can go wrong.'

Everyone nearby laughed; a welcome relief from the nagging fears now escalating everywhere. Someone called out: 'How about this? Our flight will be subject to a very short delay so we won't be departing this afternoon, but next Wednesday instead! Have a pleasant flight . . . you suckers!'

A woman stated grimly, 'I think this captain upstairs has been keeping us in the dark all the time. I overheard the purser telling someone that we've been out of normal radio and data-link

46

communications for most of the flight. But I work for Telstra in data-link comms and I know a lot about it. There are multiple methods to bypass normal circuits and send help messages in many alternate ways: satellite phones being an obvious one. Also, the purser was saying that we've lost all navigation and they don't really know where we are. So where lies the truth, and can this get any worse?'

Several women burst into tears as consternation was barely restrained from bubbling into outright horror. A man spoke up: 'Why don't they know where we are? They've got GPS satellite navigation and God-knows what else on these things. They used to have INS navigation but it's all far more advanced than that now. Even little old me knows where I am on the weekends out in my fishing tinnie. My little GPS cost about three hundred bucks and takes me straight to my favourite fishing spots every time, while these clowns can't even find Hawaii - or a place called America!'

His girlfriend corrected him. 'But Jake, you are talking about finding little fish. I'm sure these professional pilots will be able to find something the size of America - or Australia.'

'They'd better,' grinned Bob Greenly, a car dealership owner from Adelaide. 'I've got my kids here with me while my missus is back home working. She naturally expects me to bring them back safe and sound.' His children nodded a forlorn agreement: yes, they certainly expected to be taken home after their holiday – but perhaps not quite as soon as this.

'Gong!' the P.A. chimed once again. This flight was becoming an orchestration of endless P.A. gongs as a familiar voice announced, 'This is your purser, Haneed Zaresh again. The flight crew have advised me that we will be arriving back in Sydney at approximately four thirty a.m. This is during the night curfew at Sydney airport but we will have a special dispensation to land. This ETA is of course subject to any headwinds we may encounter along the way. But, rest assured, we have sufficient fuel for any eventuality, even though flight in a westerly direction is nearly always slower because of prevailing Jetstream headwinds. But if it looks like we cannot reach Sydney, then Auckland in New Zealand or Tontouta in Noumea can be utilised. Thank you . . . and now we have a superb late-night supper ready to serve you in just a few moments.'

Many laughed when the comedian crowed: 'Our last meal on death row - but would you like fries with that?'

Unamused, an American woman wailed loudly, 'How can anyone want to eat? I just want to see my little boys again.'

Maggie Silverstone looked distraught. 'I'm going to die anyway. I've got heart disease and am going to the US to see my family for the last time . . .' those beside her cast their eyes elsewhere around the cabin. It was hard to decide just who they should feel the most sorry for: her, themselves, or *all* of the doomed passengers on this condemned flight.

In the upstairs business class cabin, the atmosphere was even more unstable. Most people were staring angrily at the flight deck door which remained firmly closed. Behind that door were the crew who held the fate of them all in their hands. Feelings of helplessness were electric as heated discussions flew around the cabin.

'So why can't they navigate by the stars anymore?' demanded George Sutherland, a ninety-five-year-old RAAF veteran of the Second World War. 'We did it over Europe. Middle of winter, nothing but clouds below and all of Germany shooting up at us while those damned Stukas were diving down from above. Despite all that, our navigators read the stars and always got us back to base in England. That's why I'm still here.'

A young university student turned around, 'Celestial nav is old hat now, Pops. You need a special sextant and a highly accurate chronometer - plus a book of celestial tables. They don't even carry a navigator these days 'cos it's all so computerised now . . . '

'Yes, and that's all fine until the computers go down,' added a girl who was majoring in computers at university.

The first student added, 'And there are only two pilots these days - plus one spare for relief. No engineer. No navigator.'

'And how do you know so much?'

'My uncle's a retired pilot.'

A man stood and clapped his hands loudly. 'Big deal! Alright everybody, listen-up please! I think that we just don't have the time to sit around in this happy little discussion arena and pussy-foot endlessly about this and that. We need to be right there in that cockpit and putting very hard questions to these guys right now. My mates here have agreed to back me up. We need to be laying our deepest concerns right down on the line to these pilots. We'll tell them that we represent over four hundred passengers and we're not gonna listen to any more of their bull.'

A man asked, 'Well, how do you intend to breach that strengthened cockpit door? No-one can open them any more since September-eleven.'

The man answered, 'I used to be in the Army - the SAS, actually. I went to Iraq and believe me; I know how to get through doors – *any* doors!'

'Bull! Where's your special door-busting equipment that I've seen in movies? Or are you gonna kick it down?'

A lawyer interrupted. 'Stop suggesting highly illegal acts, you people. These pilots are doing their jobs as best they can. They've announced their intentions to fly us back to Australia, so what more can they do? Meantime, if you're not a pilot then what could you possibly know about this?'

A female office manager chastised them, 'Stupid men! It's easy to get through that door. The purser has been in there several times already, and two hosties went in there earlier with food. They must call them first on their intercom phones using secret codes or whatever. And see that camera up there watching us . . . '

'That's right,' agreed the lawyer. 'There's a wall-phone back there in our galley. The crew phone each other all the time.' A few of the rebels wondered just what secret code they would need in order to conduct an illegal cockpit invasion of an airliner, while only one other prudent person timidly suggested that they'd better have a really good excuse . . .

Listening in, stewardess Janine Hilary held up a hand at them, her eyes wide with fright. 'Now whoa, everyone! Just hold it right there, please. I will not let anyone use the intercom or attempt to enter the flight deck for *any* reason. In fact, I'm going to call the purser right now!'

The ex-SAS man snarled at her. 'So we just sit here for hours and hope these cowboy jet-jockeys can find an object in the dark called Australia before we run out of fuel? And if they can't, then what's your plan B, Miss glorified coffee waitress?'

A trainee chef added, 'Yes, and even if they do happen to find Aussie, how can they just emerge from this . . . zone of silence and land at any Australian airport without radios? Mightn't we collide with other planes in the sky? And what if there are lots of clouds around . . . or storms happening?'

Hilary had triggered a secret alarm and within moments the anxious purser rushed up the stairs, accompanied by a male cabin steward who was a huge and muscled Pacific Islander with an angry face that clearly advertised a zero tolerance of any misbehaviour.

The purser grabbed a microphone and ordered, 'Now back to your seats, everyone! I am the purser and the officer in charge of all the passengers and cabin crew. There will be no rebellious talk about bursting into the flight deck, or of any other plots or schemes to overthrow the flight crew. I must warn you all that it is highly illegal to attempt to interfere with the safe navigation of any aircraft and I will not hesitate to detain anyone . . . '

'You're not a bloody cop!' yelled a defiant rebel.

'I am up here. The captain and I are the *only* law whilst we are airborne. We can legally perform marriages and can also arrest anyone who warrants it. So just what is it that you want? The captain has already told you he is taking us back to Australia.'

'The bloody captain? He's got no instruments and he's flying blind!' The general din erupted into verbal screaming matches; surely a most foolish path to be taking at such a crucial time where a panicky crowd can quickly evolve into a treacherous lynch mob that heeds no reason. Everyone glanced around at each other while most people's hearts were undoubtedly pounding like frightened animals trapped in a hunter's spotlights.

Then, in a surprise twist for all, the flight deck door suddenly opened and out walked a tall and greying man with four gold stripes on each shoulder. The huge steward bounded to his side and bunched his fists as if to say to all: 'Go near him and I'll knock your bloody heads off!' while his bulging biceps seemed to cause his frightening tattoos to expand even further.

Captain Ray Cardin calmly introduced himself, then said, 'There is no need for any doors to be smashed down. I am the captain and I am here. Unfortunately I cannot explain why so much has gone wrong with this flight. I've crossed the Pacific and Atlantic oceans dozens of times before and have never experienced this phenomenon. If I knew only what has happened here, then I could possibly solve it. In the meantime, we are not simply wandering blindly around the ocean – as I just heard someone claim – but flying and navigating by older-type, back-up and stand-by navigation instruments, some of which are driven by spinning gyros and static air pressure valves. We were forced to quickly revert to these nav methods from the past - long since redundant - or so we thought, and now we are manually plotting our ded-reckoning position on charts.'

An arrogant rebel interrupted. 'But what does all this technical waffle actually mean? And who cares about spinning gyros – whatever they are.'

A woman asked, 'Captain: will I ever get to see my grandkids in California again? That's all what I want to know.' Many people applauded, but not all.

The SAS man barked at Cardin. 'Dead Reckoning? I reckon you're *dead* bloody lost, aren't you?' Many were peering past the huge steward and into the flight deck where they could see a man in the left-hand seat and a woman in the right. They both seemed to be concentrating fiercely ahead and this image generated some empathy among many.

Ray Cardin noticed their stares, and so did the muscled steward who glared daggers at them all. Cardin said, 'There are hundreds of dials, instruments, levers and screens in there. What would any of you achieve by barging in there and sabotaging them? Or demanding answers to complex difficulties that we ourselves are at the moment battling to overcome? We simply don't need any distractions by amateur mob anarchy; what we need is complete silence to focus on the herculean tasks that confront us. Meanwhile, people, I am the senior officer aboard this aircraft - whether you like it or not, and we are in international airspace; so Mr Zaresh and I have total legal jurisdiction here while you and your plotting conspirators have exactly nil. Sorry, but you won't be storming the Bastille on my watch. And anyway, you sir, stated that you were once an Army officer: is that how you won their hearts and minds? By smashing everyone's doors down?'

'None of your bloody business, Captain Jack Flash!' retorted the angry ex-officer. 'We got results . . . one way or another . . . '

Haneed Zaresh waved his hands around. 'Enough, I say! We don't need this treacherous debating match. Aviation laws, called the Air Navigation Regulations, are enacted in Parliament and we are legally authorised to implement them. The flying of a 747 jet requires professional pilots to operate it under the ANR's, just as other peoples' jobs require professionals acting legally within their particular arena. We are all important in our own sphere but we are simply getting nowhere here. Our captain and his two co-pilots are attempting to cope with this extreme emergency by reverting to a few older methods of flight control to hopefully guide us home, but some of you disloyal passengers are considering open rebellion which will achieve precisely nothing! So, how many in your mob of thugs know how to fly a jumbo jet, eh?'

'That's a smart-arse question!'

Zaresh countered. 'No it's not. And if no-one does know, then please just leave it to us professionals. And Captain, thank you. Now everyone please return to your seats and we will try to keep you up-to-date as best we can. Remember, we can only do our very best – like anyone.'

Fine words indeed, yet it was quite incongruous that open rebellion on this very flight had already occurred just a few tense hours ago. And it had taken place *inside* the flight deck - not out here among the frightened masses. Worse, it was initiated by the plane's first officer and heartily endorsed by none other than the purser himself.

Cardin returned to his safe haven with a thumping heart, having discarded his plans for a requested rest break because it would seem outrageous to everyone if they heard that their captain was merrily snoozing away while so many feared for their very lives. Now he felt far more alarmed than weary. While his glamorous career so far had always been one of great self pride, he now understood with no small fear the animosity directed at him.

And he had negligently voided his own authority the moment he allowed his F/O to change their heading back towards the south-west. Now he may as well be wearing no stripes on his shoulders at all while it was clear that he had no friends among the flight deck crew, and not a single passenger or cabin crew member would be cheering the daring airmanship of Captain Ray Cardin tonight. He was - to use his favourite expression, about as popular as a Cruise missile coming over your back fence. And, although they all might cheer if they eventually touched down safely, at the moment they'd probably only cheer, like Madame

Defarge in the French revolution, when his head rolled from the tumbril.

'Captain?' whispered Tom Tyson into his boss's ear. Cardin turned around. 'Can I make a suggestion?'

'Of course.'

'Well, it might sound a little crazy, even quite outrageous, but . . . '

'Go ahead. I'm listening to anything.'

'Well, we don't have any real position fixes, do we? Just our plotting charts and DR navigation. Our DG indicates the way but it doesn't give us a position fix, does it? We're really stumped without any positive fixes, aren't we, so why don't we see if anybody has a GPS on board? You know: just one of those little hand-held things that hikers and fishermen use.'

'Tom, why would they work when our multi-million-dollar global platforms don't?'

'It might be an internal problem with our plane and nothing else. But I don't know, Boss. It's just a thought. So if I asked around, surely it wouldn't hurt . . . Better than doing nothing, I suppose.'

The captain considered it. 'Hmm, can you imagine me making an announcement asking if anyone has a GPS onboard so we can find our way home? I can't think of anything more embarrassing.'

'But can you imagine if we don't?' Tom argued. 'Is our pride worth more than trying every last avenue to save our worthless hides?' Tom smiled but got no smile back from the worried captain who probably deemed the suggestion as absurd beyond belief. Ha, that would certainly be a world-first in air navigation: a lost captain pleading for anyone to produce an amateur GPS so they could find their way home. He simply could not do it. Yet infuriatingly, the idea did have some merit . . .

Tom could understand his commander's quandary. 'Boss, don't you make any announcement; I'll just go back and quietly ask around, saying 'Hey guys, anyone got a GPS I can borrow? I'll return it soon and I promise I won't scratch it.'

Cardin was rapidly succumbing to very strong urges for an accurate and positive position fix from anything at all. It was almost pointless maintaining a steady compass heading without a triangulated distance and bearing fix along their track. Actually, he himself owned a tiny marine GPS for the rare occasions when he had time to go out fishing. Although the thing was currently lost somewhere in his garage at home, he would almost *kill* to be holding it in his hands right now. Even if they produce some errors, any GPS was probably correct most of the time. But would a little satellite GPS be capable of displaying the data of a jet travelling at over five hundred knots when it was designed for an aluminium runabout that splashes along at fifteen knots? But that didn't really matter because all they needed was just one quick glance at a latitude and longitude co-ordinate for a positive fix and it would be better than discovering a gold bar in your pocket.

He finally answered Tom's request. 'Ah okay, do what you like . . . I suppose.'

Downstairs in economy, or *the sardine* class section, Tom Tyson was strolling the aisles and telling everyone that it wasn't pronounced sardine class at all, but actually *Sardinay,* where the real upper class always sat. Many people were warming to this affable young second officer and were slightly softening their opinions about the other two pilots upstairs whom they'd previously detested. Tom had a cheery persona and *surfie* blond hair. He introduced himself throughout the cabin and partially succeeded in alleviating some of the lingering fear. He eventually sat beside a young couple who were headed for a hiking holiday in America's beautiful Appalachian Mountains.

'Hi,' he said to them. 'I once hiked around our Snowy Mountains and Mt. Kosciusko with my girlfriend. She was so sweet but now she's dropped me. Anyway, we seemed to get lost all the time – a bit like this flight I suppose – and we later found out it was our el-cheapo GPS that was faulty and kept letting us down.'

Julie Page looked concerned – but not about the instrument. 'Gee Tom, do you hear from her anymore?'

'Ah no, just my luck. Anyway, I was wondering if either of you know of a good brand GPS that won't guide you up a mountain pass and straight into a grizzly bear's claws!'

The couple laughed as Allan Henner spoke, 'Tom, we always use the Garmin brand because they're American and proven to be very reliable. We've got a Garmin 490 with us now.'

'I'd love to see it,' smiled friendly Tom, 'if you don't mind.' Henner reached up into his overhead locker and rummaged around as Tom explained his plans for kayaking around the Great Barrier Reef islands – 'but not without a reliable GPS'.

As per the pre-arranged plan, the overhead P.A. gonged and the First Officer's voice announced: 'The Second Officer will report to the flight deck, thank you.'

Tom looked embarrassed. 'Sorry guys. Looks like they just can't do without me. Can I borrow this for about ten minutes, please? I'll have it sent back down to you.' The couple smiled, then he slipped down the aisle and up the stairs.

Allan Henner, an accounting auditor, wasn't fooled and whispered to his partner, 'You know, that might be exactly what they need up in the cockpit.'

Page said, 'That little thing? Surely not. We only walk at five k's per hour. It wouldn't work in a jumbo jet . . . ah, would it?'

'Maybe that's why he met us: just to get his hands on a GPS.'

'Really? Are they getting that desperate? And will we ever get it back?'

'If it gets us back home he can keep the damn thing!'

A man behind them leant over their seat and said, 'That is *exactly* why he sat down with you. They need something – anything – to find out where the heck they are. But if they get us home I'll *pay* you for whatever that thing cost. A few hundred bucks wouldn't even scratch my bank balance.'

A woman in front of them asked in fright, 'Does this mean we might have to depend on a five-hundred-dollar toy to stay alive?'

'It's not a toy, but how much is your life worth?' replied Henner.

'At least five hundred, that's for sure,' smiled another woman in the next seat. 'And to think I just complained to our local Council about our rates going up nearly $500 in one year!'

A nearby man joined in. 'How about this? My income tax jumped up by over $4,000 last year. A higher tax bracket, they said.'

Cost-of-living discussions flew around until a schoolboy footballer on holidays slightly missed the point and sneered at them. 'All you oldies! Taxes? Rates? Is that all you lot care about? Greedy bastards! What about staying alive? I might live another seventy years or more if this el-cheapo device can tell the pilots our position. And even if it does, I'll bet that by tomorrow you'll all be moaning about the cost of lipstick or beer!'

That shut them all up. Thankfully, from overhead, the cabin crew were playing pleasant music throughout the aircraft; a kind of pre-crash *Muzak*, as the entertainer who called himself Dirty Dick had announced.

Not all was doom and gloom on board the big airliner. A section of economy class had produced this professional comedian who had a guitar and could play it quite well. Everyone soon heard that he was a seasoned performer; a notorious artist who played regular pub gigs throughout NSW and Victoria. His speciality was dark humour - a particularly apt theme right now.

A helpful crew member had handed him a microphone and his croaky voice came over the speakers. 'Now my name is

Captain Crash of Last Flight Airlines, and here's what I'm gonna play now before it's all too late:

"Strangers in my pants, what were my chances,
Lovers at first glance, forget about romances
When there's strangers in my pants,
Ouch! They're just little Fire ants!

'Okay, no romance in that one; so how about this?

"If I said you had a beautiful body,
Would you accept Visa card?"

Recently-fretting passengers gathered around to the sounds of the musical outbreak. Soon they were cheering and clapping to this welcome and refreshing diversion from their frightening future.

Dirty Dick continued his new-found stardom on Flight AA200. Twenty songs quickly followed.

"I just called – to say – I hate you,
Sorry, but you're fat n ugly as sin.
So, I just called to say I hate you . . .
Hell, sorry Mum, wrong number again!"

He's disgusting!' declared an unamused woman.

A man disagreed. 'No he's not. We need a break from all this morbid weeping and wailing. Let's go down enjoying ourselves!' Aghast, the woman reeled in horror: she hadn't the slightest intention of *going down* anywhere, let alone enjoying herself in the process. If she had to die then she was determined to do it in misery.

So Dick strummed away with a huge smile.

"That lady reckons I'm disgusting,

And maybe I damn-well am.

But certainly no worse than she is,

Who is actually a short ugly man! Oi!"

The crowd roared! If this was going to be an airborne party, then some of them were prepared to go out with a bang.

The laughter was heard far above them on the flight deck of the giant Boeing as it cruised in a home-seeking south-westerly direction while the eager second officer desperately fiddled with a Dick Smith GPS unit that had been originally bought for the bargain price of only $299.

'This is completely embarrassing,' Ray Cardin complained to Tom. 'I still can't believe we are betting our whole situation on this cruddy little piece of plastic.'

'Better than nothing, Boss. My fishing mates reckon these things are as good as commercial navigating equipment. Let's see what it does now.'

'Amateur fishing aids you mean, not navigating,' emphasised the boss man who forgot to mention that he owned one himself.

Tom attached the unit to an auxiliary power outlet and turned it on. Desperately hoping that it would instantly produce a magic answer to all their hopes and prayers, the hand-held set showed nothing but a jumbled screen of crazed numerals and jumping letters. Annoyed, Tom punched all its buttons but very little changed. After a restart, he tried again and watched another spaghetti of symbols and signs dance around the little screen. Of course, the thing was simply trying to do what it was programmed to do when booting up: locate and lock on to several satellites so its processors could calculate and display the current geographical position of the unit. Tom's eyes blurred as the racing screen data failed to show anything that could possibly resemble help.

'Hell! It's all Chinese to me,' Captain Ray Cardin was looking on and shook his head in frustration as F/O Roslyn Steinhouse refused to watch and stared fiercely ahead.

'Hold the damn thing right up against the windscreen,' Cardin ordered Tom. But nothing changed until the tiny screen started flashing BATT LOW!

Another entry gong sounded and friendly hostie Ayli Gorshe was admitted. 'Captain, I've got another one. And it seems that many of our passengers have some sort of GPS in their overhead locker. Anyway, this one is for aviation, according to the man who gave it to me. He flies one of those flimsy paragliding thingies . . . have you ever seen one?'

Cardin certainly had. He'd once taken a short paragliding joyflight off the hills at Mt. Tambourine in Queensland. He hadn't admitted to anyone that he mostly enjoyed it, but still remembered watching the flickering numerals on the miniature screen which said "ground speed 27 knots." The device had been casually taped to a small wing strut and the duct tape ends were flapping in the freezing wind. His pilot was aged just eighteen while Cardin told no-one that he was a jumbo jet captain.

Cardin took another unit from Gorshe. It was smaller and more compact than the one held by Tom. He closed his eyes and moaned: 'I just can't believe I am doing any of this. We're like a bunch of little boy scouts on a camping trip. And hell, this one is about as useful as an ashtray on a motorbike!'

Undaunted, the happy stewardess continued her sales pitch. 'And there's lots more I can bring up if you like,' boasted the smiling Ayli. 'Ah, should I go back and gather them all up, sir?'

Tom took over. 'Well, not yet thanks Ayli. Let's try this one first.' With renewed hope, he switched this new one on. "BATT LOW! BATT LOW!" its tiny screen flashed.

The captain raised his eyes to the ceiling and cursed: 'Bloody wonderful! Well, all we need now is to scour the entire plane for a battery charger that fits a . . . what is it . . . *Freedom* GPS for paragliders? Should I make a general announcement?'

Tom said, 'Hang on, Boss. Let's keep trying it first.' He flicked it to POS where it should display the position of the unit. The screen was blank for a few moments, then it said *Calculating, Calculating . . .* and then a minor miracle occurred! They all stared desperately at the tiny device as the following data blinked onto the screen:

03.13.27N – 178.05.24W - G/S 504 kts

Then, just as briefly, a disappointing warning rolled across the screen. *"Unit must be recharged before further use. Also, please update your software."*

Cardin barked at Tom. 'Quick, quick! Write those coordinates down! Then get on the floor and plot that fix on your oceanic charts *now*! It sounds like it could be right. If so, we are approaching the Equator and headed for the Kiribati Islands which is just about where we should be. And a ground speed of 504 knots sounds about right, too - considering our fuel burn-off after so many hours airborne.'

Tom dropped to the floor and scribbled desperately on his oceanic chart, while Roslyn Steinhouse remained quite sceptical. She asked: 'But how can that little gadget be receiving any GPS data when our multi-million-dollar Boeing's system can't?'

'Who cares, Ros?' grinned Tom. 'At least it's something. Anyway, looks like our ded-reckoning nav might be pretty hot 'n fancy, eh?'

Roslyn looked ahead out her windscreen. 'Possibly. But look! There are lights over there to the south-west. And lots of them, too. If that's Kiribati then I've never seen it with so many bright lights shining.'

Cardin said, 'Well, we're not dropping in there at midnight to say hello. Kiribas' little airport is not for our size, and it will be closed right now, anyway. Our weight would probably break right through their tarmac if we flopped down onto it . . . and also it's not an approved alternate airport.'

The crew gazed keenly at their first sight of any human habitation in nearly seven hours. Ayli Gorshe beamed as she asked, 'I'll run and tell people to look out the left-side windows, shall I?' No-one answered her as they digested this startling windfall of a possible air fix including a priceless ground-speed readout along with a known ground sighting. This was absolutely crucial information for ongoing navigation across a featureless night-time ocean: the world's largest.

After a while, Cardin glanced over at his F/O and said, 'So, do we trust this plastic toy or not?'

Ros twisted her face in indecision. 'Our management would be having pink kittens if they knew what we are up to.'

Cardin said, 'But our management will be cheering very loudly if we return this machine back to them in one piece. Now, all we need is a few more of these toys for cross-checking and triangulating our exact position. So Tom, based on that groundspeed, what is our ETA for Sydney now?'

'Ah, 04:46 Sydney time. Which is 18:46 Zulu.'

'Okay, that's not far off our earlier ETA announcement. Obviously we've been pushing against a few headwinds here and there.' Cardin was glowing with pleasure as he watched the brilliantly-lit Kiribati islands slide below the port wing. 'There must be some sort of festival in progress down there', he said to Roslyn. Anyway, no matter how they'd done it, they seemed to be back in business. He ordered the cabin crew to round up more good quality GPS units and rush them up to the flight deck. All pride was now set aside because the potential ceremonies upon their triumphant arrival would surely overshadow any embarrassing GPS disclosures.

While waiting for more toys to play with, the little *Freedom* was tried again, but nothing was displayed except: *'You must update the software before further use.'* Another unit warned:

This Garmin GPS Map 78 does not recognize the software. You must only use genuine Garmin software.'

Eager stewardess Ayli Gorshe soon arrived back on the flight deck; excitedly lugging a plastic bag full of GPS units.

Cardin smiled at her. 'Well thank you Ayli, but we really don't need that many . . . surely.'

But Ayli enthused, 'It seems that lots of travellers carry them today, sir. They're almost as popular as mobile phones. People were nearly *throwing* them at me. And I just couldn't believe how many different uses GPS's have. Apart from most cars having them these days, some drivers have them in their cars for rallies and many truckies use them in the Aussie Outback. RV drivers use them all the time for things like pig hunting and these days most keen sailors won't go out to sea without their precious GPS. And one couple told me they won't even untie their yacht from the marina's wharf without their unit because if someone falls overboard from their vessel they can simply hit the *MOB* button.'

'Man overboard!' coo-eed Tom. 'But what button do you press if it's a woman overboard?'

His humour was ignored as Ayli Gorshe pressed on. 'Also, sports fishermen mark their favourite reefs with GPS and speed boat racers use them to follow their designated course. Some long-distance runners carry them too. Bicycle racers and motor-cross bikers have one on their handlebars, while species of marine life have a GPS strapped to them for tracking purposes.'

Tom gave her a smile. 'Ayli, are you sure you aren't a GPS salesperson on commission? Perhaps you missed your real calling in life? '

Ayli Gorshe was so overjoyed in her conviction that she might possibly be the saviour of them all, that she continued bubbling on: 'And even some golfers use the GPS – although I don't know why. Then of course there's aviation where they are used in just about everything from tiny ultra-lights right up to charter planes and big things like this.'

She gulped momentarily at the ghastly display of blank screens in front of the pilots, then continued demurely. 'Ah, one passenger said he tracks the movements and breeding cycles of wildlife, and another tracks them to shoot them! One woman straps her GPS onto the backs of hawks and falcons - along with her GoPro HD camera, then, you guessed it, she uploads it all to YouTube!'

The captain's patience was expiring. 'Ayli, please!'

'And you just won't believe this, but some parents hide them under their kids' bikes or skateboards to spy on where they've been. But how about this - and promise you won't laugh - but some jealous husbands and wives track their partners' cars for obvious reasons. Other than that, most bush walkers carry GPS these days, while geologists and mineral explorers find GPS simply indispensable. And if you ever discover a secret gold mine you can secretely mark the exact spot for later. Finally, drones are all the new rage and they navigate by GPS all the time. If they get lost, they simply fly back and land at the exact spot they took off from . . . '

'Is that all?' Cardin interrupted. 'Now give it a rest, please Ayli. And in the meantime, do you happen to wonder what all those experts down the back are saying right now about our GPS-equipped jumbo jet? If their little units can track an armadillo to its nest, or spy on their skateboarding kid, then what must they be thinking about this sophisticated aircraft that basically hasn't known where the hell it is for over seven hours? We are being made to look like navigational clowns for some unfathomable reasons, yet we are among the highest-trained navigators in the world.'

The young stewardess looked deflated. 'Oh, I was just trying to help, sir. Sorry.'

'I greatly appreciate your enthusiastic efforts Ayli, and maybe one day you'll get a top job as a GPS salesperson, but right now our priority here is to find one that isn't low on battery charge and its software is up-to-date. I need a constant read-out, if I can, of every scrap of nav data that we can gather, so let's get to it!'

They upturned the bag on the floor. 'Damn,' cursed Tom. 'This one says the software is out of date and can't be used.' He took another. 'The battery is okay in this one but it won't show any data because the software is old and unusable. That's what the first one said, too.'

'It's just weird,' remarked Roslyn. 'These three all say that, too. So how can they all be out of date?'

Ray Cardin grumbled, 'And this one is probably as reliable as a politician's promise. We just fluked that one lucky fix but can't get just one more, even with multiple units. So, do we scour the plane again for every remaining GPS on board, or will they all display the same useless rubbish anyway?'

Tom Tyson said, 'I'm just amazed how so many people can be taking GPS's to America which all have out-of-date software. Anyway, it seems that these things all tend to divert to this same default warning if they can't lock on to anything.'

Roslyn asserted her authority. 'How many units have we tried here? Ten? Eleven? Tom, please go back downstairs and ask all those GPS aficionados if their units were working properly before they left, or were they getting software update warnings then. We don't need to locate every single one on board if most were working perfectly fine before departure because their basic problems must obviously be linked to the same as our own Nav platforms - which were also tested and working perfectly before our take-off.'

Tom left the flight deck just as Suzy Tayne entered with refreshments.

'How are all our customers, Suzy?' asked Roslyn.

Suzy smiled, "Oh, it's certainly very, ah, interesting back there. They're forming noisy little groups and pockets of common interests here and there. Some Christian woman is strumming a guitar and many are singing hymns with her. And that rude guy Dirty Dick is entertaining about fifty people - he's just so funny . . . Anyway, many are furiously studying bibles which have appeared

70

like magic, and a few couples are attempting to do you-know-what for maybe the last time. Also, kids are squealing and a baby is wailing while a few people are even sleeping despite the din of general uproar. Oh, one old Asian lady keeps repeating: "What is problem? What is problem? What time I get to America?" I don't know what to do for her. I try to help but she doesn't understand a thing.'

'Well, neither do we . . . mostly,' admitted the sinking ship's captain with unexpected honesty. 'So let's wait for Tom's report and keep that chart plotting going, everyone. We can only presume that our brief flash of lat and long co-ords was mostly correct and that rare fluke may have been the one and only fix we are going to get all night. If we don't steer ahead accordingly from that prime mark, then just what reliable start-point can we base any of our nav upon?'

Puffing from bounding up the stairs, Tom rushed back into the semi-lit room and announced, 'They all claim that they had new batteries before departure; and none of their units had been demanding software updates or flashing any warnings. Basically they derided anyone who would attempt hiking or kayaking these days with a dead or outdated GPS?'

Cardin was dismayed and slumped into gloominess again. Shite! Could eleven GPS units all be wrong simultaneously? Not likely. So, if they were all fine yesterday, and so was the 747's highly sophisticated and expensive nav platform, then there must have been a complete failure of the world-wide GPS satellite system. So, had world war broken out? Well, it was always a possibility because it had happened twice before, but would such a dramatic event have also destroyed the aviation world's entire communication and data link systems just after their particular flight took-off? Possibly.

Or was it something else? Something that only affected this aircraft and no others? Some invisible barrage of radiation that uniquely affected this plane by zapping many of its electronic components? Yet most of their internal electrical lighting was still working, the galleys were still cooking hot meals and cooling drinks and, most importantly, those four giant RB211 Rolls Royce jet engines outside in the dark night were still throbbing their ever-faithful roar; thrusting them through the atmosphere.

'Tom!' Cardin instructed. 'I need you to go back down again and ask the owner of that *Garmin GPS MAP-78* unit to come up here. I want to see him now, please.' Tom vaulted downstairs like a bloodhound after bait. In two minutes he had returned with a short and nervous man who sported a handlebar moustache.

'Er, Roger Tandy. You wanted to see me, captain?'

Cardin turned around and shook his hand. 'Pleased to meet you, Roger. I'm Ray Cardin. Is this your unit, Roger?'

Tandy confirmed that the small yellow GPS was his. 'Yes it is. But is anything the matter?'

'Well, as you might know, quite a lot of things are the matter just now. But I need to know if your unit has ever flashed any warnings about software updates before?'

'No.'

'Well, look at this,' Cardin turned the unit on and the sign illuminated again. *This Garmin GPS Map 78 does not recognize the software. You must use only genuine Garmin software.* 'So the question is this, Roger: have you changed the software in this thing to non-genuine Garmin stuff?'

'No.'

'So why would the thing be saying something like that? And why would all these others here also be referring to *old* or *outdated* software?'

Tandy replied, 'I have absolutely no idea, captain; I'm very sorry. I'm just the accountant at a ladies underwear factory. I never really conquered computer concepts at all – except for basic book-keeping. I was going to fossick around the Colorado River downstream from the Grand Canyon and hoped to stumble upon a few gold particles. I just needed to get away for a while because my lovely cat died and I'd had her for such a long time. Her name was . . .'

The small man looked quite frightened as he faced the stern jumbo jet commander of his flight. He seemed to be wondering if his tiny GPS could be the cause of this appalling disaster and their imminent demise.

Cardin said, 'Ah Roger, you may have missed my point. If you've never seen any such warnings before then none of this is your fault . . . of course.'

'I hope not' the now shocked accountant trembled. 'I'm just a book keeper.'

The captain continued, 'I'm merely trying to fill in the blanks, that's all. Thank you for your co-operation, Roger.' As the accountant left the flight deck, Cardin turned and asked 'What was the name of your cat, Roger?'

'Edna. We named her after Dame Edna Everidge.'

Cardin was about to say - but didn't: 'But *she* was a man.'

'What on earth was all that about?' asked Roslyn the irate F/O. 'Cats? Edna? Don't we have an emergency here to concentrate on? And if all these GPS owners haven't had any software warnings before, then how did they all suddenly become so old or out of date today? That man's GPS is saying his Garmin doesn't even recognise the software in it, but he claims he's never touched it. So I'm guessing that our equipment was affected likewise. Yes, these little GPS's just default to their standard warning notices, but whatever has happened out here tonight has suddenly outdated our airline's exclusive software at the same time. So, no-one's software is being recognised because it is all too old.'

The arguments became further confused as Cardin said, 'Old? We are always equipped with the very latest gear in the world, so how could it possibly be deemed as old? And anyway, it all worked perfectly when we pre-flighted the aeroplane. It was also perfect for our take-off and during the first twenty minutes of our flight. Are you inferring that all our vital gear suddenly aged during the twenty minutes after we left the ground?'

Roslyn didn't seem to know and turned to her 2/FO. 'Tom, what do you think?'

Tom rubbed his chin. 'Ah, it can't be just coincidence that lots of things went crazy just then. All those GPS units along with our own expensive gear all failing together? No chance. That's no coincidence. Default warnings I understand, but I don't really know what you're getting at when you talk about *old*. Electronics don't age like we do; they just get superseded by newer models.'

Cardin said, 'Well that's what I'm trying to say, Tom. That man's device always worked before but now his thing is warning him that the software inside it doesn't even exist. So it hasn't aged because it never existed – so far as the thing itself understands.'

Roslyn Steinhouse had finally had enough. 'Really, Ray!' She rarely called him by his first name, but added 'You're not offering any solutions here. At this particularly crucial time this flight needs all the rational and professional guidance it can get from its captain. Don't you agree?'

'Yes.'

'But now you are just waffling. Your job is to hold the plane and the whole crew together through any and all emergencies, isn't it? Now you're just guessing and seem spooked by some weirdo cat lover who's into ladies underwear.'

Cardin sneered at her. 'He's their bloody accountant, for Christ's sake! He doesn't wear the damn things . . . I hope . . . '

Tyson interrupted. 'Captain, I think what Ros is trying to say is that where you're heading is pretty, ah, weird. That is, if you don't mind me saying so, Boss. That man could easily have mistakenly shoved the SD card from his X-Box or camera into his GPS, and now the thing is saying that it can't recognise the software. Of course it can't. My little niece wrecked my camera by trying to force a bit of toast into the SD slot. And all those other units: how many people fail to ever recharge their batteries or update their device's software?'

'Tone it down please - everyone,' Cardin ordered. 'I'm just exploring all the theories and possibilities. So forget the undies man; what now?'

Behind him, Tom Tyson was dancing like a showgirl, lifting his shirt up and down, wiggling his backside and flashing his underwear. The first officer was cackling and, while Cardin didn't turn around, he mumbled, 'I'll be reporting you for disrespect after landing, Tom. You'll be on report. You're not funny.'

'Well someone has to be!' declared the first officer as she scanned her fifty-year-old instruments that whirred and sucked air; then turned to Tom, removed her microphone, and whispered: 'This is deadly serious but he's covering up because he's not sure what he's doing . . . '

6.

Anyone taking even a brief glance at a map of the vast Pacific Ocean might conclude that, after passing the Kiribati Islands area, there are numerous islands and communities dotted along a south-westerly heading towards the Australian mainland, while north of the equator there's not much apart from blue water – except for Hawaii. So, once south of the great hemisphere divider, one might think there are plenty of places to land a plane, if necessary. An observer might notice Tuvalu, the Solomons, Tonga, Fiji, Vanuatu and New Caledonia. Then there's Norfolk Island and, of course, New Zealand further south.

Unfortunately, you can't land large planes just anywhere, and if your plane is a very large Boeing-747, then only some of those locations have suitable airports for such jumbos to divert to - while many don't.

So, while a map of the Pacific Ocean may appear almost crowded with printed names, in reality the area is almost endless ocean; not much more than blue water dotted with occasional volcanic outgrowths sheltering humanity's societies. And late at night, a lost pilot would probably find most of the local airports closed for business, while the surrounding water is uninviting and, of course, inky black. Of course, such islands usually have navigation beacons for any lost pilot to rely on, apart from his own computerised NAV devices and platforms, but should he have none of these vital aids to navigation operating (like this flight) then he cannot safely contemplate landing at any of these places.

The reasons are many: if he'd been hopelessly lost, how would he now know with certainty which island he was approaching to land? If he could not positively identify the cluster of lights below him, it could be anywhere. It could be an airstrip made for light aircraft such as single-engined joy-flighting Cessnas, or small crop duster planes. Also, the navaid may signify an en-route beacon only and not an airport at all. And even if he saw illuminated runway lights ahead, he would have no knowledge of the length of the runway, its approved pavement strength, or of any other air traffic also approaching to land or taking off. Between late evening and dawn, most of these locations would have no air traffic controllers on duty and therefore no instrument landing systems (ILS) turned on. So any attempt to just 'drop in' in a 747 would be begging disaster - especially if the pilot is unable to transmit his intentions by radio.

But after this approaching sunrise, when this lost flight eventually arrives somewhere over the awakening Australian mainland and its vast east coast, and if the weather is kind, then many different things could occur. The plane could fly visually at lower altitudes along the coast until the pilots identify a familiar town or city. Australia's east coast is dotted with numerous population areas along its entire length. Once again, if the weather remains friendly and there's not too many low clouds around, pilots are trained from their very early flying days to ascertain which town is which by a few simple navigation tricks.

Should a place have a wide river mouth at its seaway with many islands upstream, it could be Yamba in NSW or maybe Ballina, but it's not Coffs harbour because there's no river there, just a creek. If a largish city appears with its river flowing out to sea and there's a huge spanned road bridge a few miles upstream, it would probably be Brisbane. Sydney Harbour would be even more readily identified. Conversely, if a small village has no harbour or river, then no lost jet should waste precious time seeking a landing area there. In such a case, the pilot needs only to decide if he should turn to run north or south along the coastline until some large airport eventually appears.

This last assertion may sound somewhat cavalier, but it's true. So let us imagine a large plane like AA200 running low on fuel and approaching an unknown place on the coast. The pilots can see a long and friendly runway in the distance but they are still manacled by radio silence. Even though their transponders are still squawking *Radio Failure,* no controllers are receiving these signals. Now, the pilots know very well that this airport would be surrounded by Controlled Airspace: a cocoon of cubic kilometres where every plane, both large and small, requires special airways clearances to fly within it, so what can they do? If sunny skies prevail they might very gingerly enter the control zone while watching carefully for any conflicting air traffic, then hopefully fly along the length of the runway at 500 feet with undercarriage and flaps lowered – right in front of the control tower! Of course the controllers will be thunderstruck if an unknown 747 suddenly zooms above their main drag, but they will easily read *AIR AUSTRALIA* painted along its side.

'Air Australia?' they might yelp. 'What are they doing here? They never called us. We have no flight plan. Press the CCC (Common Crash Call) button!' Then someone will quickly decide, 'It's obviously that missing flight AA200. There's a Distress phase on it. They lost all comms and must have turned back to Australia. Now they're here. And with their gear and flaps down: that means they want to land. '

'Of course they want to land!' the tower supervisor will undoubtedly confirm. 'Flash our lights at them.'

Like road traffic lights, control towers have their own powerful hand-held signalling lights to flash at planes with radio failure. RED = don't land. Flashing GREEN = continue approach. Steady GREEN = clear to land. And that's what will happen. The pilots will welcome the strong beams suddenly glaring from the tower so they will fly a lengthy final approach to the longest runway that is facing into wind, then watch for the steady green light. Even with no NAV equipment or communications, and down to their very last dregs of fuel, their nightmare will finally be over.

This was the scenario the three Air Australia pilots were hoping and planning for with great optimism. Although it was still too dark to try this in their present oceanic region, in the morning they would descend visually to perhaps two thousand feet, wait for the Aussie coastline to appear, then follow the above plan of action.

'All is not lost . . . far from it,' their captain boldly declared over his light breakfast. 'Just a few more hours of dark remaining, then we'll all be home safe and sound.' But not everyone on the deck agreed – particularly his two assistant pilots.

Down the back of AA200, the loudspeakers were blaring more of Dirty Ditty Dick's musical recitals:

What would you do if I sang out of tune,
Would you pour your beer all over me?
What could I say if your wife ran away . . .

Soon Dick had plenty of competition: not just the Bible choristers, but now some Aboriginal passengers had actually produced a didgeridoo. With everyone trying to drown each other out, the haunting thwump-thwump-thwump of the *didge* had many people mesmerised. Luckily, surprising amounts of alcohol had recently been discovered in overhead lockers, with the consequence of the cabin crew gradually losing control of the passengers while the giant plane became an airborne festival of entertainment and mild debauchery. Whether such light decadence might escalate any further remained to be seen, but when humans are facing their imminent deaths they are often tempted to do a bit more than meekly re-arrange the deck chairs.

Too worried about their own lives, the cabin crew had long since given up policing the customers as they usually did. So, instead of the usual refereeing of silly squabbles over seat-back angles or arguing with belligerent personalities, they joined in and let the plane become a free-for-all party scene in a crazy pantomime of song and dance. They discovered that it is possible to dance in the twin aisles of jumbo jets once everyone is doing it. And anyway, who wants to be staid, boring or depressed for maybe their very last living hours when they can be occupied, exuberant and entertained? For, despite their captain making numerous re-assuring announcements about their progress of visually flying the jumbo back to somewhere in Australia, and even though Roger Tandy had assured some of them that he had personally met the captain who was really very nice, most people reluctantly realised that their number was probably up and proceeded accordingly: sex, drugs and rock 'n roll.

Adding more fun, a box of party balloons was found when an enterprising crew member snuck down in the elevator to the lower cargo deck where she also uncovered crates of Bourbon, whisky and other assorted goodies. It had already been a long night and now it was likely to become much longer. Then the sudden re-appearance of the popular Second Officer Tom Tyson was welcomed by all as he was overwhelmed with several indecent proposals from various inebriated ladies. Regrettably unable to accept any of the drinks thrust at him - let alone the proposals, he nevertheless enjoyed the party as best he could.

Eventually Tom remembered his latest instructions. Over shouted conversations, he continually tried to sell the official line that they were on track to a triumphant return home "soon."

A joyous lady gripped his arm and slobbered over him, 'You're such a handsome boy in that fancy uniform; how come your daddy let you out to play?'

The artful dodger smiled as he skated around the question, 'We got a positive fix! We really did. It was like finding a giant signpost in the middle of the ocean, but this time it was from someone's tiny GPS unit. It only lasted a few seconds but that was enough to plot our way home by old-fashioned deduced navigation.'

'Did someone say seduced?' slurred a vivacious young model from Melbourne. 'I wish someone would do that to me.' In response, an obliging man grabbed her from behind and she squealed.

'No, *deduced*!' laughed Tom as more music suddenly blared from a beat box. This time it was Rap music and half the crowd yelled 'turn it off!' while the other half roared 'turn it up!' Then a banjo was produced and a very talented girl started a new free concert somewhere near row 30. She was soon drowned out by a self-appointed DJ who grabbed a P.A. phone and announced 'Okay y'awl; let's dance the trance in yer underpants!'

Eventually Tom made it back up the stairs and onto the flight deck. Here there was no debauchery, just sombre faces and an icy atmosphere between the two pilots. Roslyn turned around and her eyes bulged. 'Tom! One side of your hair is red with rouge! And you've got lipstick all down your shirt!'

His captain was, as The Queen often says, not amused. 'That will look just great on your report, won't it Tom? And what the hell is going on downstairs? An end-of-the-world party? We can hear it all the way up here.'

Tom tried to defend his new friends. 'It's, ah, rather crowded down there. Noise? It's just the mob having fun, I suppose.'

'Well it sounds like they're all drunk!'

Roslyn stated that it made a fresh change from the usual coffin-like silences of midnight flights where snores were the only sounds ever heard above the outside airstream rushing past the fuselage.

Ignoring her, Ray Cardin reiterated their plan of action for when the coastline approached. 'Now listen up, we've all flown VFR up and down the east coast many times. It may have been years ago on your navex training but we should still have sufficient memories of it. Also, I flew VFR every day up in Papua New Guinea for two years. There, the wild terrain and low cloud keeps you right up on your toes, I can assure you. So, in case we still have no comms or nav, I intend to commence descent from this flight level down to about two thousand feet – weather permitting, starting at an estimated distance of 150 nautical miles from the coast. We will descend visually at all times if possible. So far, the approaching sunrise is showing not too much cloud ahead, but if we enter IMC then we'll descend to no lower than eight thousand before considering any further options.'

Roslyn Steinhouse shivered at those stark words *IMC*; you just can't fly IFR in IMC without instruments. Just as a brain surgeon can't operate without his instruments, flying a plane in Instrument Meteorological Conditions would herald a total disaster in their currently crippled predicament. It means 'in clouds, or other such limited visibility' – an horrendous thought for any flight with virtually no means of navigation nor communications with the ground. If this dark spectre eventuated, they may as well jump out the windows right now and be done with it. Yes, they still had their gyro-driven artificial horizons and a few other analogue instruments such as vertical speed and turn-and-bank, but to proceed into IMC when you're not even certain where is *Australia* is expecting just a little too much from Lady Luck.

"Wish we had our weather radar,' mused Tyson.

'Its software is probably out of date,' grumbled the F/O.

Cardin sighed, 'Yes, but if it *was* working the MFD (Multi-function Display) would clearly show the approaching coastline, along with river mouths and other topographical features that we usually see. You know, it still leaves me bereft why so much primary gear has completely let us down tonight. Just take that weather radar for starters: its source is not coupled with any other component; it is supposed to be completely independent. And so are all our data screens. They are all installed with no common links except that they happen to be sitting in the same damned aeroplane. So how can so many million-dollar platforms all die together? We've been right through all the possible scenarios, haven't we, but I still think that a giant solar flare hit us and knocked us for six. And even if it was that, what could we do about it? If our gear is frizzled then it's frizzled! Roslyn, what do you think now?'

"Well, remember much earlier in the night I told you that someone transmitted that we had "completely disappeared from Earth." You hated that, but why did they say that?'

Cardin said, 'It was just some nutty ham radio operator. But they didn't announce that all planes had disappeared from Earth, they only said that *we* had. So how did they know that unless everyone out there was calling us for hours with no reply?'

Roslyn felt her anger rising again. 'Of course everyone was calling us. They have a SAR phase on us. We took off then just disappeared. But it was still a weird thing to say. Many flights lose comms over the passage of a year but no-one ever broadcasts and asserts that they've disappeared from the planet Earth. And if we were hit by solar flares, then why wasn't all other air traffic affected similarly?'

Cardin sighed. 'This is just getting us nowhere. Someone might have transmitted something about something. So bloody what?'

Tom asked, 'Well, if we did have a comms failure, then how did we hear that broadcast when we haven't heard another thing all night."

'I don't damn-well know yet, do I?' Cardin yelled at them.

Roslyn glared at the captain once more. 'And after two hours without comms, we should have simply turned back - as I said before, Ray. Anyway, I have written my objections in the aircraft log book.'

Cardin barked, 'I don't bloody-well care if you've written a new version of *War and Peace* in the goddamned log book! I made my decision and proceeded accordingly.'

'Based on what?'

'I've had previous outages . . . '

'For how long?'

'Look, at the time we were too damn heavy to go back and land. You should know that!'

Roslyn argued, 'We should have returned westwards and dumped fuel along the way. If necessary we could have orbited and dumped even more. I asked you about that but you were too mesmerised by all this solar flare mumbo-jumbo.'

'It doesn't bloody-well matter now, Roslyn! We've burnt up all that excess fuel now, and when we get back we'll have a near perfect all-up landing weight.'

'Yes, meantime we've blown half a million dollars worth of the company's precious jet fuel on this ghostly joyride right around the Pacific Ocean in today's times of critical fuel conservation and rising global fuel prices.'

Cardin turned red and yelled at her. 'Now listen here my girl: just who the hell are you now? The company's chief friggin' accountant? Will you have to pay back this precious jet fuel out of your own damn wages?'

Roslyn screamed back at him. 'Don't you dare *my girl* me! I am not anybody's *girl*! And don't call me *my dear Roslyn* either.'

Tom bravely interrupted this latest flare-up. 'Whoa! Hey, excuse me everyone, but we're still not working together as a team, are we? Part of my job is to act as a go-between and a mediator in cases of dissent in the front row. I'm the junior officer here but also the third vote if we face extreme discord. I have peaceful suggestions to make but you two won't stop attacking each other.'

Cardin turned around and screwed up his face. 'Alright Mr United Nations Peacemaker, ask that friggin' army SAS guy to come up here. He knows how to resolve any confrontation: he just blows the crap out of everything!'

Tom pleaded. 'Please, let's just ease up a little. Look out there, the horizon's getting lighter. Not long to go now. Let's sign a peace treaty and we can all laugh about this when get interviewed on the Midday Show.'

'Can I be on it too?' smiled Roslyn.

Grumpy Cardin grunted. 'Yeah, yeah, and happy days will be here again. In the meantime we need to agree, if possible, on plan-B in case we don't stay visual on the descent. If still in cloud, then eight thousand is my lowest limit because no terrain is higher than that anywhere in Australia; but after that we have to let down all the way sooner or later, don't we? I suppose it's a bit like going to the toilet: sometime it eventually just *has* to be done.' Roslyn almost gagged at his crude analogy, but she and Tom nodded.

'Okay. So, if stuck up at eight thousand we need a positive fix over some town,' said the captain. 'Even if we have to fly inland all the way to Ayers bloody Rock to see the ground, we do it. Once it's identified we check our WAC charts and note the elevation. Then we continue in VMC - hopefully, to below eight thousand feet and follow roads and railway lines if we have to – just like in the old days!'

This would certainly be an aviation first for a Boeing-747 to descend over an Australian rural region and ascertain its name by identifying a local feature, then charge off towards the next grain silos along the wheat line. But Sir Charles Kingsford-Smith did all that a century ago, and so did Bert Hinkler. The trail-blazing Smithy also conquered the mighty Pacific using mostly ded-reckoning while rain poured in his open window. That was the way of the past and in these days such primitive rural navigation might need someone to watch out for flying drones, not crows.'

'Happy, everyone?' asked Cardin. 'No more dissention. So, just repeating, if we don't see land at our estimation of the coastline, we don't descend below eight thousand feet but continue west. Eventually we *must* see some land - unless we've really drawn the short straw. But when we see something, we pop down and do what we've just agreed: VFR flying all the way back to the coast and then to some airport big enough for us to put down – somewhere. If there's no suitable airport anywhere then I suppose I'll just have to put us down in Farmer Jones' paddocks because it *must* be done sometime and somewhere – as I said earlier. Any questions?'

Tom joked, 'What goes up must come down, eh?' The flight deck fell silent, then Tom grinned: 'Old farmer Jones might be used to crop dusters zooming past his barn at ten feet, but he might be slightly surprised if a Boeing-747 suddenly touches down among his scattering stock. Let's hope he's got long paddocks . . . '

After a silence Cardin added, 'However, we're most unlikely to fluke it and simply pop out of the haze and there, lo and behold, lies the beautiful city of Sydney dead ahead, and with its vacant 13,000-foot runway just waiting to embrace us. But we turned around half-way across the ocean in some God-forsaken twilight zone and high-tailed it all the way back to here, so I reckon we definitely deserve a break at some damn stage.'

Tom laughed. 'Maybe not. It could be like the old sailing days, Boss. Many of them believed that if they sailed too far they might sail right off the edge of the Earth! They even had maps with printed warnings saying: "Here there be dragons!" '

'Thank you Tom for that invaluably optimistic contribution. Meanwhile, I assure you there won't be any dragons but let's just hope that some slick navigating finds us reasonably close to our planned track.'

Tom smiled, 'If that happens then it will be the greatest feat of aerial navigation since Santa Claus delivered dissolving bikinis to the Playboy bunnies!'

Roslyn laughed. 'Now that really *was* funny.'

Even the captain chuckled. 'I've never heard of dissolving bikinis,' he smiled at them, then added seriously: 'Speaking of bikinis, we will all sink or swim together in this, as you know - and all those behind us, too.'

Tom added, 'But if we do make it, most of them won't even remember that they were lost. They'll be too drunk to know if they were in Oodnadatta or Parramatta!'

Business class stewardess Janine Hilary was discovering that not all on the plane's manifest were partying like there was no tomorrow. Far from it; Mrs Cheng Xingu, an eighty-year-old Chinese grandmother, was beside herself in grief over her own uncertain destiny. Sounds of raucous celebration coming from all around her merely added to her confusion and distress, while Hilary could think of nothing to alleviate the woman's misery. It was hard enough for Janine, with a lump in her throat, to contemplate what might happen to herself quite soon, let alone to maintain a professional smile for this stranger in what may be everyone's final hours. Janine's priority was her one-year-old son back in Melbourne, and her loving partner who was at home babysitting for the five days she'd be away. Before her departure, he had begged her yet again to give away this modestly-paid *air hostessing* as he called it, and become a full-time mother to their baby who cried every time she was away. She could almost hear her little boy wailing now, just like this old lady before her, and she cursed her puzzling insistence in defying her partner's repeated and justifiable pleas.

Janine muttered to herself that the teary-eyed woman knew no English, so she spoke aloud: 'Just why on earth am I fretting over any of my passengers at all when I really should be spending what may be my last chances to hold my lovely baby's photo and pray?' But perhaps the woman *did* understand what she'd said because, in response, she pulled several family photos from *her* bag and thrust them at Janine. Janine glanced at some unknown Asian children smiling at a candle-lit birthday party.

'I don't know them and I just don't care about them,' she muttered in selfish misery. 'They will live for another eighty years and I won't. I just want to hold my baby again!' The attractive stewardess burst into tears but the Chinese lady thought that this kind stewardess was actually concerned for *her* grandkids. The old lady hugged Janine and thanked her profusely.

It was a confused world on AA200 this long and agonising night where the sweating and frightened crew weren't the only bewildered souls on board. In First Class, businessman Rod Appleby was the wealthy owner of a Great Barrier Reef game fishing outfit. They operated ten luxury cruisers with overnight five-star accommodation for seriously rich marlin hunters. 'Yes Stuart, business sure is booming', he explained to his fellow traveller. "Fifteen thousand bucks a week is no problem to some of our customers. So I'm doing really well . . . at least I was.'

Stuart Rhys was a physics scientist with Australia's CSIRO. 'I've never caught a fish in my life, Rod,' he smiled. 'But I hope to retire soon, so how much for a half-day out on one of your luxury launches?'

'Free for you – if we ever get out of this . . . ' Appleby forced a grin. 'So what do you think might happen to us, Stuart?'

The scientist rubbed his chin, deep in thought. 'Absolutely no idea, I'm afraid. I've spent my life developing chemicals for crop spraying with pesticides, etc. Then I went into Biology and now Particle Physics. But I can't even fly a kite, let alone one of these enormous things. I just hope and trust that these pilots will know what to do in these awful circumstances. They are professionals, as we are, and should be trained for all eventualities. Surely they must have emergency checklists to guide them through any contingencies. We certainly had them aplenty in case of chemical spills or explosions in our labs.'

Rod Appleby sighed, 'Well, I know nothing much about flying either, so I'm of no help to anyone. We're just helplessly at these pilots' mercies - like newborn babes, really. Even though we often work with the Reef's helicopters when they ferry customers out to us, I have no idea how a chopper stays up in the air - let alone this monstrous thing.'

Rhys replied, 'Anyway, in the final analysis I suppose some consolation is that the two of us have been pretty clever, haven't we? I mean to get where we are in life?'

'I started out with nothing,' boasted a proud Appleby.

'And my parents owned a greengrocer's shop,' said Rhys. 'I was the only person from our whole family tree to ever get into university.'

Appleby countered, 'The only fish I ever handled were the flathead that I sold on our jetty at weekends. And some of them I had to steal from the nearby fish shop because we never had any money. Now I've got millions because I worked damn hard, but just where has that got me now? I'm sixty-five and should be allowed a few more luxury years before I toddle off, don't you agree?'

The scientist thought deeply. 'Allowed? I'm not sure if we are automatically *allowed* anything. If you are sixty-five then that's many more years than lots of people get. Some humans die when they are just infants. Lots more die in wars. We all have an allotted life span and maybe our spans have now been reached. And anyway, we are all living much longer than humans once did. Did you know that the average age that Australian men died in the year 1900 was just 51?'

'So, should I be happy and grateful that I'm 65 and on this death ship right now?'

Rhys laughed, 'No, but we should be feeling privileged that at least we're riding in the Death Ship's First Class!'

Appleby grinned, 'Oh goody: I'm going to die in First Class! Much more preferable than dying in Business Class . . . and certainly an absolute *joy* compared to the sardines in Economy!'

The scientist tried to smile. 'So Rod, what the heck can we possibly *do* about this awful hell that we're in? Just go down with the ship?'

'Demand refunds on our tickets, that's what we can do!' This caused hearty bursts of laughter as a few despondent passengers glanced over to wonder what could possibly be considered even remotely humorous at this wretched hour. Then Appleby asked, 'Hey Stu, are you religious - although I suppose it's too late now?'

Stuart Rhys replied, 'Nah, it's incompatible with science . . . much like trying to mix Nitro with Glycerine.'

94

7.

'What's the latest from military radar, Harry?' asked the Sydney SOC controller.

His assistant checked his data readout again. 'Well, nothing significant. Our RAAF say they've got some spurious paints out to sea here and there, but, as you said hours ago, if all those engine transponders went off the air at the same time then we know what must have happened. And if they miraculously happen to be still airborne somehow, then they're way out in the eastern Pacific – God knows where. My guess says wreckage might be found one day washed up somewhere south-east of the Hawaiian Islands - bearing in mind that hardly any positive wreckage from Malaysian 370 has been discovered after several years.'

'But Harry,' the SOC persisted, 'I still hold hope that Ray Cardin might have pushed on to Hawaii. I know him and we had a barbecue at his place recently. They've got a little baby. I just know that Ray is strong-headed and persistent, even though he's in a flying ghost ship if neither he nor his plane has sent out any signals all night. Yes, the US airforce might pick up their primary paint, but it would just be a green blob with no associated data on their screens. But can you imagine such an unknown target rapidly approaching Hawaii or the US mainland like that? A radar paint travelling at jet speeds but refusing to answer any calls or transmit any ID data at all. This is the part that worries me. Even if interceptors flew beside them and saw it was Air Australia, how would they know that the 747 wasn't under the command of a dozen hijackers with bombs and whatever else? Yes it's a nightmare, but I still feel that somehow Ray might barge his way through.'

'Okay Sam, so if they're still airborne then it sure has been a long night for them. But what reception could they expect if they've headed back towards Australia? Our own RAAF is on high alert just in case. What would your mate Cardin do then? Head for his home-town Sydney to land here in total radio silence?'

'Hmm, the airspace is way too busy around here; especially around mid-morning. But I doubt he would have the fuel to about-turn over the eastern Pacific and make it back to here.'

Well, if he *does* happen to turn around, where else in Australia could he put that thing down apart from Sydney?'

'Well, Brisbane, I suppose. Amberley is quite long – but that's military. Then there's the new airport near Toowoomba; it can take 747's. But when do our guys run out of fuel?'

Harry Felds jotted down a few figures. 'In about four hours. Of course, just exactly where they find themselves at that awful moment will depend on any headwinds encountered during the night. Strong winds could easily prevent them from ever reaching the coast at all.'

'Do you think their NAV displays are still working? If not, can they possibly know where they are?'

The SOC, Sam Hughendon, scratched his beard. 'Hmm, basic analogue navigating? It's possible, I suppose. But if their screens are still working then they should have landed in Fiji or maybe New Zealand long ago and our data links would be alive with the tales of their survival. It's just this damn total silence that's killing us – killing everyone. The world's media and the families left behind are screaming for facts and official statements from me, but I don't have a single fact, good or bad, to offer them.'

'At least we haven't lied and covered up to compound wishful guesswork like the Malaysian disappearance. By the way, I suppose attempts have been made to contact the passengers' mobile phones and laptops?'

'I have an officer co-ordinating all that, but nothing has been received yet – just silence. If they suffered a massive electronics failure within the plane then it's possible that all the passengers' gizmos went down as well. But it's all just guesswork and has left us completely stumped while the awful truth is that this doomed flight has probably vanished.'

The assistant SAR co-ordinator, Harry Felds, looked glum. So many safety improvements had been made to airliners worldwide since the 2014 dramatic and tragic disappearance of Malaysian MH-370 over the Indian Ocean that authorities today, such as the international aviation governing body ICAO, were confident that such a disaster should never recur. These innovations were essential because surely nothing could be worse than bereaved families being unable to retrieve the remains of their missing loved ones because they don't know where they are. In fact, in the case of MH-370, no-one is even sure in which *ocean* the remains might lie.

But despite the best plans and finest intentions of many, this scenario certainly had recurred. Sam Hughendon was the Senior Operations Controller in charge of all this and was now facing the gnawing spectre that AA200 would join MH-370 in becoming another frustrating aviation mystery where nothing was ever found and unbridled speculation was all that remained.

Just then, another SAR officer rushed into the Search centre to dramatically announce: 'There's been a development!'

Sam Hughendon spun around in surprise. 'Really? What?'

'They're not all dead - at least they weren't dead seven hours ago. Not sure about right now, though. Anyway, a smart computer hacker who won't reveal his identity has contacted authorities in India about an email he intercepted seven hours ago . . . '

'India? Hell! And seven hours ago?'

'Well, he's a hacker and they don't normally rush into the public arena with revelations of their tools of trade for all to see. Anyway, apparently he's some Indian computer geek who hacked into a brief email that appeared to emanate from the southern Pacific Ocean about seven hours ago . . . '

Paul Sarange paused for emphasis, then blurted out,' It said: "The service on this airline is okay, I suppose, but this weird old woman next to me said that our plane is lost and is going to crash! I hate crazy people like that, but what can you do when you're plonked next to them for hours?" '

After a silence, Sam asked, 'Is that all? And just how does this hacking genius know that the message came from AA200?'

'How do they know anything? They hack it, that's how.'

'So why did he sit on this all night before releasing his news?'

'I suppose at the time he didn't know that any planes in the world had gone missing.' Hughendon digested this speculative and flimsy information that was probably more GIGO: garbage in, garbage out, with which the www world-wide-web can be infamously awash; i.e. many of the mountains of web rumours are true, while many are not. But in this case: which was correct?

Sam consulted his assistant and many others on his hotlines that were relayed by satellites around the world. Then he decided, 'If any of this is true, this unknown passenger's email was intercepted by some Indian of doubtful authenticity who illegally hacks emails. Why should I place credence in him? And just who was the email sender anyway? There must be an email address that can be traced. And how could they send emails at all if they were suffering some communications blackout? Here in this very room there are some busy times when I can't send or receive any emails myself because it says "Cannot contact server. Please try again later." Ha, at least they say please. But anyway, the real significance is this: it means that the timing of the message, if genuine, is crucial. It means that this flight was still airborne for some hours after its departure and they didn't crash into the ocean after all. Do you agree, Harry.'

'Yep.'

'Okay, if that's the case, then just where the hell are they now? And why haven't they used their satellite phone to call in?'

Harry looked glum. 'It's here being repaired.'

But the email remained a puzzler. Hours of eager investigations ensued in various parts of the world to obtain more information about this curious email, but the hacker had gone to ground; selfishly more concerned about concealing his online whereabouts than assisting grieving families to locate their lost loved ones.

Outside Sydney's Search and Rescue Centre, a bustle of media journalists jostled with cameras and microphones to harvest any morsel of news from whoever was brave enough to pass by. Most walkers ignored them, but a lone university student was eager to face the press and declared with sincerity that aliens from the planet Krypto had enveloped the missing jumbo and simply "taken it away."

'But where to?' barked the reporters. 'And why? And just where is Krypto, anyway?'

'Up there!' explained the young woman as she pointed skywards. 'Do you think I'm stupid? They've been taken back to Krypto. It's simply common knowledge . . . '

Watching from nearby was a group of three worshippers who shivered in the cold dawn air while holding up signs that said, 'IF IT IS GOD'S WILL THEN IT MUST BE ACCEPTED' and 'THE DEVIL ALWAYS WELCOMES SINNERS.'

Sam Hughendon looked out his window and shook his head in contempt. 'Look at that! I wonder just exactly what wicked sins those innocent passengers and crew onboard AA200 have committed? Business people, ordinary workers off to the US for a holiday; students, parents, little kids, babies . . . Apparently it is

God's will that some people must die in terror as they plunge into the sea at over five hundred knots!'

But Sam still wondered about that eerie email? Passengers must send thousands of messages via satellites from en-route planes. Many of them would be routine or trivia, and some might be sheer silliness like: "Oh my God, we're gonna crash! Only joking . . . no we're not."

Travel is customarily quite boring on long-distance flights, especially on this route from Sydney to Los Angeles which is one of the world's longest non-stop flights and usually takes over thirteen hours. Often it can be even longer on the return journey because of prevailing headwinds from the west called the Jetstream. To relieve some of the tedium, travellers tap on their electronic devices to amuse themselves. So: was this email sender also fooling around, or was he or she unknowingly transmitting the last distress message from inside an unexpected communications cocoon – a Twilight Zone? In truth, the message could have come from any one of ten thousand flights criss-crossing the world at that very time. Hughendon reminded himself of the astonishing fact that at any one time, and on any day of the year, there are more than *one million* people up in the air.

8.

As with many headline stories, they often originate as media leaks. No matter how secure, high-interest stories usually manage to leak out to the public. While some may trickle out over months, like the Watergate scandal or the Lindy Chamberlain case, others positively burst forth onto the public who are always eager for the latest *goss*.

And along came the case of AA200 which - like blaring trumpets - woke everyone in their morning news with horrific headlines about *Australia's Death Flight!* Then, even more spectacularly: *Desperate email plea from doomed passenger!*

The fact that the email in question merely said "This weird woman next to me said that our plane is lost and is going to crash" was awarded little attention by journalists. Firstly, the person referred to was probably described accurately as *weird,* but the media omitted that word. Secondly, it didn't say that the email writer asked any official crew for corroboration of the claims, and lastly, the writer said that he/she remained stuck beside this weirdo for hours – and again the word "weirdo" was substituted with "person." Nevertheless, all of Australia and indeed the world, now knew that Uncle Joe or little Daisy's plane was a *death flight* and that it was undoubtedly lost because the media had solemnly declared that it was. Quietly in the background, however, no tabloid dared mention that the email might have been faked or could have come from any point on the entire globe.

Nevertheless, the plane in question was definitely missing so the public was blowtorched with non-stop coverage of this prime-time saga as TV hosts adopted appropriately glum faces, repeating endlessly how everyone on board AA200 had by now plunged - or *plummeted* - at supersonic speeds into the very depths of the vast Pacific Ocean. And despite two official denials and statements of caution from senior aviation officials like Sam Hughendon, the whole public now knew differently and joined the nationwide commotion about "officialdom and its transparent cover-ups." Consequently, repeated scenes of grieving family members outside the Air Australia departures terminals in Sydney and Melbourne were enthusiastically shown in favour of scheduled advertisements.

'How do you feel?' prompted a young TV reporter who'd located a wretched woman crying because she'd probably lost her whole family. But the woman was unable to answer through tears, so the journalist pounced again. 'But how do you feel? Really bad, eh?'

Still getting no answer, the reporter turned to the camera. 'Yes, she feels really, really bad!' Following this, an ad could not be ignored any longer so the screens flashed to a commercial for dog food that apparently "keeps Fluffy happy all day!"

Far away, and over a distant ocean of pitch black, on a plane which the world believed had definitely crashed (even though its fuel load had not yet been exhausted), the on-board party on AA200 continued without pause.

An elderly Salvation Army couple had retrieved their tambourines from *above* and were jiggling them in time to *Nearer to God are we,* while a few rows away Dirty Dick competed with a seemingly bottomless reservoir of his own joyous hymns for the masses.

> *Oh I met an ugly dancing lady,*
> *And she was rather fat,*
> *I said I'd rather kiss your dog*
> *But she said here's my cat! Oi !*
> *Then our pilot said that we're not lost,*
> *We're headed for Australia*
> *But now it's all a hell of a mess,*
> *And a great big bloody failure!*

A crew member was recording the entertainment and conveyed it up to the flight deck for approval. 'Such coarse but accurate tributes to the chequered tapestry of life,' remarked the real captain who was naturally pre-occupied with saving the souls of all those brave humans behind him, and, not the least, himself.

'Well, at least they're having fun,' remarked Tom the second officer. 'Better than armed insurrection, I suppose.'

'Wish *we* were having fun,' rued Roslyn Steinhouse, glancing at Tom who had finally changed his lipstick-smudged shirt.

Roslyn was seated in the jump seat behind the pilots, rubbing her aching neck. She'd spent a large part of the night manually steering this great ship of the air under a star-filled sky using primitive ded-reckoning navigation - or *dead* reckoning, as some insist on spelling it. Of course, she'd had great assistance from the mighty auto-pilots and therefore didn't always have to struggle with the control wheel using raw muscle power alone, but auto pilots always some need human input to feed them a compass direction to maintain, otherwise any auto-pilot will dumbly steer a plane straight into a mountainside if that's how the human in control sets it.

World aviation disaster records reveal numerous ugly examples of such blunders over the history of manned flight. Too many pilots have fallen asleep and never known why they suddenly ceased to exist when their auto-pilot dutifully steered them straight into unyielding objects like mountains or high terrain – and often at speeds of two or three hundred knots. In 1979, a sightseeing Air New Zealand DC-10 flew at 240 knots straight into the ice-covered slopes of Mt Erebus; a 12,000-foot active volcano in Antarctica. The pilots weren't asleep but wide awake and, incredibly, dangerously far below their lowest safe altitude.

Worse, they were blissfully ignorant of the sudden and deadly *white-out* phenomenon that can occur on that great iced continent, and failed to see the approaching mountain right in front of them. When their GPWS ground proximity warning system suddenly claxoned *Pull up! Pull up!* they didn't leap into startled action but the captain casually ordered "Go round power, please.' A quaintly polite but futile request considering that all 239 persons on board the jet were dead just four seconds later.

In the current case of Air Australia flight 200, manual pilot input to the auto-pilot was absolutely crucial because they had no source of electronic data to generate a flight path. Even though they had mostly flown at 39,000 feet all night - and this was easily high enough to avoid all the highest terrain in the world, auto-pilots are still basically dumb – as starkly illustrated in the previous paragraph. In this case, just a one degree error in AA200's magnetic heading for the whole night could result in the plane drifting hundreds of miles off course - and all while the auto-pilot (and human pilots) might merrily think that it was doing a grand job. So Tom's manual chart plotting, along with Ray Cardin's constant assistance, plus the one quick fix they obtained from that cheap GPS unit was all utilised together to help Roslyn guide the plane.

'And don't forget the magnetic variation, Tom,' Cardin ordered.

But now Roslyn had steered enough and her eyes were becoming blurry. She slumped in the back seat. Modern airliners were never engineered to be flown manually without the elaborate Nav systems with which they are equipped. Only small, light planes can be hand-flown for a few hours here and there because their relatively modest speeds don't allow them to wander too far off track. But the faster they travel, the more off-track they will quickly become. A vehicle driving at 100km/h will quickly go a lot further astray in the bush than another one doing

50km/h; so a plane doing 930 km/h is obviously a wild card indeed.

Roslyn performed more muscle stretching exercises until her latest headache abated. She rubbed her forehead and thought of all her friends back in Melbourne and her parents in rural Victoria. She'd had a few male friends over the years, but none just at the moment. Now it might be too late. Her frequent absences from home had ensured that any relationships were usually brief and fractured. Most international airline pilots lead disruptive home lives where wives, partners, children and friends exist only in temporary spurts in which any bonding is regularly fractured upon each departure.

Roslyn had initially decided to enrol in university after high school and felt her path in life should be in education. She considered it only fair that she should teach, just as others had taught her. But one weekend at the age of sixteen she went flying in her father's single-engine Cessna-182 and it changed everything. Airborne, they soared over sunny Shepparton for only half an hour but Roslyn was instantly sold! Terrified of gripping the control wheel for the first time, she nevertheless marvelled at the freedom, the power and the spectacular views from above. She told her father right there that she would love to become a pilot.

'Look, there goes an eagle!' her dad had pointed suddenly. They were at eight thousand feet as a large black shadow streaked past her wingtip. 'Do a steep right turn and follow it,' he ordered. With some help, Roslyn banked around steeply, but the big bird had gone – probably chasing more rising thermals.

'What's a thermal?' she asked.

Her devoted father smiled at her. 'You will have a lot to learn my dear, won't you?'

Now Roslyn frantically wondered how her ageing parents would be reacting to this morning's nation-wide news about her Air Australia flight. Their plight was sure to get saturation coverage, and in any case the Steinhouse's always kept up-to-date with her flight schedules; eagerly following each flight on the internet. Roslyn wept as she realised that Martin Steinhouse would be blaming himself for ever getting his daughter into aviation; after all, it was he who had enthusiastically egged her along every step of the way; paying out thousands for her flying lessons at the Shepparton Aero Club; then paying more for advanced training at Essendon airport in Melbourne. Today, her sick mother would be distraught while Roslyn wondered if her Mum would ever recover should anything have happened to AA200 and their precious and only child.

'You look dreadful, Ros – if you don't mind me saying . . .' Tom Tyson stared at her. Tom was nice, and Roslyn was pleased that he was onboard today, but Ray Cardin was 49 and his grating personality was uncomfortable to be with - especially when under tremendous pressure such as this, while she herself was plunging in and out of despair over their ghastly predicament. Soon, no matter what, they must descend and find somewhere to land because, as Tom had dryly noted, what goes up must eventually come down. So, if they finally burst into clear visibility but out of fuel, only to discover to their horror that there was nothing below but empty ocean, then they would have to ditch it in the sea. Such a spectacular slow-motion crash was just too horrible to contemplate.

Actually, ditching a jumbo at sea would be a quite delicate event at first, where they would need to ditch along the lines of wave swells and not across them; as their emergency manuals ordered so matter-of-factly. Swells? Pleasant lines of one-metre waves gently rolling onto tropical Pacific island sands? These might daintily appear on holiday postcards, but rarely in the exposed open ocean. Three-metre walls of water were much more likely in the historically misnamed *Pacific*. And sometimes they can rise up to eight-metre brick walls! In big storms, mid-ocean waves have been fifteen metres or higher and can capsize ocean liners and huge freighters in a brief moment . . . and they only travel at about 25 knots. A huge plane smacking into such hard walls of moving water at 140 knots would ensure its instant and complete destruction and of all those who travel upon her.

Tom saw her reading the emergency manual. 'So are you up to it?

Ros answered, 'No, it's sickening. It all sounds so fine and dandy in theory, but we may as well cut our throats than attempt that.'

'But if it has to be done then it just has to be done,' Cardin stated nonchalantly.

'But Ray, in the dark how do we determine which is along the swells or across them? And has any 747 ever done it?' Ros asked.

'With our landing lights on, that's how we do it. And Tom, you are our resident historian: has it been done before? '

'There were plenty of large types that ditched during the wars,' enthused Tom, a keen aviation history buff. 'Four-engined stuff like B-29s, Lancasters, etc. There's dozens of 'em still lying on the bottom of the English Channel. Some crews made it and some didn't. But they all broke up on hitting the drink, and only those that put down beside an allied naval ship recorded any successful escapes. Anyway, we won't conveniently find a lovely cruise liner to alight beside and hop aboard without getting our socks wet, and they wouldn't want something the size of us crashing right beside them, anyway. And no: I read somewhere that you can't properly see the swell lines at night – landing lights or not. And if it's raining or foggy you can kiss your sweet butt goodbye.'

'Gee Tom, thank you for such sparkling optimism,' remarked Cardin. 'So would you both prefer me to gently land on some nearby cloud and we shall disembark from there?'

Roslyn ignored him. 'Oh God, it says here that upon a water impact - even with the undercarriage retracted, we would most likely rip the wings right off. Then the plane would probably cartwheel end-over-end before sinking immediately.' She grabbed her mouth and felt like vomiting as a deathly silence ensued on the flight deck. It was starkly apparent that land must be reached at any cost and that the spectre of thumping down in

Farmer Jones' bumpy paddocks had now become almost appealing, while his fleeing stock would just have to take their chances.

The crew of three glanced at the time yet again. They now had about three hours' fuel remaining in the voluminous multiple tanks, so in three short hours they would definitely know their fate - one way or another. And this approaching grand final performance was finite: it had only two inescapable and inflexible ends. The worst outcome was an eternal blackness for them all, while the best was a possible landing somewhere . . . anywhere, and maybe a walk away to incredible triumph and heroism. But which would it be? Roslyn Steinhouse quietly cursed the bald certainty that she should have stuck to her original ambition of teaching instead of flying, while Tom Tyson sorely wished he'd persisted with his vague dreams of becoming a surfboard riding professional. Unlike them, Captain Ray Cardin had never held any ambitions other than to fly, and could not contemplate any different occupations from this one that had led him to the dire straits they were in right now. But whichever way the cookie eventually crumbled they could all clearly foresee that it was going to be one hell of a final ride!

In fear, Cardin realised that, of the hundreds of passengers and crew behind him, every single one of them would now be cursing that they were on board this particular flight. They would be regretting their present occupation or holiday plans or the travel bug that had bitten them; indeed, any quirk of fate that had led them to board this death flight and into this intractable predicament. And nothing could ever prevent the inevitability that, one way or another, this flight would terminate very soon while the combined but desperate wishes and prayers of all their families and friends back home would, in the end, "not amount to a single hill of beans" as the Americans often say.

And on-board, neither the banging of tambourines nor whoomping of ancient didgeridoos nor a beseeching of the gods would evade their ominous outcome. It wasn't predetermined or a plot, it was just fate; a deathly spin on the roulette wheel of life. It could be compared to the weekly drawing of the unlucky or lucky Lotto numbers: either an undeserved cruelty that would nevertheless prevail if it so desired, or a joyous escape to freedom and a second life. Meanwhile, the cabin crew under Purser Haneed Zaresh were actually fortunate that total anarchy with violence had not yet broken out – although the potential was always there while the uncaring clock kept ticking away mercilessly.

It happened earlier than Zaresh thought. A group of men suddenly approached him from behind then heavily tackled him to the ground. Zaresh struggled for air as scattering passengers screamed around them. One of the men loudly declared, 'We are taking over this plane! We've had enough of all the promises, the dumb excuses and the bullshit! I have flown light planes before and reckon I can land us on the very next little island that we see, okay? It's better than stupidly wandering around the bloody ocean until our fuel runs out . . . '

Bang! A large metal frying pan crashed over the vigilante's head. He slumped to the floor as stewardess Ayli Gorshe cheered at her own bravery under fire. The world's shortest mutiny was over already and the other red-faced mutineers were hurriedly shoved back into their seats by a group of angry men. But panic had now clearly bubbled above the surface and openly signposted that another three hours of this acute tension was sure to be not only highly volatile, but probably intolerable.

Gong! The overhead P.A. soon sounded once again and made everyone jerk upright and take notice because this time it actually sounded quite angry. Many worried passengers whispered, 'This is bound to be trouble, for sure.'

They were right. The sombre announcement began: 'Ladies and gentlemen, boys and girls, this is your captain speaking. Now I'd like everyone to listen to me very carefully, please. You won't hear any more of our promises or weak excuses about our situation because this is for real. So far, in this most difficult flight of my career - and perhaps the worst in any airline pilot's career, we of the flight tech crew have been absolutely baffled by the current events in progress. Multiple critical system failures have occurred which are not only unknown to Air Australia, but probably unknown to any other airline in the world. I'm sure that not even the Boeing manufacturers themselves envisaged this appalling predicament in which we currently find ourselves and which were caused by unknown and unforeseen events. Consequently, we pilots were not trained to overcome simultaneous losses in digital navigation along with all our communications. But we *are* highly trained and competent in partial impediments to navigation and we are therefore proceeding accordingly with makeshift navigation methods as we head back towards Australia.'

Failing to mention his original headstrong opposition to turning back, Cardin continued: 'I did not proceed towards our planned destination in America due to that nation's numerous airspace considerations; not the least of which is the hellish danger of blundering blindly and unidentified into heavily defended American military air defence zones. I must point out that the USA is the world's mightiest military power and does not treat unknown invaders - whether by land, sea or air - lightly. So, a few hours ago we turned around and headed back towards our homeland of Australia. The crew concluded that a vagrant Air Australia plane would be more likely welcomed into Australian airspace than elsewhere. This was our decision and is not open to discussion and you will simply have to trust us here because, unfortunately, you have no choice.'

'Now folks, the next few hours are absolutely crucial to all of us - not just for we of the Air Australia crew. Here are the bald facts so far: we absolutely cannot and must not run out of fuel over the sea because that is simply not an option. So, we will continue on this basically west-south-west compass bearing until arriving over landfall somewhere on Australia's East coast. We should all remember that back in 1770 Captain Cook was also somewhere around here and sailing his *Endeavour* westwards, seeking the vague and unproven rumour of a "Great South Land."

'Fortunately, Cook did not face any mutinies from doubting crews or untrained usurpers but was aided by nothing more than a sextant, a chrome compass and a finely polished time-piece. Eventually Cook discovered that Great South Land, just as Sir Charles Kingsford-Smith also found it in 1928 - and just as our Air Australia flight two-hundred will also find it today.'

Applause was heard throughout all cabins as the captain continued. 'Now, most disturbingly, I have been informed that some of you planned to take over this plane. Well, everyone listen-up very carefully while I say this to you all: No you bloody-well won't ever commandeer this plane because even if you did manage to succeed you still wouldn't know what the hell to do with the damn thing!'

'Similarly, I bet you wouldn't you allow a group of competitors to take over your own plumbing business back home; or let a troop of enemies to take control of our Army. No? Well we won't allow similar treachery either. I am not deriding your various professions by asserting that we pilots are any better than you, I am simply informing you that if you ever desire to get back down to Mother Earth again from this extreme predicament then you must trust it to the designated pilots.'

'Again, if you are still contemplating taking over this aircraft and you somehow don't comprehend my message, then I suggest you definitely consider another career choice because I can positively guarantee that you won't be able to penetrate our EDS shield system which electronically defends our flight deck.'

'And anyway, who the hell ordained upon any of you that you are suddenly competent to fly this thing? You may be experts in your own fields back at home where some of you might competently run your own factories, or perhaps you stylishly model clothes on the catwalk, while gee, we can't do those things. Or you might be a great pastry cook or an expert bottle washer while we're not. Or perhaps you act in movies or TV dramas while we can't do any of those things either. Maybe you teach classes of students, or are a doctor or a chemist or a bank teller while we sure aren't because we are only pilots. Heck, you might even be a fantastic child carer or the Federal Minister for Agriculture or the best chef in Australia while I can't even flip a burger at Maccas and neither can my two co-pilots. And if you are the biggest rock star or the best footballer in Australia, then we most certainly are neither of those.'

'Ah . . . I've just been advised that some people are still whispering among themselves, so everyone please sssh-up right now, pay attention and listen very carefully while I whisper just what I *am* – apart from being a parent of a young one like many of you. I am your captain and a fully qualified Boeing-747 pilot, and so are my two co-pilots. Therefore I am the legal master of this aircraft and the master of all your current destinies - whether any of you are prepared to accept that or not. So, now that I've honestly confessed that I couldn't mend a shoe or strum a guitar or do comedy on stage to feed myself, you also know that what I most certainly *can* do is to attempt to save all our bacon here today and get us safely back down onto the ground and home to all your families.'

'Meanwhile it is just an undeniable fact that no-one else ever can - or ever will - extricate all of you from this ghastly black hole in the sky except this current flight crew. You can even write this down if you like: *"**We will save all your lives while no amateur opportunists or headline-seeking band-aid commando heroes in their own damn letterboxes ever will!**"* To clarify further, if we of the crew are still not exactly sure just what the hell is wrong with this plane, then how on earth could a bunch of clumsy buffoons ever know how to fix it? Do you understand all this? Or, to quote Clint Eastwood: *Did ya get ma drift?'*

'Now, I'm not at all sorry if I happen to be repeating myself here, even though my second officer is waving at me and indicating that I am, but we pilots intend to land this plane *somewhere* sometime, whereas none of you can and none of you ever will land it *any bloody where!*

'On the other hand, I wish to sincerely thank all our loyal on-board entertainers - whether famous or not - for contributing to the mostly general harmony during this severe crisis – as opposed to those few treacherous skunks who conspired and exacerbated our general terror. There is nothing more therapeutic than good humour and music to relieve dark moments in such times of crisis. So, we will certainly try to attend any concert or show to be held by you in the future because you real stars know how to do it and we don't because all we do is land big planes . . . as I probably said *ad nauseum*. Again, thank you to everyone who has contributed to our success so far.'

'And finally, to those conspirators and amateur confederates who stupidly chose not to participate in helping us defeat this thing, then you are not part of our winning team and we are certainly all watching you! Remember, there are only four of you bastards against four hundred and seven of us decent citizens and we will definitely be remembering you after landing where you will be facing numerous serious charges . . . won't you? So, that's all: did everyone get my drift because this outfit is not called Mickey Mouse Airlines, this is Get Real Airlines . . . so *get real*, team!'

After a few breathtaking seconds of silence, all the passengers enthusiastically cheered and applauded as eager discussions erupted, then a team of African-American basketballers leapt up and slapped each with hi-fives: 'Yo man! How cool is this captain dude!'

Around the cabins, many asked: could this be the greatest speech ever made over a plane's P.A.?

Up on the flight deck, Ray Cardin beamed a wide grin as Roslyn Steinhouse congratulated him and shook his hand. 'Wow Ray, that certainly was socking it to them! But I should ask just what are these EDS shields, because I've never heard of them?'

Tom Tyson enthusiastically agreed with the F/O's compliments while dancing around and applauding wildly. 'Jee-zuss-H on a boogie board! What a fantastic speech, Boss! Maybe you should run for parliament one day because not even the Gettysburg Address was better than that!'

'Or longer,' quipped the first officer.

Tom added, 'Anyway Boss, I'm wondering too. Just what are these flight deck shields? I've never heard of them either.'

The captain grinned at them. 'And neither have I because I just made that up. But in the meantime let's ensure this door remains firmly locked and alarmed at all times, just in case they try again. Remember Captain Bligh? He only found out about the mutiny on his HMS *Bounty* in 1789 when it was all too late. Then he was forced to sail an open long-boat for three thousand miles to safety in Java. So once they burst through that door we're finished.'

All three of them turned to stare at the gray flight deck door. Strengthened, alarmed, monitored and specially wired, that narrow door was all that remained between possible salvation and total anarchy. A cockpit intrusion was the very last thing that anyone needed just now when they might possibly be within spitting distance of victory. Such a Dante's Hell would be as disastrous as a mutiny on Captain Bligh's open long-boat.

'Check arms!' Cardin suddenly ordered. They all reached for their concealed under-seat holsters which contained Taser guns - among others. These weapons could certainly come in handy, but a wild shoot-out with intruders in this tiny cabin would be fraught with danger and a last desperate gamble.

Once again Cardin switched seats with Tom who returned to the front row. Cardin slumped back in the jump seat. His may well have been a grand speech: offensive but essential and to the point, because his crew simply must not suffer any more rebellious actions by the passengers. Cardin shivered at the thought of so much danger all around him, plus the Herculean tasks ahead when and if they spotted Australia's coastline. And what a total farce it would be if a gray coastline appeared on the horizon just as he was desperately wrestling for the controls with fanatical cockpit intruders. He recalled the horrifying tales of the fourth plane hijacked on September eleven, 2001. It was apparently destined to crash into the White House in Washington but the pilots were later heard on CVR recordings grappling with the hijackers in a deathly struggle. Ultimately, neither side won the struggle and the plane spun out of control and plunged vertically into a farming field near Shanksville, Pennsylvania; burying itself deep into the ground.

Gulping in horror, Cardin could clearly envisage a similar band of amateur desperados overpowering him and his two co-pilots with a resulting vertical dive straight into the deep blue sea far below. He recalled once flying to beautiful Lord Howe Island north-east of Sydney; a dot in the ocean which they hoped they would be overflying soon. He discovered that the fishing there is just incredible; especially the Lord Howe Island Kingfish which are said to be different from mainland Kingfish in that they are classified as "deep sea" fish because the waters immediately adjacent to Lord Howe are an amazing 13,000 feet deep. Gulping; it certainly was a lovely island to contemplate, but Cardin had no wish to plunge that far down to his final grave after having already tumbled out of the sky from 39,000 feet! This was simply incomprehensible as he had always been wary of any water after nearly drowning twice as a child.

Cardin covered his eyes and thought briefly of his wife Alicia and their two-year-old boy, Jamie. There was so much convoluted horror swirling through his mind that he'd hardly had a chance to think of them this night, but if something very bad was about to happen then he would cherish some final fond memories. He'd been forty-seven and a late starter in the marriage game when he finally decided to take the leap into matrimony with an Air Australia stewardess, nine years younger than him. Their baby had arrived two years ago and now he was a father of a young family while next year he would turn fifty. Since his son's birth, his wife had often suggested he change to domestic routes with AA and discard his endless circling of the Earth on the international roster. He had a responsibility to be a Dad and to be available to his boy; to take him to the local park and push him on the swings, and for . . . just everything. Cardin had considered Alicia's earnest requests but ultimately decided to fly one more year on international, then go domestic.

Now perplexed, he pondered just what on Earth was his skewed rationale behind that rash decision? Was it his addiction to international flying, or just his love of the mighty Boeing-747? It was hard to pin down, but if you've done a job that you love for over twenty-eight years then you generally just stick with it. Also, he'd never envisaged a baby coming along so late in life, so lifestyle changes were up against entrenched habits that most of us find discomforting to change.

As today had proven, his decision was ultimately and disastrously wrong. He could clearly see his beloved Jamie asleep in his cot right now while lovely Alicia would be sitting alone, watching the appalling news on TV. Soon she might have no husband and Jamie might have no father. What would she tell the boy when he grew older: that his Dad preferred going away all the time to staying home with his little family? His only son would never remember him and grow up fatherless, like so many others these days. And worse, the growing boy would not fondly worship his Dad's memory because he'd been a glamorous jumbo jet pilot; instead he would curse him for never being at his school plays or never cheering at his weekend soccer. And just where was this parent when he needed help with homework, or attendance of both proud parents at his high school graduation? He was dead. His father's plane had become lost for some mysterious reason and was never found. And great horrors: his Dad wasn't just on board that plane, he had been the Captain. It was his own father who had killed all those innocent people . . .

At the end of the day, airline management generally blames the captain for any crash. Even though a flight may have run short of fuel because the refueller pumped the wrong measurement of litres (instead of pounds) into the wing tanks (Air Canada), it will still be the deceased captain who wears the final noose of shame upon his memory because he always shoulders the overall responsibility for just about everything. Should a plane crash from iced-up wings or from hail stones destroying the engine fan blades, it will be the captain who was legally negligent because lawyers can't sue the weather but they sure can sue a deceased captain's estate. At the end of the day, the buck always stops at seat 1A: the front left-hand seat on the flight deck.

In 2006 a Greek Helios Boeing 737 crashed near its destination in Greece and all 121 on board were killed. Radio contact had been lost with the plane since shortly after take-off, but it still dutifully flew to its destination city then entered a standard holding pattern - exactly as its auto-pilot had been programmed to do. To scrambled military jets flying beside it, it seemed that the pilots were asleep, unconscious or dead. We might reason that surely no pilots could be at fault here because it was highly unlikely that both of them would be deliberately culpable in such a negligent act as sleeping on the job. But in the subsequent investigation it was regretfully determined that, just before departure, a company ground engineer had been inside the 737 conducting checks on the cabin pressurisation system. To do this he switched the CAB PRESS setting from AUTO to MAN. He conducted his tests but then forgot to switch it back to AUTO; a serious omission for such a professional person.

Not long after, the plane taxied out and the pilots went through their usual pre-flight checks – but missed one. Disastrously, in their haste they forgot to check CAB PRESS and so it remained on manual. When the plane passed through ten thousand feet on climb to cruising altitude, the cabin pressurisation system deemed that the cabin was still below ten thousand feet and provided minimal pressurisation accordingly. Consequently, with further gains in altitude, all on board became

123

slowly deprived of oxygen and drifted off to sleep - then into unconsciousness followed by death. The 737 was declared a ghost ship when interceptor planes eventually circled it and could see most of those poor souls inside (except for one) apparently asleep or dead. Ultimately, it was not the ground engineer who wore most of the blame, but the captain, of course.

So, no matter what eventually happened to AA200 or where some wreckage might wash ashore one day, Captain Ray Cardin would surely bear all the responsibility, with his name forever tarnished and reviled by the families of all those on board. Cardin's reputation would, fairly or unfairly, be apportioned to this mysterious disaster while the world's media would forever uphold the slander, safely secure in the knowledge that dead men can't fight back.

Another gong to the cockpit brought news from the purser that the few remaining sober passengers were desperately wondering just when "things" might actually start happening? Also, how far from Australia were they now? How much fuel was left and when would it start to run out? What should they expect then? Should they don life jackets and oxygen masks now? What about protecting their children before they brace for impact? Or should they just start saying their last prayers right now?

Cardin thought deeply before replying: 'Please tell them that we will proceed just one step at a time. I will announce clear instructions for all these events in due course. It is simply unproductive for anyone to be fretting furiously at this stage – or at any stage. They should all remember that the flight crew intends to bring this plane down safely *somewhere*. Let them not dwell on bracing for any impacts at this time, or protecting their children. Or alarming everyone by donning frightening fluoro jackets and horrid face masks. This is not a horror movie and we hope it never will be. We are not doomed yet. So how about more positive attitudes back there, Haneed? This might be the grand culmination of all your training. In fact, I think that no purser was ever quite this lucky to be granted this situation, don't you agree? You'll be a bloody hero when we land. Ah, Haneed, are you still listening?'

Cardin heard a burst of laughter in the background. He wondered what he'd said or done to generate this merriment, then realised that someone had probably told a joke. Oh well, laughter was like gold tonight on Air Australia flight two-hundred, and if any group of people ever deserved comic relief it was right here and now.

In the first class lounge, Maggie Silverstone quietly reflected upon her own cruel fate. She'd left America when she was nineteen to see the world. She discovered the delights of Australia and stayed, then got married and made very good money in fashion design. But she and Warren had no children and since Warren had died in an accident at only 41, Maggie was diagnosed with a rare and deadly heart condition. She was headed back to Florida to visit her American relatives for the last time, but now the plane had turned back! She could feel herself spiralling down a dark tunnel with no-one to comfort her. Here, the non-caring passengers around her were all too preoccupied with their own imminent fates and had already forgotten about the woman who'd announced she was dying. 'Perhaps it is better this way,' she sobbed in ultimate despair, just as someone blasted a trumpet into a microphone. As party balloons popped everywhere and drunks chanted dirty ditties, Maggie lay down on her row of four seats and cried to herself.

Just nearby, marine tycoon Rod Appleby tapped on his dying laptop, pointlessly reviewing his now irrelevant profit and loss accounts. He focused on a serious gap in cash flow that he'd long suspected was caused by his business partner, Will McFarlane. For some time he'd been considering confronting the man and shouting about the missing half million dollars, but unhappily conceded that his old buddy would now get away with the lot if this plane went down.

Appleby heard sobbing and glanced over his seat-back to see Maggie Silverstone in tears. He muttered, 'Well, she'll just have to get used to it, won't she. Just like all of us.' He considered comforting the distressed woman but decided that as no-one was consoling him, then why bother to comfort this stranger?

A long way rearward in Economy, Roger Tandy of women's underwear fame was forcing positive thoughts to occupy him. If they somehow got away with this - and their captain, who he'd recently met, had assured them that he and the other pilots were doing their utmost to get them back home, then he would simply walk away from the grind of ledgers, accounts and tedious paperwork in his stuffy office at the factory, and buy a motor-home to travel around Australia. He might even buy a new GPS for bushwalking and exploring – one where the software was up-to-date, of course – and simply disappear from society. On reflection, he couldn't believe that he'd endured a self-enslavement of thirty-eight years keeping the books in a horrid little office overlooking hundreds of machinists down below who all seemed as miserably bored as him.

On a brighter note, it appeared that he'd made good friends with Julie Page in the next seat; a divorced housewife travelling to Disneyland on her own. 'What will you do if we, ah, get out of this?' he asked her. 'I've decided I'm going to retire and travel around Australia. I'm not going to waste another minute, are you?'

Page answered, 'Ah, I'm really not sure. I certainly won't be going back to Disneyland because I'll never step into another aeroplane ever again. And, on reflection, this trip seems so pointless anyway. I mean, walking around a theme park by myself for a week? Watching families have fun? I don't know why I even contemplated this silly journey. But now it's back to suburbia . . . if we can somehow get away with this.'

Tandy took a deep breath and rushed in. 'I, ah, don't suppose you'd be interested in travelling around Aussie with me? It wouldn't be anything special - no obligations or anything like that. I know I'm just a boring accountant in a boring factory, but that's only because I tied myself down to monotony and convinced myself that I actually had a fulfilling life sweating over dusty ledgers. And yes, I've already heard all those women's underwear jokes a million times!'

Page laughed. 'Well, thank you Roger. I think I'd actually *love* to travel around with you. You seem so nice. And I desperately need to get away from . . . everything. I booked this trip without even thinking, and now . . . well, I've got some money from my divorce from Ralph. Maybe I could go halves with you in that motor-home. Would that help?'

Tandy smiled happily. 'I might be boring, but I do know how to handle money efficiently. No, thank you anyway, Julie. I would just be delighted to have your company. But first let me tell you about my big meeting with the captain. You just won't believe it.'

Julie Page replied, 'Oh I just feel so sorry for that poor man now. He said he's got a wife and small child. And such terrible responsibilities with everybody on board cursing his hide no matter what he does. Surely it can't be his fault that all this technical stuff isn't working.' She gripped his hand and they embraced as Tandy related his meeting with the captain.

Other couples weren't quite so content. Bryce and Matilda Kennard were having terse words about she being the original disseminator of rumours about their plane.

'Matilda,' he chastised his wife, 'I never told you to blab to that woman next to you that we were about to crash, did I? I simply said that I overheard that hostie called Suzy gossiping to the other one that our plane had communication and navigation problems. But you went ahead and told her that we were about to crash! Then she asked the purser about it . . . in a loud voice which everybody heard, and *now* look at the place! It's total mayhem in here. It's like a damn booze hall . . . or a bordello. An airborne street party! And now there's been rebels trying to take over the plane . . . Hell, what next?'

His wife wiped a few tears and protested. 'I only asked her if she'd heard anything curious about this plane. I never expected her to broadcast it at full volume for the entire cabin to hear.'

'Matilda, I told you it was probably nothing but silliness and gossip.'

She argued, 'Yes, but we *do* have some big problems with our plane, don't we? The Captain admitted it himself.'

'He never said we were going to crash.'

'They never would, would they? Only when it's too late . . . '

Bryce said, 'Well it seems that after you squawked to that purser he rushed straight up to the pilots' cabin and confronted them with it. They all had a big argument then it spread like wildfire around the whole plane.'

Matilda Kennard sobbed some tears. 'Why are we even arguing, Bryce? At a time like this . . . and after all these years? You know how it upsets my diabetes and blood pressure.'

Her husband sighed and hung his head. This was not a time or place to be at each other's throats after forty-one years of matrimony. They should instead be devoting any remaining quality time to fondly remembering their three children and five grandchildren. Besides, Mrs Loud-Voice next to his wife was still peering intently at them; possibly waiting with bated breath for the next morsel of salacious gossip to relay to the masses. 'Oh, what does it all matter anyway,' groaned Bryce Kennard as hugged his wife. 'We should have just stayed home and painted our house like we intended, then we would never have been on this cursed death flight.'

Just then, Purser Haneed Zaresh swept past, obviously on another rushed mission. But he spared a second to enquire if they were okay.

'Wonderful, thanks. Just bloody wonderful!' answered Bryce Kennard as he stared at the blank movie screen in front of them. 'Hell, we can't even have a last movie to watch!' But Zaresh had disappeared down the aisle.

Scientist Stuart Rhys was strolling the aisles; sometimes tripping over people's feet and rubbish that lay around. Surprised that he was actually rather calm, the research biologist and particle physicist was utilising every ounce of his intellect to control his emotions. After a lifetime of training in how to analytically examine every factor of a complex equation, he was nonetheless failing to rationalise this ghastly predicament. And it was all his fault because there had been no need in the first place to accept this free trip to the USA in order to lecture at various universities in three states. There'd been many others keen to go but Rhys had pulled rank on them and now it had become not only the worst but the last mistake of his life. There was no scientific approach to this dilemma, nor any magic formula to evade the appalling spectre of their immediate future. A brilliant man all his life, his clever advice to others had always been: 'If in doubt, take the scientific approach. You will always find a solution.'

But there were no simple solutions to this horrifying equation merrily bubbling away in test-tubes. The plain fact was that they were all trapped in this giant metal can that would soon fall straight out of the sky. And after it did, there would be no grieving mourners at Stuart Rhys' funeral service because, quite simply, he had no family or friends; his test tubes and microscopes being his only kin. He had evaded a social life since his earliest days at university where he avoided all those who he considered of "lower intellect" than himself. Yet he wasn't a vain person; he was a boffin who'd been admired and respected in his field where he'd simply kept quietly to himself. And now it was far too late to change anything because neither he nor anyone else on board could reverse back up this one-way street.

9.

Seventy metres away at the forward end of the big Boeing-747, yet another critical discussion was taking place. This was just one of dozens of such summit deliberations that had taken place on the flight deck this long night. Second Officer Tom Tyson sat behind his captain and spoke from the jump seat.

'Okay, it says here Boss that in the necessity of critical range or endurance flying, one or even two of the engines can be shut down so the flight can proceed with greater range - although at a lower altitude and slower speed.'

Cardin answered without conviction. 'Yes, *can* be, and that's the operative word. But I'm not going to do it, Tom.'

'And why not?' interrupted Roslyn Steinhouse who again glared at her captain in anger. 'I strongly support that idea. We should be doing absolutely anything and everything that might help us get home'.

Tom bravely queried, 'Yeah Boss, why not?'

'Because the cabin down there is verging on complete pandemonium. We've already had insurrection and a near take-over with an assault on the purser. As our time gets more critical the tension will surely rise - maybe to a boiling point from which there will be no escape and no relief valve.'

'So what's your point?' demanded the irate first officer.

'The point is this, Miss Roslyn: if we were to reduce or shut down the power to one or more engines, the passengers would certainly notice the sudden decrease of engine noise from outside. Additionally, some will notice the deceleration as we slow down. This will be followed by the perceptible feeling of pitching into a descent, as happens on every flight when we reach our top-of-descent point – as you both know. But this time they would know that we are still flying over a horrible ocean and assume that *all* the engines are starting to fail, signifying that this is their final death knell and we pilots couldn't be bothered telling them about it.'

'Well, why can't we just explain honestly what's happening,' suggested Tom.

'They won't believe us. It would start a riot.'

Roslyn sat fuming in silence as Cardin continued. 'And in that case, pandemonium is next. Actually, I can't think of any word that would adequately describe the hell that would erupt.'

Sensibly, Roslyn said, 'How about utilising the concept of *honesty*, Ray? Passengers have had enough of pilots' lies when things go wrong. As Tom hinted, we simply state that very soon we will be saving critical fuel by shutting down one or two engines, and to please understand that this Boeing-747 can fly perfectly well with just two engines turning - although at a lower altitude and slower speed . . . "

'A bloody slower speed!' Cardin screeched. 'That will send them insane with fury if they are told that we will be flying slower so they'll be trapped up here in this flying coffin for even one minute longer than they expected – let alone *hours*! They just want to get the screaming hell out of this thing now . . . and so do

I for that matter. So just one extra minute trapped in this cigar-shaped nightmare will be one too many for them. And most people won't heartily accept the concept that some of those huge motors hanging off the wings out there were pointlessly shut down by their detested pilots so their nightmare will be extended for even longer when we are already as unpopular as suicide bombers at a wedding party.'

Tom Tyson argued, 'But surely this isn't a popularity contest? They should just accept what they're told, Boss. If we had an engine fire we'd tell them straight away that we're shutting it down because it's on fire, wouldn't we? We would then descend and continue on three.'

Roslyn backed him up. 'Exactly! And very well said, Tom. They must do what they are told by the crew. And anyway, they wouldn't know the difference between endurance flying and pink elephants flying - especially now that they're all half sozzled.'

'Now listen you two!' barked Cardin. 'A sudden reduction in power along with a lowering of the outside engine noise will be like setting off an explosion in here. Can you imagine if ten of them came bursting through that door at once. Do you realise what they'd do to you . . . to the three of us? When humans are threatened by grave danger and an imminent and horrible death they are capable of *anything* . . . anything at all! And if they do manage to take over this plane then we are all definitely dead because, as I told them earlier, they wouldn't know what to do with the damn thing anyway. Do I make myself *clear*?' There was silence.

134

'And, my dear Roslyn, with all due respect I realise that you've got a few thousand hours of flying experience, but I've got nearly twenty thousand. And if you are thirty-one years old then I already held a commercial pilot's licence when you were born. Tom, you are twenty-three and I had probably crossed this ocean dozens of times before you even started pre-school. So I don't want any more of this debating contest. Our passengers are already on a knife edge so I won't initiate anything that upsets them any further and tips them right over the edge. And lastly, if we leave all four of those big Rolls Royce fans running, we'll all get home safe and sound much sooner, won't we?' The other two pilots shook their heads in silent disagreement with their commander.

But Cardin wasn't finished yet. "So Roslyn, answer me this: if we descended to a lower level after shutting one or two off, might we strike stronger headwinds or weaker?'

The F/O considered the question. 'Ah, without any input data it is difficult to say.'

'Exactly. And you know that sometimes the Jetstream can be stronger a bit lower down - although I admit it is usually less. But it's just a guess, isn't it? Imagine if we descended to, say, flight level 270 and we struck some new headwind component while we are already handicapping ourselves by flying slower on two engines. We might dash any remaining chances we ever had of reaching the Australian coast. Have you thought of that? How about you, Tom?'

Tom thought deeply. 'Ah, in general we should expect reduced headwinds lower down when flying westwards. But it's always a gamble and we can only take rough chances without reliable data input. And anyway Boss, I was only quoting from our official Air Australia Emergency Procedures Manual, page 114. I can show you if you like.'

Cardin bragged that he had digested "all that crap" while Tom was still in nappies. And anyway, it was compiled by senior pilots long ago for a flight that was *not* lost all night over the ocean and was *not* reaching its fuel exhaustion point. It was written for *normal* flights where all onboard equipment was serviceable but might be getting just a little low on fuel reserves and were aiming towards tidying fuel usage to comply with laws and to please management on arrival.

Roslyn Steinhouse sighed in anger. 'So what's the answer, Ray? How can we do or plan anything without any data? We can't even ask anyone in the whole world for assistance. Meanwhile, I just don't see why we can't make a polite announcement like Tom suggested, then very gradually reduce the throttles on two engines so it doesn't surprise or frighten everyone. What else can we do? If we strike stronger winds lower down then we could be stuffed. If we stay up here at 39,000 feet like this we're probably stuffed. And if we pretend all this will just go away some time, then we are definitely stuffed!'

Tom held up his hand. 'I know, Boss! Let's hold a concert!'

Cardin exclaimed, 'What the flying . . .'

As the captain turned around in amazement, Tom was excited. 'But Boss, at the moment they're all sitting around chewing their nails and waiting for any damn thing to go bump in

136

the night, right? But we don't want them panting on hot bricks with their ears peeled for the tiniest movement or sound; what we really need is to make heaps of distracting loud noises, don't we? Yelling, singing, thumping music, banging pots and pans . . . anything . . . Eh Boss?'

'Have you gone totally mad, Tom?'

'Hope not, Boss. But if we create the loudest party of the century then they shouldn't hear or notice it when you carefully reduce the throttles to slow us down. So why don't I go downstairs and stir them up? I used to play in a band at the Maroubra Surf Club so I can sing and put on a noisy show. They're already partying so I just need to create one gigantic party for us all so we can pump up the volume, eh Boss? And a few more drinks in them will oil the wheels of mischief. I'll even put on a ballet tutu and dance the Sugar Plum Fairy if necessary.'

Cardin grinned for the first time in hours. 'And exactly what page of our Emergency Procedures manual is that on, Tom?'

Roslyn giggled, 'Yes. That just might work. How would we do it, Tom?'

'Well, I'll prance around down there and wind up the noise and then when it's at its very loudest, I'll grab an intercom phone and send you a code Delta. When my Boss-man answers I'll whisper *Geronimo* and he starts retarding the throttles very slowly and gently . . . '

'Geronimo?' squawked the astonished Captain. 'You mean a hairy male ballerina in a tutu will whisper *Geronimo* and then we'll all be saved? Can someone please tell me I'm dreaming?'

The first officer threw a heavy look at Cardin and asked, 'Got a better idea, *Captain?*'

Tom jumped up and practiced a few ballet swirls around the cockpit, making sure to kick his legs high as he had seen in that ballet movie, *Billy Elliot.* As Roslyn hid her mouth in laughter, Captain Ray Cardin asked just where Tom might happen to locate a ballerina's tutu in a lost jumbo jet over the Pacific Ocean.

This was no problem and Tom grabbed the P.A. mike and pressed the *Gong* button.

'Gong! Hey ladies and gents and kids. This is Tom the surfie; your friendly Second Officer. Guess what? We're all gonna have one big party. But no ordinary party: the party of the century! Now let me warn you that attendance is compulsory. There will be no drop-outs or no-shows. No wet blankets. Everyone must dance, sing and have a great time. We already have several brilliant musicians and performers on board so there'll be no excuses from anyone. Before this, all our artists were performing separately, but now they'll all be going at it together as in a real concert! The wildest party in the sky starts in ten minutes so be there or be square! Oh by the way, can any nice lady lend me a spare dress – or the one you're wearing now might do. I might need some lipstick and make-up too . . . '

Captain Cardin shook his head and stared at the wall of blank screens in front of him. "I don't friggin' believe this! I'm quite sure AA's founding fathers never envisaged Sugar Plum Fairy Airlines.'

'Don't worry, Boss,' laughed the number-three pilot. 'You never know guys, after we make it home they'll probably make a movie of this after I write the book.'

Roslyn pleaded, 'I want to be in it, please! But I wonder what they could call it?'

Smiling Tom suggested, 'How about *Flying Low*?'

The captain upstaged him. 'How about: "They All Flew Off The Cuckoo's Nest." '

After the astounding announcement had been made, and throughout the many cabins of the stricken jet, most passengers were coming to the stark realisation that their flight crew and cabin personnel were only human after all. It was plainly obvious that if this ship went down, then so would the crew with it. In 1912, Captain Smith of the *RMS Titanic* was recklessly negligent by taking a short-cut through a reported ice field, so he dutifully went down with his ship. But that was long ago and it was not credible that any crew member of this flight deliberately, negligently or even accidentally interfered with or sabotaged any equipment on board this aircraft. And why would they? They flew these routes routinely. This was their lifetime's work and so far they had done their utmost to ensure the safety and comfort of all passengers on board AA200. And despite much passenger resentment and anger so far, the entire affair seemed to be nothing but sheer bad luck: rotten fate that had mangled their destinies to the extent that these may be their very last hours on Earth – or above it. And their captain, who was so despised before and who may have made some wrong decisions and perhaps some correct ones, was nevertheless a family person like most of them and was obviously doing his very best.

So now there was to be one grand party: their last hurrah. After all, if you've gotta go, then why not go out with a bang! Most people felt sure that the plane's young second officer would enhance exactly that.

At just about the time that someone found a trombone - of all things - in an overhead locker, several senior search operations officers flew to the MARSAR marine centre in Canberra for another emergency conference involving over a hundred aviation specialists. Here is where any signals from emergency ELT beacons would be received if your little dinghy or yacht capsizes too far from shore to swim. In fact, any vessel at all can have their distress signals relayed by satellites to Canberra and other locations. Large ships in the middle of the ocean receive the same service as an overturned runabout just off the Australian coast. And should any aircraft be so unfortunate as to ditch into that vast ocean, it would certainly take some time for rescuers to reach the scene but at least the ditching site would be precisely pinpointed by Canberra to give any survivors some chance of survival.

Since Sir Charles Kingsford-Smith (Smithy) paved the Pacific way in 1928, millions of airline flights have since crossed the world's oceans without loss. While several have suffered various engine and communication problems over the years, there are no recorded instances of any heavy aircraft being forced to ditch in peacetime. And just as well, because not only would such a hairy escapade be fraught with danger, it would have about the same chances of success as an elephant walking across the Grand Canyon on a tightrope.

In Canberra, Sam Hughendon and Harry Felds talked to their American counterparts once again via video hook-up. The FAA officials confirmed the worst: that AA200 had still not entered U.S. airspace even though it should have done so many hours ago. Further, they assured the Australians that it could not have simply *snuck* into their airspace on any covert mission, or whilst under hijack, because their AWACS surveillance planes and satellites can detect just about anything in the skies apart from stealth aircraft in training . . . and even then, some of those are detected when they believe they haven't been.

So, the long-overdue Aussie jumbo had either suffered a catastrophic failure and plunged into the sea, or had turned back from its course and diverted to heaven-knows-where to put down. But where? There are several locations dotted over the Pacific such as American Samoa and Nauru Island that could possibly take a jumbo jet, but many of these would not be suitable to an unannounced arrival in the middle of the night where they may not have their runway lights or glide-scope T-vasis guidance lights illuminated.

Also, it was agreed that fuel burn-off rates on AA200 would be a big consideration, while any headwind factors and their current ability to navigate was very much in question and basically unknown. It was agreed at the conference that since the flight had not emitted any radio or data link signals at all, it was therefore quite likely they could not receive signals either. But if they could in fact receive basic nav guidance, then they should have put down somewhere long ago.

The many nations of the Pacific group had volunteered all possible assistance hours ago, but Australian authorities could not offer them any clues as to the whereabouts of the flight, even though the Australian airforce and navy were scouring the ocean east of New South Wales along the expanded flight planned track line. But no other maritime search and rescue efforts had put to sea or to air because it was impractical to conduct a blanket search based solely on raw guesswork over an inconceivable watery expanse of sixty-four million square miles.

To do so, some clues would be needed first: primarily their last known position - and this flight's last known position had been just half an hour north-east of Sydney - a very long way back. A painful silence descended on the delegates from both sides of the Pacific during which most of them were reluctantly forced to conclude that the plane was undoubtedly lost and would never return.

Sam Hughendon, however, wouldn't go that far yet. During their coffee break he declared to anyone who would listen: 'I'm not giving up until fuel exhaustion time. After that . . . well, what can anyone do?'

But actual fuel exhaustion time can be quite variable and open to interpretation. When the airline company dispatcher lodges the flight plan it might say *E/1510*, meaning fuel endurance is fifteen hours and ten minutes. That is how long the plane can stay in the air at normal consumption rates. But if the pilots close down one or more engines for any number of reasons then it should stay aloft for quite a bit longer than that - but fly slower. In effect, with two fans shut down the same plane might now have twenty hours' endurance, but it might also, at a slower speed, take twenty hours and one minute to get somewhere. Similarly, a truck might drive from Melbourne to Darwin at half engine power. It might use only half a tank-load of fuel along the way but would probably take twice as long to get there.

So the GMT time that Sam Hughendon had determined when all would be lost was not entirely clear-cut, while perhaps he was overlooking human spirit, ingenuity or resilience. For many hours Kingsford-Smith was quite unsure just where his lonely *Southern Cross* was out over the untamed Pacific and, even though he confidently carried an American navigator, the man turned out to be not an aviation navigator at all, but a naval navigation officer who'd only ever charted ships' courses at plodding maritime speeds. Undeterred, Smithy's bandwagon pressed on with he sitting in his wicker cane chair while torrential rain often poured through the Southern Cross's open windows. Miraculously, their ded/dead reckoning navigation saw the Fijian islands eventually appear on a distant horizon through morning mists. While Smithy had perhaps throttled back for a while to conserve precious fuel and thus took longer to arrive; arrive he most certainly did.

It was now nearly thirteen hours since AA200 had taken off then vanished into wispy clouds to the east of Australia, and due to volcanic media coverage there would scarcely be a person in Australia who hadn't heard about it by now - especially the families and friends of those on board. It soon became a media Cinerama as most morning TV shows were now displaying a morbid countdown clock superimposed on their screens. This death clock brazenly informed everyone that in exactly two hours and eight minutes the mighty jumbo would finally run out of fuel and crash – if it hadn't done so already. Meanwhile, assorted aviation "experts" were bustled in front of cameras to present their wild theories often tarted up as established fact. One such expert had, until recently, been the network's gardening guru, nonetheless he seemed to know all about this flight because he'd once travelled to L.A. himself – as a passenger! Next, an off-duty cabin stewardess from Qantas was given a whole twenty minutes of prime-time exposure in which she informed viewers just exactly what each person on the ill-fated jumbo would be doing right at this minute – assuming, of course, that they weren't already providing the ocean's voracious marine creatures with their breakfast menu down in Davy Jones' locker.

One person in a Sydney street almost became a celebrity because he claimed to know the wealthy Rodney Appleby from Sunrise Marine who, the person claimed, still owed him a substantial sum of money. 'But now I'll just write it off,' he boasted magnanimously - while failing to mention that the debt in question was actually the other way around.

Quickly, an avalanche of commercials inundated every channel while network bosses hadn't enjoyed such morning prime-time ratings since the last Hollywood star died from an overdose. For the gasping viewers, the grisly ticking clock did not disappear - even during the screening of endless tortuous ads. Not to be missed, it was apparently vital for viewers to know exactly when 411 of their fellow countrymen would die. With luck, you might just get time to take a quick shower and grab a coffee before the momentous occasion actually arrived . . . proudly sponsored by some pet food company.

In Melbourne and Sydney, it was pompously announced that some trains and buses would be delayed for a while during the morning peak hour to allow commuters to gawk up at wide-screen TV's at the final bleak moment, and many media commentators insolently implied that workers and students shouldn't be penalised for being late today because, after all, this was in the national interests, and 'They're our Aussie mates up there, you know!' Meanwhile, a few savvy viewers, aghast at the bizarre orgy of it all, got the distinct impression that if the stricken plane suddenly turned up and all was somehow fine and dandy, and then the lost passengers themselves triumphantly marched across the TV screens trumpeting *Oh when the saints go marching in* - then the ratings would instantly plummet!

Meanwhile, the networks ran regular updates on the latest Hollywood gossip during the breathtaking wait for the 411 deaths.

Far away and interred on the stricken plane, it wasn't exactly a fun park of joy but a few alert passengers noticed a slight lightening of the sky behind them as the sun blinked its first rays. Then, looking ahead, some people could just make out a long dark shape lying along the distant western horizon. Could that be Australia, they desperately wished and hoped; or just another gray line of distant cloud banks? 'All will be revealed,' as the magician said. But the waiting was utter agony for some while the wild parties in the aisles merely camouflaged many gnawing fears.

Bringing some relief, many cheering people agreed that Second Officer Tom Tyson looked quite fetching in his floral red dress and matching lipstick as he pranced up the aisles, noisily tooting a trumpet. He was pursued by dozens of street dancers who threw at him anything they could get their hands on. He dodged ice cubes, sandwiches and fruit while the jumbo's cabin soon resembled a suburban Cleanaway truck. But no-one seemed to care very much; after all, there would be no cleaners to complain about it *post party.*

Soon the noise was deafening throughout *Party Airlines,* as someone had renamed it. Just about everyone had joined in, while only kids slept through it all. Eighty-year-old Cheng Xingu neither slept nor partied, but peered out from a business class window in puzzlement. Travelling alone, she had not understood a single announcement from the crew all night and was restricted to frightening guesswork as to her own plight. But she'd travelled the world quite a lot over her eighty years and could feel every bump and grind of these planes - especially the lowering and raising of the flaps and undercarriage, plus the familiar feeling of deceleration whenever a descent was commenced. Although she had little idea what all these manoeuvres actually were, she understood that they were essential occurrences at certain stages in the manipulation of the plane.

So when she felt the plane decelerating then its forward end tilting slightly down, she had no-one to ask why this odd angle was occurring when they were still way out over a black ocean. Not that anyone was really interested in an old Asian lady anyway – especially with Dirty Ditty Dick beer-halling loudly in the aisle just near her:

>Oh when we wake up in the morning
>We're all be bloody dead!
>And just when you thought my name was Daisy,
>It's actually bloody Ted! Oi!

This was quite humorous to all except Mrs Xingu who shook a woman's shoulder while pointing desperately out the window. The woman nodded then laughed and leapt up to join the dancing Conga line as a banjo and fiddle duet fired up some foot-tapping' country hootenanny, proving that the American contingent on board weren't going to bow out without a real rootin' shootin' and bootscootin' ho-down. Overall, the standard of entertainment was judged to be really quite good and, considering it was free, even better!

But just who might have to pay for all this booze? 'Ask someone who cares!' laughed Dirty Dick into the P.A.

Unhappily, upstairs at the so-called *pointy end*, a miserable Roslyn Steinhouse felt like she was shackled and manacled to Ray Cardin to share what could well be their very last hours on this final flight. Cardin had agreed with Tom's logic to very gently reduce power on numbers one and four engines; then shut them both down. This was after the agreed code and password of *Geronimo* was whispered over the crew intercom, guaranteeing that the raucous party noises of the cabin drowned out any reduction of the airstream noise from outside. Tom's idea was an absolute winner: there was no other way in normal times to conceal such a change in the aircraft's configuration and attitude - a technical word that is often confused with *altitude*, but refers instead to the angle that the planes' wings slice through the airstream and how the famous bulbous nose adopts a certain snobbish *angle of attack*. But this time it seemed that they had gotten away with the moderate change in attitude so Cardin thanked whomever that things would continue to remain relatively peaceful for as long as possible.

But had the recent changes gone completely unnoticed? Undeterred, the inquisitive Mrs Cheng Xingu managed to fight her way up the aisle past inebriated passengers in various states of undress, and towards the nearest galley. Inside was Business Class stewardess Janine Hilary who clearly wasn't in any party mood, but was quietly shedding a few private tears as she unthinkingly diced carrots into a porcelain bowl. Sobbing, she had no idea why she was doing this because none of the rabble out there were drinking carrot juice, nor would they ever do so again.

Straight Vodka or whiskey was mostly the product of choice on this eleventh-hour Party Airlines flight.

'Hello! Hello!' a croaking voice made Janine glance up. She pretended to be interested but her job was over: indeed her *life* was over!

'Hmm, yes?'

'Ah, I not have the good English, you see. But why this thing slow down and go like this?' The old lady sloped her hand down towards the floor at 45 degrees.

Janine recalled this woman from hours ago when she'd proudly produced her family photos. Now she gulped again as she thought about her own one-year-old baby back in Melbourne. But something sparked her fear as she stared at the woman's hand pointing down. Holy hell! Was their plane really starting to go down? Was this it? The very end? Right now? Her own demise was now imminent and her baby girl would never see her mother again? And would the final impact really hurt? Of course it would. Janine stared at the galley floor; yes, it seemed to be sloping down slightly, just as she'd seen and felt hundreds of times before. Yes, they *were* now on descent because the fuel must have finally run out - just as it inevitably would. She remembered Tom Tyson once laughing when she asked him if it was hard to fly a plane. He grinned handsomely and boasted, 'Nah, what goes up must come down!'

So now they were finally coming down and the Chinese woman obviously knew it and could feel it. Meanwhile, the rest of AA200's passengers apparently felt nothing, and how lucky they certainly were.

Naturally it didn't occur to Janine that perhaps the pilots had simply shut down a couple of engines to save fuel, but a few of the revellers gawked at the strange old lady standing with her hand sloped towards the floor as the Business Class stewardess watched her in fear.

Mark Dekanic, a Melbourne high school maths teacher, also noticed the Asian woman pointing towards the floor. He craned his neck but there seemed to be nothing on the floor to be staring at, and no reason for the stewardess to be following her gaze. Or perhaps the woman was angling her hand down, rather than pointing? Dekanic taught geometry and decided that, yes; maybe the woman was indicating an angle of some interest. But an angle of what? Just what was angling down? The truth hit him in the chest and he sucked a breath in pain. Of course! It was the plane itself that seemed to be angled slightly down after thirteen long hours of flying level, but he'd heard no announcements about this from the pilots. Normally they announced when they'd commenced descent then stated their estimated time of arrival. But this flight was anything but normal and a descent could mean only one thing: the plane was running out of fuel now because their time had finally come. This was their grand Armageddon and the cowardly pilots were remaining silent. Anyway, what could they possibly say?

So this was how it was going to be . . . .

Ray Cardin consulted yet another emergency manual and declared to his F/O: 'This says Flight Level 270 will give us max endurance for range flying.'

'If the winds are favourable,' Roslyn reminded him. 'Oh, this is all so . . . horrible. It's just guesswork, isn't it? Everything we've done all night is nothing but rough estimation.'

Cardin gestured his hands upwards. 'Well, what the flying hell else is there, Roslyn? We head towards Australia. We find it. We look for somewhere to put this thing down. End of fairy tale. I want you and Tom to be scouring the landscape from the minute we break visual to determine where we are. It will be pure VFR navigation so see if there's an old WAC chart in the map locker and get familiarised with every damned inch of it. When we see anything at all that looks like a reasonably long runway, we go for it. As you know, this thing usually needs at least 2,400 metres to land but we're desperate and I don't mind running off the other end if we have to.'

Roslyn looked miserable; her lovely face in pain. 'If we make it – I mean *when* we make it, I'll be quitting flying.'

Instead of cursing again, the captain seemed quite surprised. 'Ah, will you really?'

'Yes. I'll go and teach something – anything - as I should have done in the first place. What about you, Ray?'

'Hmm, I'm definitely finished with international. Domestic rosters for me. I want to see my son grow up - and Alicia needs me too, of course. Anyway, if this will be our last landing in a seven-four, then we better make it a bloody good one, eh Ros!'

'Yes, I agree with that,' declared Roslyn Steinhouse in one of few things to which she'd agreed with her captain all night.

Cardin wished he'd been much nicer to his pretty first officer, and to all the crew in general. And he quietly cursed again his stupidity in persisting with international flights after becoming a father so late in life. He'd already enjoyed decades of being a young single pilot crossing the world's oceans and continents, living it up without a care. And now, in the next few hours, if he pulled off a miracle landing it would finally be time for him to *get real* - as he had so righteously lectured everyone else.

Upon reaching their new flight level of 27,000 feet, Cardin gingerly pulled the fuel cut-off levers to no.1 and no.4 engines; the two outboard engines. They had been windmilling and providing partial thrust throughout the descent and now they would stop altogether. He felt a further deceleration and heard another slight decrease in airstream noise and desperately hoped that no-one else would notice it. Downstairs, most passengers seemed *not* to notice anything at all because the party was still going strong, but here and there a few Bibles wavered in shaking hands while many eyes were closed in fervent prayer.

Tom Tyson paid a brief visit to the morgue-like atmosphere of the flight deck where the airflow over the windscreen was now about half its usual roaring self. 'Did it work, Boss?'

Cardin turned around, pleased. 'Yes, Tom. I think so. How about downstairs? Do you think anyone noticed our descent? And ah, do you normally dress in a floral skirt and bright lipstick?'

Tom hopped into the jump seat to undress. 'Um, not all are partying. Some are very quiet . . . religious, I suppose. But most of them are still fired up and enjoying the biggest and loudest party ever held on a plane. But yes, I think we may have gotten away with our ploy.'

'Have you been drinking, Tom?'

'Yes. One tiny sip. Does it matter?'

'Well, of course. I still need you up here for the final grand performance which will involve intense VFR flying because we have to find a landing area soon.'

Tom smiled. 'I used to fly shark patrol Cessnas all up and down the east coast of NSW. I know it like the back of my hand. Mind you, they were all mostly flown at five hundred feet.'

'In that case you should know every damn landing strip, runway, and area of long paddocks along the entire coast. But this time you won't be flying; you'll be sitting firmly in that seat with the WAC chart in your hands and directing us the very best you can. We're all in this together, Tom.'

Tom gulped at the truth of it. 'I know. Meanwhile, I'll ah, just go back down for a short while because there are a few nice ladies waiting for me, okay?

Cardin ordered, 'But when I page you I want you back up here like a shot, Tom. Remember that if we dive into the drink they might find our black box CVR tapes one day and will transcribe them word for word. Even if we're dead, it won't look good to your family if investigators ask: 'But where on Earth was the second officer? We haven't heard a peep from him on these tapes. Was he even on the flight deck at the time?'

Interrupting, Roslyn Steinhouse said, 'Well Ray, I don't mean to be rude and in-your-face, but if they ever do examine our cockpit Voice Recorder tapes then they might also hear our earlier discussions – or arguments – in which Tom and I could foresee our peril and strongly suggested we take this present course of action, while you bucked against it for quite some time. And if they do, maybe your son will grow up one day and get to hear about it all.'

Cardin was stung. 'Oh really, Mrs Nostradamus? Well I wasn't aware that you knew every damn thing about flying and I didn't. I simply based my opposition to *your* commandeering of *my* plane upon a whole career of flying these things – as opposed to you two who have about one quarter of my hours and experience between you. I just couldn't think of any way we could shut those things down without too many stickybeaks noticing it.'

'I think a few may have noticed it by now,' said Tom as he exited the flight deck once again and prepared for battle and final goodbyes to several lovely ladies. He winked at the captain. 'Now I have urgent appointments, Boss – if you know what I mean.'

Cardin grunted after him. 'Yes, that's the right attitude, Tom. Groping a few passengers is far more important than preparing to save us all.'

Roslyn said nothing. What was the point of bickering to the very end? Actually, just what was the point of anything?

10.

In a vast chunk of oceanic airspace east of Newcastle, New South Wales, a lone FA-18 fighter jet from the local Williamtown Airforce base had been conducting night flying training over the lonely and bleak ocean the previous midnight. Within this military restricted area called R689, Flt. Lt. Steve Howland flew solo this night. He hadn't quite completed his full certificate to graduate into the *Tigers* squadron so the squadron leader ordered him to fly two more hours – alone.

'This flight might be a little different,' smiled his commander before take-off. 'And this time you'll have no-one to ask for help.' Howland was puzzled but was also on the verge of becoming a fully-fledged Airforce fighter pilot; his life-long dream.

Soon after, the supersonic FA-18 streaked into the night sky and headed east and out to sea. There will be no-one else out here, he had decided; not even civilian air traffic because they won't be cleared through the military restricted area while I'm here. Wary of what surprises his testing officer might suddenly throw at him, he casually threw a few joyous barrel rolls, loop-the-loops and Immelman turns – easy tasks to an FA-18. He switched his radios to MUTE; this was a night for radio silence in preparation for war zone training.

At 150 nautical miles east of Williamtown and still waiting for the unexpected, Howland soared and dipped while travelling at twice the speed of sound. Pulling up hard and gritting his teeth under several crushing G-forces, he was suddenly face to face with red and green nav lights hurtling straight at him. It all happened in less than a second and the pilot had no time to even commence an evasion. He missed the other plane – thank God – and Howland whistled a shrill of relief. But who the hell was that? Was it a Hercules from his base, or a huge C-17 from Amberley?

Howland broke radio silence to call on the discrete MIL-SEC channel and get the intruder identified; but he got no answer. He needed to report this "act of war" or he might fail his test. He called the base for fifteen minutes without reply. So that was his big test, eh? 'Pretty dumb test, then,' he decided. 'Just what did that achieve?'

Suddenly all his glowing data screens went blank. He had nothing but engine power thrusting away. Then, in the receding distance, Howland spotted the 'intruder' again, disappearing towards a rising Moon. Its strobe lights were going *blink blink blink* away from him, then they suddenly vanished. Howland was unnerved: unless this enemy had decided to turn off their strobes for evasive purposes, then something really weird had happened out there. Then all his warning horns went off at once. It was a shock. He felt like electricity had surged through him. His training and raw instincts kicked in as he hauled the nose up towards the stars and lit the afterburners.

At fifty-five thousand feet, Howland was flying so high he could have seen the curvature of the Earth had it been daylight, but he was shaking with fear in a totally blackened and silent cockpit. In curiosity he took a quick glance at the billions of stars in the Western sky, then violently rammed the control wheel forward while streaking west. Just then, a massive flash filled the black sky and made Howland pass out.

At 2½ times the speed of sound, or Mach 2.5, he awoke just as everything abruptly changed. All his console lights suddenly illuminated again and barking radio controllers were berating him for being off the air for almost twenty minutes! But he hadn't — he'd been calling *them* all the time. After a high-speed landing back at *Willytown,* Howland demanded to know the results of his test flight. The OPS officer refused to tell him but informed him that he was grounded for a fortnight. It was not revealed what F/L Howland had encountered that night, and the pilot soon forgot about the other mysterious plane that simply disappeared *out there* . . . That is, until the next morning when he turned on his TV.

Angrily, Howland stomped off to the OIC's tiny office and lodged official complaints about last night's mysterious events. 'I don't mind being tested, but I won't be lied to . . . sir.'

His OIC argued, 'We never quite got to that testing stage, but something else happened out there last night, Howland. We don't know just yet what it was, but it was right where you were for a short while . . . '

'What was it, sir?'

The Intel boss pointed to an oceanic map. 'Look. Right there is where this missing Air Australia 747 disappeared. It is the same place as you were . . . briefly.'

'But how could they have been there in R689 without a clearance?'

'They weren't.'

'Huh? You just said they were, sir.'

'We've gone over the radar replays for last night. You weren't out there last night and neither were they. Something massive happened last night but no-one knows what it was. That's when we ordered your RTB (return to base).'

Howland thought this over for several moments, then declared 'I saw it, sir.'

'Saw what?'

'That huge ghost plane. I nearly collided with it. I can confirm that it was either a C-17, a Boeing-747 or an A380 because it had four engines. It missed me by just metres, then it disappeared towards the horizon.'

'And then?'

'I saw it again for just a second, and then its lights vanished, sir. Like it had never existed - just as you said.'

The OIC mulled it over, then declared that the Base C/O would never reveal a single word of this civilian mystery in case the big military bosses became entangled in a nightmare of official enquiries and were threatened with budgetary cutbacks. And what could be worse than that?

Steve Howland went back to his bachelor's hut and watched the TV media circus again. Unbelievably, some people in Sydney's streets were running a betting book on what would eventuate, both before and after "fuel exhaustion." But what had *really* happened? The more he thought about his flight track last night - which had been plotted on maps that had now been confiscated - the more he became sure that both he and AA200 were in the exact same spot at the same time. And what was that enormous flash that he glimpsed just before blackening out? Lightning? If so, it was one hell of a lightning flash that illuminated the entire night sky and Howland could only think of one thing that could do that . . .

It just *had* to be a nuclear explosion. But who would do that? What country would detonate one of those apocalyptic monsters without informing its own military planes and civilian airlines? Enemies would. But who? Australia was not at war; especially not some nuclear war. So it must have been a nuclear test that was conducted at 150 nautical miles east of the coast. Seeking secrecy, authorities must have ensured security in that it occurred well over the horizon so no people living on the shoreline would see it - even if they happened to be staring in that exact direction just after midnight.

But surely seismometers would have recorded it? On the internet, Howland clicked on a site that divulged any recent seismological activity, especially near New South Wales. These devices record any earthquakes or other events of small or great magnitude. There was nothing.

The young Airforce pilot desperately wondered who else in the world he could contact to ask about this? The answer was no-one at all. All RAAF pilots were sworn to secrecy in all aspects of the defence of his country, and Steve was only twenty-four and in his third year of flying training; a junior. Now he was grounded for a fortnight and he could almost guarantee his own instant dismissal if he attempted to blow this baby right out of the water – especially at a time of national grief such as this. So what could he do: secretly whisper to someone that he was the last human to see AA200 and that he observed it just before a massive nuclear explosion took place that no-one else happened to see? In such a case, he might as well join the crazy *alien* brigades in the streets. And his wild theory could never be shared with any of his RAAF comrades who might also be prosecuted or discharged from the service if they propounded such lunacy without military approval. So his flight apparently never happened and his pilot's log book had already mysteriously disappeared to be magically replaced with a new one where last night's flight did not appear.

Thinking further, neither did Air Australia flight two-hundred ever appear. He knew this because his OIC had told him so.

11.

On board the Air Australia flight that may have never taken place, there nevertheless was a grand party in full swing right now. Dirty Dick with his dark humour was leading a conga line of devout followers as they chanted:

Oh send us up to the Spirit in the Sky,
That's where we wanna go when we die,
When we die and they lay us to rest
We're gonna go to the place that's the best . . .

A grand old rock song from the seventies and only remembered by a few, this was nevertheless a big hit again tonight which pulsed its way upstairs to the flight deck. At the aft end, someone's beat box was churning out a bass thump as laughter and frolicking was tonight's theme of the dream. Dirty Dick, in his greatest-ever performance, bragged that this was also his cleanest-ever performance and he thanked everyone for attending and being his final and most captive audience. Innocently, a few young children, unaware of the actual circumstances, eagerly joined in the merriment and danced in the aisles.

But how long could this party last? Even though inebriated, it was presumed that most of the 411 on board understood that the spectre of the Grim Reaper would inevitable arrive soon; attired in a black cloak and wielding his trademark scythe. So, it was really down to which song would be playing when this flying coffin took its sudden and final plunge into oblivion, while most wondered just how hard would it collide at super-high speed with either the water or hard ground?

Back up front, Captain Ray Cardin and First Officer Roslyn Steinhouse were peering anxiously forward through their heated windshields for any positive signs of land. From both chart and air plotting, they had reached their estimated time when they might hopefully see their homeland ahead. Would they spy a familiar river mouth and then a known town near it, or would it be the miraculous image of a city to emerge from the gloom of dawn?

Then at last, glancing down from 27,000 feet, a vague gray line appeared, running north to south on the dawn horizon.

'Could be just a cloud bank,' cautioned Second Officer Tom Tyson; now back on duty in the rear jump seat.

Roslyn squinted her eyes in fear that this was not so. 'I'm not sure, but I hope it's land. What a pain that the sunrise is so slow when we're flying from east to west. It must be twice as long as heading the other way against the rising sun.'

'It is,' Ray Cardin confirmed. 'Anyway, full sunrise shouldn't be too much longer now, folks.'

Tom interrupted with light conversation. 'Hey everyone. You know when they're flying on the International Space Station; they orbit the Earth about every ninety minutes. So when they're heading east, the sun doesn't just come up, it absolutely *leaps* up at them, suddenly blinding them with its glare. It's like someone has switched on a huge searchlight!'

162

Cardin didn't seem to hear him and spoke again. 'Because of our lower altitude we'll see the coastline later than we would have. But we can only do our best and, ah, I wonder if we should commence a further descent after passing this cirro-stratus layer . . . what do you think, Ros?'

The F/O was startled that the captain had deferred to her opinion after quite some time. Not expecting him to ask her anything at this most crucial time, she nevertheless realised that her answer must be entirely right. 'Ah, I say we should wait a few more minutes considering we're only on two engines. Any altitude we throw away now will not be regained if we're wrong.'

'Exactly!' agreed a temporarily happy Cardin. 'We'll have plenty of time soon to be joy-flighting around at lower altitudes. But damn it all; if only we had some weather radar or DME readouts. Or some GPS data instead of this . . . nothing! Radar would tell us what is land and what is not. And while we can squawk our transponder ident till we go blue in the face, what bloody use is that without radios to receive a confirmation and identification of our position? Christ! Just look at all those damn things sitting there dead!'

No-one wanted to hear that awful word just now (dead), and no-one desired to attain that state by never arriving over dry land at all. An imminent ditching would herald their death knell, while all Cardin could do would be to peer down at the waves below and attempt to roughly estimate the sea-level wind direction and strength by any whitecaps on black waves – a futile exercise, as Tom had sombrely warned him.

163

And even if he was able to determine the wind, the captain would then attempt the highly questionable manoeuvre of ditching into wind while also flying *along* the heaving swell lines, and all this in the bleak half-light of dawn. In any landing configuration the final impact would be horrendous as a massive wall of water would surge up hundreds of feet, with the pilots' windscreen either being smashed in or drenched in water and giving them nil visibility. Worse - as Roslyn had already warned, all four engines would likely shear away from the airframe – just as they had been carefully designed to do so utilising special shear-off bolts - then the wings could also be ripped away. Then the fuselage would be mortally holed and sink rapidly, while no-one on board could expect to survive. And even if they did: where in the world would they swim to? Where would they be, anyway? They might be near land and safety, or hundreds of miles from terra firma. In any case, who could contemplate or actually attempt a long oceanic swim after the violence of a massive plane crash into water? And even if you did happen to survive it, a life vest might keep you floating, but to where?

On the land, heated internet social networks continued to run riot with speculative rumour and wild guesswork about the ill-fated Air Australia flight-200, especially after Australian Navy and Airforce search organisations had so far found no trace of any debris in the oceanic area in which the flight was last plotted.

This mystery, although appearing similar, was actually somewhat different from the missing Malaysian Airlines Boeing-

777 flight MH370 which had reflected primary paints and secondary SSR radar returns to ATC for some time, then, once out of range, continued to transmit "handshake" beeps from its engine transponders as it wandered away in a puzzlingly opposite heading from its flight plan, far out into the Indian Ocean. The intrigue surrounding that flight, as yet still unresolved, soon centred on emotions of the flight crew - and particularly the captain, a man rumoured to be privately troubled by his divorce and perhaps other personal worries.

Also facing scrutiny was the young Malaysian first officer who proved to be somewhat of a playboy with female passengers - although it was hard to spin such normal behaviour into suicidal catastrophes when it was rather unlikely that he was the only male in the world like this.

Of further intrigue to some investigators was the fact that two Malaysian male passengers travelling on stolen passports and who were seated together on this flight, were mysteriously given scant attention by mainstream authorities or world media. Strangely, this became a contentious avenue that was hastily dropped for 'sensitivity' reasons because they were Muslims.

But these factors hardly pertained to AA200. The two flights held scarcely any similarities except that they both disappeared. For example, AA200 hadn't made any sudden turns off track, but was last radar identified as being "right on track." Then their primary radar *blips* were not seen at all after 80 DME Sydney, and no secondary SSR radar or digital transponder beeps were received after 150 miles. Far worse, all Satcom and CPDLC data links stopped transmitting about there, so the plane basically ceased to exit at this point. And, although scrutiny of the passenger manifest failed to disclose any suspicious persons on board, investigators could never preclude the possibility of such.

As the flight had been headed for American airspace and a landing in the USA, the FBI, the FAA and the US military held powerful defence interests in any and all aspects of this case. It was always possible that the plane had been commandeered by hijackers/terrorists and was forced to dive low over the waves and race towards US territory as an approaching silent killer. After all, this was precisely what the Imperial Japanese Navy/Airforce had done so successfully at Pearl Harbour on December 7th 1941. And now, although intense military and satellite surveillance had located nothing as yet, a maximum security alert had been declared over much of the vast Pacific Ocean.

Privately, US authorities believed that the flight had crashed into the sea many hours ago and was therefore an Australian predicament, but the ocean-wide alert remained in force until evidence ultimately proved otherwise and thus made the alert no longer necessary.

An interesting theory, however, suddenly appeared on Twitter concerning what one science writer referred to as "gravitational ripples." Just discovered on this very day, these waves are tiny ripples in space and time that are formed by the merging, or coalescence, of two black holes. "The ripples have recently opened up an entirely brand-new field of astronomy so we Earthlings can expect a flood of gravity wave signals arriving here over the next few years as our detecting devices are improved," the writer asserted.

"The stronger the gravity an object has, the greater the deformation of space and time it causes," he assured all readers. So whatever that actually meant, or whatever the implications for us all, could these coalescing dual black holes have anything to do with the disappearance of a passenger plane at the same time? Was it downed by these gravity waves and ripples in space and time?

This theory was soon lost amongst the jumbled swirl of all the others, especially the eternally ripe "little green men" theories, but many leading scientists world-wide did a sudden *heads-up* and seriously wondered about the amazing co-incidence of these two events occurring on the very same day.

On TV and talk-back radio, fiery debates choked the airwaves as the ghastly "death" hour approached. And suddenly it seemed that everyone claiming credibility was either an aviation "expert" or an occult guru to be heard and taken seriously. Suspiciously, some who claimed to be "retired airline pilots" didn't seem to know the difference between a Boeing and an Airbus, while one assured us that a 747 has two engines. And pushing their uniquely mystical barrow, several fortune tellers confidently predicted that the missing flight would re-appear "sometime" and that the answer was already written in the stars.

Even more vocally, while the usual fire-and-brimstone brigades were blaming the sins of all blaspheming mankind for this catastrophe, it remained silently unexplained why tens of thousands of other global flights every day, also presumably full of such sinners, successfully reach their destinations safely and without a scratch.

As the new day dawned near the International Date Line, eager locals ran to their sparkling Pacific shores to enthusiastically scour for debris from the missing jet. And in some places their frantic searchings bore immediate results with hundreds of pieces of *suspicious* metal fragments being gently washed ashore by small waves – just as they are every other day of the year. Claiming success, almost every island community started reporting that "parts of the jet" had been discovered in their waters.

Similar to when parts of MH370 were purportedly found scattered across the entire Indian Ocean from the Cocos Islands to the Chagos Archipelago, from the Maldives to the Seychelles and from Madagascar to Reunion Island, now it was Pacific islanders' turn for their brief moment of fame. Miraculous discovery claims flooded in from areas as far flung as Noumea to Samoa and Tonga, and from Vanuatu to the Solomons and the Gilbert/Kiribas islands. Even the remote Cook Islands on the way to Tahiti filed a report of a metal section that was definitely part of the jet's "wing flaps." But, while a ditching plane might leave a trail of pieces a mile or so long, these latest areas of alleged "finds" were encompassing a whopping section of the Earth's surface larger than the whole USA – surely one incredibly long splash! And on isolated Easter Island - not even within coo-ee of the flight planned track, a local radio station assured listeners that "parts will be found soon."

It was a bonanza, and the world media gleefully seized upon each new claim like feverish Alaskan miners who once shrieked *gold!* from the Klondike. But this time it was all fools' gold and hardly the Real McCoy. Without any confirmation or verification, experts nevertheless pronounced all these lumps of metal and floating debris, which tumble from the world's shipping every day, as indisputable evidence of AA200's final resting (or floating) place.

In truth, today's world's oceans often resemble seven gigantic garbage dumps which signify mankind's disgraceful contribution to world pollution. In storms, entire container ships (or their contents) often spew into our oceans and seas. Many of these containers soon break open from wave motion and their cargo inside - be it bicycles or cars, machine parts or Buddha statues, are gobbled by the waves – some to wash ashore in time, scattered across thousands of islands.

And the very worst of all this pollution are water-borne plastic particles which are a devastating curse upon Earth's struggling oceanic environment and its vast trove of living species. Thousands of miles long, linked up and spiralling throughout all the seven seas, satellites look down at what is smugly referred to as the *plastic soup.* This ugly soup comprises snaking trails of floating doom; an endless conga line of plastic bags and every imaginable plastic item known to us, all twisted and fused together and choking the existence out of marine life everywhere - especially turtles. Some once-beautiful beaches at tropical lagoons like those found at the picture-postcard lagoons of Tahiti's legendary Bora Bora lagoon can be nothing but unsightly garbage dumps today where large metal objects often have *Toyota* or *Samsung* or *Sony* stamped on them. Or *Made in China*. And to confuse plane crash spotters everywhere, the floating tides of the plastic soup often contain many plastic parts from fittings that are routinely installed inside airliners.

But even though none of today's finds had *Air Australia* or *Boeing* stencilled on them, they were nevertheless claimed to be genuine proof of the mystery plane's watery graveyard. Much of this galloping conjecture escaped even before the real flight's fuel had finally depleted; i.e. while it was still in the air and probably thousands of nautical miles distant; near the Hawaiian Islands or mainland USA. Or perhaps on its way back to Australia . . .

Happily and profitably for some, all this alleged *proof* was guaranteed to sell serious numbers of newspapers and chunky blocks of air time.

12.

Not everyone following the drama was sympathetic towards all of those poor souls on board the missing AA200, and attention was now quickly turning from a mild dislike to a powerful hatred of the plane's captain, Ray Cardin. Along with a stern-faced and very unflattering photo of him plastered in every newspaper and on TV news screens in Australia and probably most parts of the world, Cardin's once-fine reputation was now being shredded through the ugly meat grinder of uninformed, unjustified and irrational public opinion with headlines such as:

> *Kaptain Kamikaze!*
> *Did he take his woes out on them?*
> And, *captain's failed marriage!*
> *Oh no! Not another suicide captain?*

Despite Mrs Alicia Cardin holding her crying child and fronting a wall of cameras outside her Sydney suburban home while attempting to deny there was anything at all wrong with their marriage, reporters yelled and irate mobs screamed vengeful insults at the frightened woman whose life had suddenly erupted like Krakatau. In fairness, a few decent commentators on morning TV spoke up for her husband and revealed that this all started innocently enough when someone Tweeted: 'Maybe his marriage has failed?' Then another had added, 'Just like that Malaysian pilot, eh?' And so, like a metastasising cancer, the gossip snowballed from there into the frothing hatred so often a hallmark trait of the arrogant lynch mob mentality.

An Air Australia PR spokeswoman quickly fronted a wall of microphones to deny that Captain Ray Cardin's marriage suffered even the slightest hiccups, but the news juggernaut often finds it rather inconvenient if the truth threatens to derail a really juicy story. So, while people everywhere were soon gossiping in trains and buses and breakfast cafes "Did you hear that the captain was suicidal and crashed them into the sea? Fancy doing that!' . . . Mrs Alicia Cardin was huddled inside her home in sheer terror; afraid to ever emerge again. The most unjust part was that she loved the tall pilot who married her at his age of 46, and their marriage was quite good and they were both devoted to young Jamie. Unfortunately for her, such boring normality never makes headlines.

When Cardin's friends and family finally turned a vengeful blowtorch onto the vile rumours about the allegedly suicidal captain, slick media attention conveniently skated sideways to the very attractive first officer, Roslyn Steinhouse, whose smiling face was emblazoned into the public's awareness as though she had just won the Miss World contest:

Was lovely Ros bullied by him?

They were Cardin's orders: she HAD NO CHOICE!

"Our lovely Roslyn Steinhouse," previewed one popular women's magazine article about to rush into print, 'has one of the cutest hairstyles we've seen in a while. But what has happened now to poor Ros? This is our Aussie glamour girl who only ever wanted to teach children, but her strict father insisted she learn to

172

fly flimsy little planes. Please come back to us soon, Ros. We all miss you.' The magazine's glossy front cover showed glamorous Roslyn in uniform; gripping the controls of a 747 while smiling beautifully at the camera. This cover would eventually sell millions.

But even this diversionary angle was soon surpassed by journalists who, refusing to surrender, hoisted second officer Tom Tyson up onto the public chopping block. His cheeky grin on a front-page photo showed him shirtless and muscled with hair askew, drying off after surfing at Bondi Beach in Sydney.

Surfie Airlines takes a wipe-out! Was this long-haired surfie hunk to blame?

So, in a land where the law purportedly declares "Innocent until proven guilty" Captain Cardin had already been pronounced guilty and hopefully executed, First Officer Steinhouse had been canonised into martyrdom and Second Officer Tom Tyson's jury and admiring female fan club were both still out.

Soon the relatives, friends, and sometimes dubious acquaintances of the entire manifest of ill-fated passengers and crew were thrusting themselves before TV cameras; relating heart-rending tales of how young Tyler had always been such a good boy at school, how Caitlyn was easily the best singer in the choir, and how Margie was always going to be a doctor "if only she'd had the chance." Curiously, with about four hundred passengers on the flight, it seemed as though each one of them had suddenly blossomed a legion of loyal friends willing to testify to their doomed friend's holiness, purity and kind-heartedness, but when someone mentioned Dirty Dick the pub singer no such glowing tributes emerged. Apparently Dick, real name Richard Rendy, didn't qualify for martyr's Heaven – but Hell only - although a few devoted fans laughed and said:

"I bet he could sing a dirty ditty about that!"

> *Now, when I went down to the Devil's tomb,*
> *Way down under the sea,*
> *I met a young mermaid in a lovely room,*
> *And guess what she showed to me . . . . Oi !*

13.

Sadly, the young and innocent are often involved in any major accident, and AA200 was no exception. Young Corrie Newnes was aged just six and her brother Slater was four. Having recently escaped from a tragic house fire in Melbourne where they'd lost both their parents, the two orphaned children were being taken to America to live with their only known relative: their aunty Jennifer in Phoenix, Arizona. While this aunt was enthusiastic about adopting them both, she already had three children of her own so it was going to be somewhat crowded. But there was little else she could do: Jenny's deceased sister's children had nowhere else in the world to go.

On this day, with all the relevant documents approved and stamped, professional chaperone Jane Grayling was accompanying the newly-orphaned children on AA200. While Grayling was a kindly and wonderful hostess to unaccompanied children on long flights, and had done so many times before, she was nevertheless quite wary of flying itself; only tolerating it because it was part of her job.

Now with this horrific scenario facing all on board, the chaperone almost needed a chaperone for herself. Trying to disguise her gnawing fears while denying the stark truth to these two bereaved children was certainly the hardest chore Jane had ever encountered. And all this occurring whilst confronting her own looming demise. So, should she simply surrender to grief and betray the innocent childrens' last hours, or pretend that life was normal and sing more merry songs with them?

'But what's wrong, Mrs Grayling?' inquired perceptive Corrie.

'Oh, nothing darling. We'll soon be there,' assured the chaperone.

'But why are so many people crying? And why are all those others laughing and singing and doing funny dances?'

Jane answered while wiping a tear away. 'It's, ah, hard to explain, Corrie. Maybe some of them just want to have fun and the others don't, so they might have had a little fight over it. You know how kids sometimes fight over crayons or swings . . . things like that.'

Young Slater trustingly gazed up at her, never saying a word and permanently sucking his thumb while remaining unaware that both his parents had gone forever. Corrie considered Mrs Grayling's words then whispered, 'But I wish our mummy and daddy were coming with us.'

'Now Corrie, I've explained to you before that they have gone away for a very long time. You remember when your house was on fire that night and those brave firemen came and saved you and Slater? Well, after that they didn't have any more time to save your mummy and daddy so they went up to Heaven. Okay?'

'But mummy was fun and daddy told us lots of stories.'

'Aren't I fun?'

'Yes, but why are you crying like them? That's not fun, is it? Did you have a fight too?'

'Ah no, I just have sore eyes, that's all.'

Thankfully, the girl's short attention span wandered to other matters then she asked, 'I can't remember my Aunty Jenny's face, but will she take us to Disneyland when we get there?' Jane Grayling shuddered over those words "get there." The cabin crew were now cautious about making announcements concerning *getting* anywhere because everyone knew their plane was probably lost and could not communicate with anyone or anything in the world. And that's not supposed to ever happen, is it? Aren't all these modern planes fitted with more electronic gadgetry than you could ever imagine? While Jane hated planes and air travel but loved her chaperone work, now she was to lose absolutely everything – even her trusting charges along with her own life. It just wasn't fair.

Then she had an idea. 'Why don't you two jump up and dance with all the people, Corrie? Come on Slater, you too!'

'Yay!' cheered little Corrie on what could well be the last night of her brief and tragic life. 'I love dancing! We learnt dancing at my Kindy school when I was only little.' The two kids joined a snaking line of chanting and inebriated adults and were soon the stars of the show, while scared little Slater firmly gripped his sister's dress as though she might fly away. Once they were down the aisle and out of sight, chaperone Jane Grayling burst into uncontrollable sobs.

Things weren't much better at the front of the plane as Roslyn Steinhouse felt a burning in her throat along with overpowering urges to break down and simply *lose it all*. But that's exactly *not* what pilots are supposed to do; they are programmed through rigorous training - mostly in flight simulators, to react to every conceivable emergency in a split second. And not just react, but to respond with precisely laid-down procedures in the most professional manner possible - like robots.

This is all grand in theory and within those million-dollar simulators - no matter how realistic they are - but none of the crew had done any training for a complete failure of almost every vital component that they flew with. Yes, they'd practiced a total loss of all their main panel screens and had to press on with the old basic analogue dials, but in the simulator they still had radio and data communications to report their predicament and request assistance. Then the simulator had failed their data links and left the main panels working. Next, their radios died so they simply communicated through their data links until they had finally passed their sim checks for another six months. Fair enough.

But this real crisis situation wasn't even slightly fair.

'It's just not bloody fair!' Ray Cardin angrily banged the console with his fists as he glared out the window. 'We've done every damn thing exactly by the book tonight, but every damn thing has still gone bloody wrong! So will someone please tell me just what the hell I have done wrong?' His frantic eyes peered forward through the windscreen, desperately seeking any signs of land ahead instead of the endless gray stretches of water below. They had reached their projected ETA for making landfall - according to their trusted chart plotter, Tom Tyson, but only long gray cloud bands could be glimpsed on the distant western horizon.

Roslyn asked, 'Ah, could Tom be wrong? He can only estimate any headwinds and obviously they were stronger than we allowed. Tom, have you checked it all again?'

'Again and again,' was Tom's despondent reply. 'But I used an average wind because it's no use cheating and pretending we're in Fairyland.'

Cursing the whole world again, Cardin continued his fiery tirade to whoever would listen. 'And just how many goddamned times have I crossed this friggin' ocean and not a single thing went wrong? Fifty? A bloody hundred? And no-one else . . . absolutely no other flight that I know of has ever had to cope with something like this! None! Yes, planes have become lost. Some have had nav losses plus comm losses. Even data link losses. Some lost an engine - or even two. But no poor bastards were ever as unlucky as we've been tonight. We've been airborne for about fourteen hours now and have not sighted a single object, aircraft strobe light or speck of land – except for those lights on Kiribati. They were probably the only things we saw after taking off from Sydney. Last things we might ever see, too. Je-zuss! If I ever find out that someone was responsible for all this . . . '

He noisily pounded his fist again just as Roslyn fondly recalled those lights from hours ago and spoke: 'There was something unusual about those lights . . . ah, did anyone notice?'

'Huh?' Cardin remained infuriated by their miserable luck.

'Well, there were just so many lights down there,' Ros said. 'It's only a few weeks since I flew over there last time and there was nothing like that sea of lights we saw tonight . . .'

The captain roared. 'Jesus Ros, we're trying to find bloody Australia, not some damned light show on friggin' Kiribas! I told you back then that it was probably just some religious festival going on. What could it possibly matter, anyway?'

It all mattered to her. 'And earlier there was that voice that claimed we'd disappeared right off the planet Earth . . . so just imagine if we really have?'

Cardin spun around to Tom and gave him a fierce glare. 'Wonderful, just bloody wonderful! Tom, could you please relieve Miss Starry-eyes here from her post? Just when I need her assistance more than ever, she's gone off with the fairies on the good ship Lollipop!'

But Tom didn't budge because some of it made sense - in a rather abstract sort of way. He disregarded the captain and asked her, 'What do you mean about those lights, Ros?'

'I mean that I stayed there for three days last year, and even though Kiribati is spread over 3½ million square kilometres of ocean while their population is only one hundred thousand, there were only a few lights on each island apart from Tarawa, the capital. But even there, no way was there anything like the million or more lights I saw down there tonight. It was huge – like looking down on Melbourne - and unless we were wrong in our identification of Kiribati, then it has quadrupled in size since last year.'

Cardin sneered. 'So the damn natives got a bit restless, that's all. Not much else to do down there at night, I suppose . . . except making little babies.'

'You made a little baby recently,' she smirked.

Cardin was unamused. 'And what about your mate the ham radio operator, Roslyn? Some nerdy teenager in his bedroom in northern bloody Bogistan announces that we, on the other side of the world, have disappeared right off this planet instead of *he*, in his insanity, being the real one floating in a celestial wonderland!'

'This is getting us nowhere,' interrupted a disappointed Tom. 'And we went through all this before, ladies and gents. So, how about any sightings of shipping down there? Yachts? Fishing trawlers? Let us please remain focused here . . . and I shouldn't have to remind anyone of this.'

Surprisingly, the irate Cardin quickly forgot about keelhauling his officers for treason and quietly joined them in scanning the seas below. Perhaps if several freighters or tankers were sighted all heading in roughly the same direction, then they might be pointed towards land and a harbour somewhere. And most places with a decent-sized harbour also have a reasonably-sized airport, too . . . although this surely was dead reckoning at its barest bones.

Incredibly, it was just moments later that a huge vessel like an aircraft carrier was spied, smashing the waves far below. 'It's enormous,' Cardin observed. 'US Navy, I suppose. And look at those cross runways on the deck. See that? The thing's got huge runways going lengthways *and* sideways across it. Never even heard of that, have you?'

'I don't suppose we could pop down on it for lunch?' smiled Tom.

'Ha! No such luck,' Cardin cursed. 'It's big alright, but not *that* damned big. If we approached them they'd shoot us down then cook us for lunch rather than invite us to land on it.'

But Roslyn wasn't wasting any breath on humour. She keyed her PTT mike button and broadcast to the warship on all emergency frequencies: HF, VHF and military UHF. 'The aircraft carrier heading west towards the east coast of Australia with the crossing runways on the deck, this is Australia two-zero-zero, do you read?' She repeated the call many times without success, recording yet another painful frustration for them all.

Tom sighed and also cursed their luck. 'And we can't even follow it. It's sailing at maybe forty knots and we're doing 450!'

Cardin's only response was to punch the console again. 'Shite!'

There was a light tapping on the flight deck door. Tom sprang up, full of suspicion. He'd decided that anything at all could happen tonight and he wasn't about to take any chances; especially right now when the pilots needed maximum attention and concentration during this: perhaps their very last chance at escape.

There was another soft knock. Tom panned the CCTV camera around but saw no-one outside the door. He picked up the intercom phone but no-one was there. Then he checked the overhead alarm panel and no warnings were flashing or sounding.

'This is serious stuff!' he decided with heart pounding. 'Hey Boss, someone is tapping on the door! Can't see anyone, but maybe they're lying down and waiting to pounce . . .'

Cardin spun around and snapped. 'Oh what joy! And just what I friggin' need at this particular stage of my brilliant career. Not only a hijacker, but a stupid bloody hijacker! Does he think we're having a party in here too and will welcome him in? Where are our party hats?'

Cardin gonged Purser Zaresh and barked at him, 'Security alert! . . . as if we need another one. Haneed, get your arse up the stairs faster than Ussain Bolt with diarrhoea! There's someone at our door. Bring your Taser gun and any help you might need. I hereby authorise you to take any actions necessary to overcome this threat. Now move it!'

As if the flight deck crew weren't already on high alert, now they most certainly were! The pressure and strain of it all had become simply too much . . . until Zaresh called them on his discrete two-way radio and said, 'All clear, captain. Code blue zero-ten. I am here and have a special visitor to the deck. Would you like to meet her?'

Cardin almost choked with rage. 'No I bloody would not, thank you for nothing Haneed! What is this: Halloween? Do you think I have nothing to do at the moment? Do you realise what stage we're at now? When you become a purser again in your next life you can conduct free tours of the entire plane for everyone all day!'

'But captain, she is only six years old and she'd like to give you some flowers . . . '

'Flowers!' yelped Cardin. 'Have we gone down already? Is this Hell? We need more than bloody flowers in here . . . don't we, Tom?'

Tom squinted into the CCTV and spied Zaresh holding hands with a little blond-haired girl. There was no-one else in view and no threats apparent. Tom raised his hands in question: 'Ah, okay Boss?'

'Okay? Yes, I suppose it's bloody okay. And it's also okay for the whole AC/DC rock band to waltz in here and give us a free concert. And while we're at it, why not invite the Tierra del Fuego Philharmonic orchestra to grace us with their presence . . .' Cardin was still flapping his arms in hyperventilation as the purser entered with a lovely smiling child adorned with pink ribbons in her hair.

The girl stared at him in puzzlement. 'Um, hello Mr Pilot. Someone told me to bring you these flowers and to say thank you for saving us all. They are only plastic but we had ones like them at our kindergarten and I loved them. Do you?'

Cardin slumped down, embarrassed. 'Ah, that's very nice of you little girl, but we are kind-of really busy in here right now. Ask nice Mr Zaresh to bring you back another time.'

But the first officer was delighted at this refreshing change of scenario and turned around to smile, 'Hello sweetie. What's your name?'

'My name is Corrie and my little brother is Slater and he's only four. Ah, why do you have those funny stripes on your shoulders?'

Tom Tyson whispered cheekily, 'At last: someone sane on the flight deck!'

Cardin snapped at him. 'What did you say?'

'I said there were some planes on the flight deck of that aircraft carrier.'

The visiting princess smiled her winning smile again and announced, 'As soon as we get to America we are starting a whole new life. Did you know?'

'No, but that's just fantastic, Corrie,' Roslyn smiled. 'Is your whole family moving there?'

The little soul looked downcast towards the floor. 'Well, our mummy and daddy died in our big house fire last month, so we are going to live with our lovely Aunty Jenny. It should be really fun there and she has three children of her own for us to play with. But first we hope she'll take us to Disneyland before we start our whole new life. It will just be so exciting . . . I hope.'

The flight deck went silent. No-one knew where to look so Cardin stared at his blank screens. Roslyn Steinhouse covered her eyes with her hands while Tom Tyson suddenly considered the overhead console of five hundred switches to be conveniently interesting.

Cardin stood up and thanked the girl for bringing this welcome and refreshing ray of sunshine into their gloomy tomb in the sky. He accepted her flowers then stumbled over his parting words as he gave her a hug and assured her that her whole new life was just up ahead.

'But up where? When?' Corrie asked.

185

'Ah, we can't quite see it yet, Corrie. But soon . . . I promise.'

The girl looked at him strangely, then pointed eagerly forwards out the windscreen. 'Well, there it is right there. See?'

The three pilots and the purser spun around and gawked forwards. There, on the distant horizon, a blackish lump had emerged from the scattered low clouds. But this time it wasn't a false cloud layer, but a headland! Genuine solid earth and surely the greatest sight ever seen by any of them.

Stunned and amazed, the pilots realised they had flown right through Hell and back into the real world again. And the first person to spy it was a charming six-year-old who casually announced, 'Anyway, my real name is Coralie, but you can call me Corrie if you want. Oh well, I have to go back to Mrs Grayling now. But I like aeroplanes, too. Do you think I could be a pilot lady when I grow up?'

Cardin nodded, then before the door closed he forced a grin, 'Yes, I hope so. I really do . . . '

'*If* she ever grows up,' whispered Tom, which made Roslyn weep into a handkerchief. Before exiting, the angry purser threw them all a contemptuous glance which obviously blared: 'So how come it took a six-year-old to find some land?'

Roslyn peered intently forward at the dark blob far away. She'd never been so relieved in her life as the moment that little girl had pointed the target out. There was nothing to worry about now; they were "home and hosed" as the saying goes. But how and why did it all go so dreadfully wrong in the first place?

14.

Throughout Australia, people everywhere stopped to watch or listen to the appalling news that the Air Australia Boeing-747 had surely come down somewhere because it would now be out of fuel. With 411 souls on board, that meant a lot of families and friends to not only commence grieving, but to loudly demand what went wrong.

Perplexingly, this tragic loss was much more frustrating than the Malaysian triple-seven in 2014 because at least that plane emitted pulsing electronic beeps to satellites which showed it veering wildly off course, then wandering inexplicably far across the Indian Ocean to its ghostly doom. But in this instance there were no trails to follow and negligible clues to investigate. On the ground, it was now full daylight in eastern Australia where a partially cloudy sky hid the morning sun. But no adverse weather had been forecast or observed by the Bureau of Meteorology during the night, and no thunderstorm cells appeared on satellite printouts where the planned track of AA200 lay. And it wasn't cyclone season so this avenue of pursuit was bare; Mother Nature was most unlikely to be the villain here.

All that was positively known was that the flight departed from Sydney airport, flew for about 25 minutes along its planned track line, then simply disappeared. If it had kept going it would have arrived somewhere on the North American mainland by now. And that was the operative word: *somewhere*. If not, it should have at least reached Hawaiian FIR airspace hours ago.

But it hadn't. Sadly, no news from America was bad news indeed. This only heaped more frustration upon search and rescue SAR organisations everywhere. Meanwhile, the bereaved families were left with little hope while politicians made condolence speeches of commiseration that answered nothing and eased no-one towards any closure. And while the downed engines - wherever they lay, were probably still warm, communities were already drawing up plans for mass funeral services with extravagant shows of public grief. In the background, the media, trading in the misery, were exuberantly rearranging TV program schedules so not a single thing would be missed.

On TV, a nervous Air Australia CEO, David Turnbull, issued a lengthy statement which strongly praised Captain Cardin and his flight crew as "the very finest of professionals who would have battled courageously through to the very end." Hearing this, some astute viewers thought that his halting and awkward words were certainly stirring but embarrassingly premature because there was still no proof that the plane had crashed yet, while most other viewers just *knew* that it had crashed and remained convinced that Captain Hopeless or one of the others had accidently pushed a wrong button somewhere along the line. Oops!

'But we'll never know one way or another,' was the most common public expression, while savvy social networking sites boasted that they already knew exactly what had happened and continued to *go viral* with "genuine" sighting reports that the big

Boeing had landed in either Acapulco, Alaska, or the dusty plains of Kyrgyzstan, while much-maligned aliens were, once again, copping most of the blame for this. When the plane subsequently could not be sighted at these locations, those in the know proclaimed that it had already, conveniently, taken off again to perform another dramatic death plunge elsewhere.

So it was scarcely noticed when a young Australian Airforce pilot suggested on Facebook that something "cataclysmic" had occurred over the ocean the previous night, and that he *knew* what it was because he had inside information. But his claim received no Facebook *likes* and was mostly derided for spreading falsehoods. Curiously, no-one thought to query him on just what was the particular inside info to which he referred. Dismissed into oblivion, he was quickly overridden by paranormal witch doctors who managed to command the list as the number-one experts on the subject.

As the day progressed into night, some intelligent observers remained unconvinced that a huge plane can take off then simply vanish without any trace. Unlike the Malaysian Boeing which trailed behind it a virtual digital blitz of electronic clues for radar and satellites to absorb and record, the AA200 plane, apparently, just quietly ceased to exist – and so did all her unfortunates on board. One minute they were there, and the next they were not . . .

The following day on daytime television, Captain Cardin's wife, Alicia Cardin, appeared for an interview with popular Midday hostess Hailey Goss. Although she now possessed a new-found wariness of the media, Alicia usually enjoyed watching Goss at midday and felt she could trust her. Besides, she sensibly decided that she might very well need the generous appearance payment offered by the network. It was not that her husband was an underpaid worker - far from it, but rumours were swirling that if any professional negligence were ever proven against her husband then his final payout could be substantially reduced – despite AA's hasty assurances to the contrary. And she had a two-year-old child to consider - as her mother reminded her frequently - while the costs of raising a child these days were enormous. Further, Ray had left her with a house only partially paid off. She might need every cent . . .

On this note, she needed to bear in mind that legal proceedings against the airline - in this case represented by Captain Cardin and his crew - were already in motion and lawyers everywhere were backed and armed with the combined anger of over four hundred irate families or associates of the passengers who were all angling for their slice of any possible litigation payouts.

In the TV studio, the cameras flicked on and Hailey Goss smiled and offered her condolences to the tall and dark Alicia Cardin, then said, 'This won't be easy, Alicia, but all those families really need to know just why their loved ones simply vanished . . . and how.'

This was a tactless start and a surprised Alicia Cardin eventually replied, 'How the heck would I know that, Hailey? I'm not a pilot or an air accident investigator. I was just a stewardess.'

Goss said, 'Yes, but they just can't reconcile how all this could occur if nothing was reported as being wrong with the plane and there was no adverse weather along the route. The pilot said nothing and then *whammy,* they were just gone!'

As much as Alicia had previously admired Goss for her show, she was tolerating none of this line. 'Firstly, Hailey, airliners have at least two pilots. But you said "the pilot." On airline flights there is not just *a* pilot, but several in fact.'

'I'm sorry,' apologised Goss.

Alicia Cardin continued, 'Hailey, I hate the way the media always says *THE* pilot did this, and *THE* pilot did that. As I indicated, on international flights they are a team of at least three fully qualified airline pilots who work as a team to fly the thing. And sometimes there may be four of them if a check captain is on board to check someone out. No-one ever flies airliners around the sky by themselves.'

This early turn of events seemed to be slipping out of Hailey Goss' control; something that she dreaded. Her firm policy during interviews was always to keep the upper hand, but if a guest showed hostile defiance in any way then she would immediately divert them off track so that she, the host, always won. This was why she was paid so handsomely.

Goss smiled crookedly – possibly like a cobra about to strike. 'About your late husband, Alicia: was Ray a good husband?'

But this captain's wife was a most determined ex-stewardess who was apparently not just a glorified coffee waitress - as many assert. Alicia fired back: 'He is *not* my late husband, Hailey, because they aren't even confirmed dead yet! Gee, how tasteless was that question?" Alicia glanced at an off-camera director in a glassed

191

booth who made a gesture of slitting his throat as she bravely pressed on.

'And I won't be diverted by you because I know where you are leading. Our private life is of no concern to you or anyone; but what is of great concern are these vile rumours flourishing everywhere that my husband somehow stuffed this up and killed all these people - maybe by pressing a wrong button, or whatever. But let me tell you that I've spent hours talking to pilots on flight decks and I know . . . '

Alicia was astounded that Goss was no longer listening to her but appeared to be whispering into some concealed microphone down her blouse. Finally Goss came up for breath and neatly side-tracked her. 'Alicia, what about some stories we're hearing that Captain Cardin is not very well liked at Air Australia?'

The pilot's wife burst out: 'You don't have a clue what you're talking about! A captain doesn't need to be liked; he just needs to be respected.'

'Thank you Alicia,' interrupted Goss. 'Ah, we need to cut to a commercial break just now . . . '

'No we bloody-well don't!' spat a fuming Alicia Cardin while the furious director slashed at his throat again. 'You asked me to appear on this show so I will finish what I was saying. My husband has enormous flying experience. And for everyone's info, there is no single button or device on a 747 jumbo that can suddenly destroy it or make it plunge to the ground. There are, for example, fuel shut-off valves that could be pulled, but not without loud claxons and warning bells going off. And everything else is also alarmed and controlled by on-board monitoring so that no inadvertent use of anything can take place. Or do you think that brilliant Boeing design engineers would have placed Armageddon buttons in stupid positions so that stupid or negligent people could stuff it all up?'

The canny Hailey Goss wasn't beaten this easily. 'Ah well, the Germanwings suicide pilot did exactly that just recently . . . '

'He did it when the other pilot left the flight deck for the toilet. And there was no magic button, he simply locked the captain out. Also, it was a domestic flight where they only carry two pilots.'

'So, perhaps your Ray ditched his jumbo into the Pacific Ocean and they are all still safe?'

Shocked, Alicia Cardin hadn't even considered this nightmare. 'Ah, I'm sure you can't land that huge thing in water.'

'Well, Captain Sully had no trouble ditching his plane into New York's Hudson River.'

Alicia was a mother; a former stewardess. She had never envisioned this friendly chat on live TV degenerating into a star-chamber bitch session about advanced aviation technicalities. She glared daggers at the smirking host and spat: 'Smart arse!'

Goss quickly grasped that she had lost face here again, but took one last stab at salacious or scandalous victory. 'Well, I really don't know as much about aviation as you, Alicia – of course - and I understand the grief you are suffering right now, but I had rather preferred that we could amiably discuss your home life with Ray. '

'Rubbish!' exploded Alicia Cardin. 'Your only preference is to dig the dirt. And I am not suffering any grief because I firmly believe that my husband and all those people are still alive. Meanwhile, this tacky show is for lay people like you who wouldn't know the front end of a 747 from the back end, and to make snide insinuations about matters of which they know absolutely nothing.'

And she wasn't finished yet. 'Do you know how many times Ray has flown a jumbo jet across the Pacific Ocean? I looked in his logbook yesterday and it says *sixty-six.* Yes, sixty-six is the number of flights he has safely and successfully navigated across to America and back – plus around the world to Europe, Asia, and most everywhere else. So why would a highly professional pilot like him suddenly make a crucially fatal mistake this time after almost twenty thousand hours of perfectly safe flying time? But no-one ever thinks about this when they open their big . . . '

Goss smirked, 'But has he ever shown any signs of depression?'

Furiously, Alicia Cardin stormed off the set and thus became Goss's very first walk-out. The interview was promptly terminated with the enraged director's voice-over assuring viewers that their guest was quite okay; it was just that her grief had, quite understandably, overtaken her.

It was time for an important commercial: "Does your pooch suffer from fleas?"

Later, opinion polls recorded a majority of viewers who stated that they didn't particularly like 'Mrs Smarty-Pants-Captain's-Wife', as against a loyal few who sympathised with her plight. In a street interview, a very large and angry woman called Froggy told the camera that "You could see on that lying bitch's face that she's hiding something,' while a heavily-tattooed backpacking tourist from Argentina assured us all that 'Her star sign just doesn't align, man.'

Only one old man in the street was graciously awarded a few seconds of air time when he remarked, 'That US AIR Airbus was only about half the size of a 747. And it ditched onto glassy river water in nil wind. There is no comparison with those lucky people and a huge 747 putting down into the massive swells of the mid-Pacific Ocean. And anyway: what a gutsy girl. Go Mrs Cardin!'

The man waved his fist at the cameras just as the uncaring reporters lost interest: 'I know what I'm talking about. I was in the aviation industry for 43 years . . . ' but any further remarks were swept away by gusty winds and would not have sold news copy, anyway.

15.

There once was a lovely but sad song that went:

Well even the longest night won't last forever,
Too many hopes and dreams won't see the light.
And even the brightest star won't shine forever . . .
But there is something in the air . . .

And so it was for the exhausted passengers and crew on board
Air Australia flight two-hundred. This night could not last forever,
but something most certainly was in the air: *they* were still in the
air!

Up there, the party to end all parties had raged away for
almost ten hours and now most party-goers had danced
themselves to a standstill. And, disastrously, the booze had run
out! Crates of liquor and beer that had been found downstairs in
the cargo hold had been attacked without mercy and now the
cupboard was most definitely bare. And if Dirty Dick had still been
conscious instead of flaked out in the middle of a Business Class
aisle, he probably would have sung:

Well, even the best free grog won't last forever . . .

Now there were bodies strewn everywhere; not at all like the
neat midnight arrangement on *normal* flights where everyone tries
to doze sitting up; this was more like a battle zone after the last
bugle had faded away. Many revellers who had noisily declared
that they would be staying awake to the very end had instead

collapsed after their body clocks decided that sleep time was many noisy hours overdue.

Always trying to help, airlines often issue polite warnings about consuming too much alcohol on long flights. This is mainly because cabin crews don't want to be battling belligerent drunks for hours, but also because aircraft cabins are generally not humidified. That is, the ambient humidity is quite low: the direct opposite of a sweltering tropical afternoon in monsoonal Calcutta. So when humidity is very low, excessive drinking of alcohol dehydrates a drinker even faster than it usually does - sometimes to a dangerous extent.

But it would be unsafe if the pilots on the flight deck were also dehydrated over many hours, even though they certainly don't imbibe alcohol when flying. Because long stretches without adequate moisture in the air can cause many nasty medical risks to crew, the flight decks of many long-haul airliners are specially humidified while the passenger cabins are not . . . cost being the official half-true reason given.

So, if you've partied heavily all night long in a dry passenger cabin you can easily become severely dehydrated and even pass out, while all your declared vows and intentions to rage forever will fade away with you.

This is how Purser Haneed Zaresh found most of his customers after returning from the flight deck. He gently lay little Coralie Newnes down on some cushions as she fought her tiredness. 'My real name is Coralie,' she whispered to him, 'but I like Corrie best. Do you?' Zaresh nodded then bid the friendly child goodnight while desperately hoping he wasn't saying a final farewell to her. But, if it was to be, then he held back a few tears and prayed that she would have sweet dreams.

Back on the flight deck where the air was comfortably humid, the crew seemed to be succumbing to an insidiously different fatigue. They'd all been counting on a rest break during the flight but only Roslyn and Ray had snatched brief naps while Tom Tyson had none. And extreme stress for many hours takes a wretched toll: perhaps even worse than dehydration does, so the three pilots now felt desperately wearied and seemed to be suffering from tingling and fragile nerves.

'I absolutely forbid anyone from falling asleep again,' ordered the captain as he wagged a warning finger at them. 'Although I feel I could drop off right now, this is the very last thing any of us can afford to be doing. Apart from all those trusting souls behind us, we owe it to ourselves to be absolutely one hundred percent on the ball. Eyes wide open and brains in top gear! After we land on some country road or in Farmer Jones' paddock we can sleep for the next month if we want - but not now. Everyone copy that?'

So, in essence there were three half-zombies in a semi-conscious state who were planning to perform a miracle landing after locating their position in the world through sheer guesswork and primitive visual reckoning. While a landmass the size of Australia certainly is massive, it is almost minute when compared to the whole Pacific Ocean, so this crew needed more than a mere stab in the dark to find it and then to pull off the landing of the century on something that might not even be suitable for light planes.

In the jump seat, a sleepy Tom Tyson found himself imitating Dirty Dick as he sang quietly . . .

If Farmer Jones goes out in his fields today,
He's in for a big surprise . . . .

But it was perhaps another eerie force that enveloped all those on the ill-fated Boeing early that morning. Yes, long hours of unbearable tension, the black spectre of imminent death, and too much drunken revelry certainly took its toll, but now the great ship of the skies itself seemed to be lurching along, strangely handicapped. Unknown to all, the giant jumbo was approaching the area where they last had contact with the *real* world; where they unknowingly and narrowly missed a collision with an airforce fighter jet by just a few metres, and where an enormous flash in the night sky behind them had seemingly illuminated the entire world.

Captain Ray Cardin fought his drooping eyelids with an almost ferocious zest, but knew he was losing the battle. Glancing over, First Officer Roslyn Steinhouse already seemed to be asleep – even though Cardin had warned the two of them about sleeping. He tried to turn around to check on Tom Tyson, but found he could not. Damn, this was the most crucial moment of his whole career - and indeed his very *life*, and he was carelessly slipping into sleep. Not now, please. Not bloody *now!*

But Tom was still awake – just. Cardin heard Tyson's voice in his headset singing something silly about a farmer. He sounded groggy and confused. Nevertheless the thought slowly dawned to

Tom that maybe their cabin oxygen supply was faulty? So should they don their OX masks?

Tom mumbled, 'Boss, I think I've saved some more fuel. I, ah, did another fuel trim and pumped a fair bit out of the auxiliary tanks and, ah, maybe it gave us an extra hour in the air. Don't forget that with only four engines running . . . I mean with only *two* engines running, we are now ah . . . gee, what was I saying?'

Cardin slurred, 'Stay on the ball, Tim . . . I mean Tom. We need you.' He glanced across at his F/O. Although her glazed eyes were open and staring forward out the windscreen, she appeared to be asleep and unmoving. Cardin felt sudden alarm and forcibly shook himself to attention before fading away again.

Tom sat bolt upright. 'Boss! Boss! Check our pressurisation for leaks! Quickly! It's sleep hypoxia - I'm sure of it. Remember the Helios plane and that golfer's private jet? We absolutely must not end up like them. Boss, check your hands to see if the skin is wrinkling. If it is then it means hypoxia and we must drop the passengers' masks now!'

Getting no response, a hand gripped Cardin's shoulder and shook him. 'Hey Boss, we've gotta descend . . . like right *now!* We're at twenty eight thousand and we must get down to ten. Boss?'

Cardin's foggy brain could hear his second officer's pleas, but he struggled to comprehend. But yes, the urgent voice was right. This could be somewhat like explosive cabin decompression following a major rupture somewhere in an aircraft's pressurisation system. This usually causes a catastrophic loss of oxygen for all on board. The only action that can be taken, apart from activating everyone's drop-down masks, is to institute an emergency dive down to ten thousand feet or below, otherwise all those on board will soon stop breathing permanently.

In this case where the plane itself seemed to be gradually dying, it could be a slow leak; an insidious but deadly loss of air which may have been caused by a pressure pump running low on fuel, or a weakening of electrical power because the engine that produced it was no longer operating.

Yes, a slower loss, but certainly not one to be casually ignored. American pro-golfer Payne Stewart lost his life when his private Learjet suffered a pressurisation failure not long after take-off in 1999. Similar to the later Helios flight of 2006, their auto-pilot became the only thing flying the plane as all those on board fell unconscious and died while the jet flew itself right across America to finally run out of fuel and crash in a South Dakota field.

Now it seemed the same thing was happening here. Because Cardin was so slow to react, Tyson reached over to punch the auto-pilot button in front of their groggy co-pilot. A loud warning *Whoop! Whoop!* heralded this action, then he reset the assigned altitude dial to ten thousand feet. While Roslyn Steinhouse still failed to react at all, the famous bulbous nose of the 747 gently pitched down and headed towards the brightening shape of a distant headland and home. Tom then activated another switch and four hundred oxygen masks promptly fell from the ceilings above every passenger.

16.

Across Australia, solemn (but premature) memorial services were held for all those unfortunates on board AA200; the plane that had apparently ceased to exist. And for shift workers and others who had missed the live TV broadcasts, they were re-run numerous times later.

Then the fireworks started. Lawyers needed someone to be declared culpable, the media needed someone to demonise, and the bereaved families needed a target to hate and litigate for their losses. Newspapers, blogs and virulent social networking sites were flooded with eager volunteers who thrust their often wild theories into the buzzing public arena. Not an hour passed without another "retired airline pilot/aviation expert" donating his or her "valuable expertise" and thus confusing everyone even more. And every one of these posts went *viral*, regardless of their accuracy or otherwise.

Adding to everyone's frustration, the hunt for a smoking gun could not even find smoke, let alone any gun. On TV, an Indian airport ground worker in Melbourne where the flight had actually originated, and who had loaded some of the cargo into the freight hold of AA200, told enthusiastic interviewers about a strange smell wafting from the pallets of freight just before he closed the cargo doors. No, he had never smelt anything like that before and his family ran an Indian restaurant where they were accustomed to numerous cooking smells every day. He himself had been brought up to work in their kitchen from the age of nine so he could recognise most smells.

'See!' yelled viewers at opinion pollsters. 'That's obviously what it was: the plane was blown up by something that smelt suspicious in the cargo hold. This forced airline officials to reveal that the odour was just a load of fresh seafood bound for parts of Canada which had a current shortage of such. Curiously, it wasn't revealed that the Indian's family restaurant had never sold seafood.

But as fast as Air Australia's CEO and other company spokespersons issued official denials to hose down one impulsive theory after another, the public bayed for their blood, claiming that the company would deny just about anything if it meant evading crippling litigation. Normally, an airline's liability is limited to about $US85,000 per deceased passenger - and they have insurance for that, but should professional negligence ever be proven in a court of law then only the sky is the limit.

In the case of the notorious Air New Zealand DC10 crash of 1979 - mentioned here earlier, the New Zealand Government itself was revealed as the actual owner of the airline. After the crash, the government discretely calculated that if they officially admitted to any negligence at all then the resultant litigation could possibly bankrupt the entire nation of New Zealand. So the government attempted to cover up their guilt in a blatantly theatrical stance of denial that their own Royal Commissioner ridiculed and blasted as "a predetermined plan of deception and an orchestrated litany of lies."

And now in the present day, Air Australia was terrified of going down that same deceitful road as ANZ. This time every piece of evidence and data would need to be presented to forthcoming investigations as one-hundred-percent *watertight*, especially the captain's entire life. The other two pilots would also be thoroughly examined, but it is always the captain who bears the ultimate legal burden for absolutely everything that takes place on his flight.

So, like dogs chasing their tails, the nightmares continued to swirl around and around; fuelled by wild speculation, uninformed rumour - and occasional truths, of course.

But surely the group with the most vested interests of all in this whole raging affair were the passengers and crew still flying on board the Air Australia flight two-hundred: the flight that *hadn't* crashed. Most of them were now well and truly asleep with their blank faces and mouths drooped open. Although every one of them had personally vowed to stay awake to the *very end* – after all, who would want to sleep away their last few hours – most had unknowingly succumbed to the twin coma-inducing forces of alcohol dehydration combined with sleep hypoxia caused by a struggling pressurisation pump in the starboard wing.

Down the back, two stewardesses, Ayli Gorshe and Suzy Tayne, found room to snuggle up together on the galley floor in Economy. They'd been dancing the Conga line and imbibing the free drinks with everyone else all night. It had been Party Central and they'd raved with the best of them while they'd found it hard to believe how many musical instruments had been produced from the overhead lockers, and how many talented musicians were on board.

The two women had gone to school together, lived together, and joined AA on the very same day together. These days they regularly bid for parallel roster lines so they could work and travel together. Now, on this gray and cloudy morning they were asleep, side-by-side and blissfully uncaring that they'd been drunk while on duty while also unaware that they could die from hypoxia even before the final crash.

Meanwhile on the flight deck up front, Tom Tyson struggled with grogginess to stay alert as the plane seemed to be taking forever to descend to his new selected level of ten thousand feet. Ten thousand is the acknowledged altitude where humans can usually breathe normally, but eight thousand is considered better. At jet cruising altitudes the air density is much too low for human breathing, so cabins must be pressurised – usually equal to about eight thousand feet. So no matter what the outside air pressure or temperature, a jet's cabin should always remain at a sustainable pressure while the outside temperature, usually a bone-crushing and unsurvivable -56°C, should remain at about a standard and pleasant +24°C inside. Of course, jet engines were specifically engineered to operate in ambient temperatures of around -56°C where the rarified air density is precisely what they thrive on.

Tom stared at the analogue dial in front of a comatose Roslyn Steinhouse. Curses, he'd set the VSI rate of vertical descent to only one thousand feet per minute! But they needed to descend from 28,000 to 10,000 as rapidly as possible without overstressing the wings or airframe from excessive speed, but over the last ten minutes they'd only come down to 18,000 which was not nearly low enough for everyone to breathe safely. He angrily punched the button again through blurry eyes and watched the VSI needle dip down, tripling their rate of descent. With increasing trepidation, he hoped his error hadn't caused the deaths of anyone on board as he shuddered to realise that he was now the only person flying this ghost ship.

Suddenly he berated himself: 'Speed brakes, you idiot!' He had overlooked this vital action and angrily hauled on the captain's speed brake handle. Outside, huge flap-like panels dutifully leapt up from the giant wings and formed a kind-of barrier fence that defied the racing airstream and soon killed off some of their excess speed and lift. The plane sank down further.

Tom cursed again, realising that he needed to be flying this thing from a pilot's seat and not while perched precariously between two limp bodies. He urgently needed to drag one of them from their seat and chose Roslyn because she was probably the lightest. With uncaring roughness he managed to relieve her of her duties by dumping her heavily on the floor. She didn't stir while he remembered to re-attach her oxygen mask, then adjusted Cardin's mask once again. In shock, he glanced at his own hands to reveal white and wrinkled skin as though he'd been surfing at Bondi all day.

Now frightened, Tom realised that both these pilots had been barely conscious and perilously close to never waking again. It had been pure luck, he supposed, that his own mask had functioned perfectly while others can deliver mixed results when tested.

Finally strapped into the right-hand seat, he glanced at the altimeter once again: passing fourteen thousand feet. Good. At the new descent rate of four thousand feet a minute, they only needed one more minute to reach the magic level of ten thousand. Upon reaching that point, he reset the assigned altitude once again to eight thousand feet which was Cardin's originally planned descent profile, then, with more luck, everyone should start breathing normally again – that is, if they weren't already oxygen-deprived to serious levels. Tom had now become a solo aviator where he was making all the decisions in this bizarre little room full of switches, dials, blacked-out screens and levers. Sweating, but now breathing without his oxygen mask, he hauled on the speed brakes again to slow them down even further before reaching eight thousand.

Surprisingly, a jet can't speed below ten thousand feet like it can above it. The lower air is too dense and airframes are only engineered to certain tolerances of stress levels; depending on altitude. But novices can find it hard to see why a jet at high altitude can cruise at 1,000 km/h yet it faces speed restrictions lower down - not from police on patrol but firstly from air traffic controllers who impose a general speed limit of not above 250 knots under 10,000 feet for the purposes of traffic sequencing, and secondly to protect the plane's airframe itself which, as already mentioned, requires several different speed limits for many different events and airframe configurations. For example, a merry pilot can't simply bang the wheels down at any old speed just when he feels like it because he could easily rip them right off! He needs prior airspeed braking to slow down to the published indicated air speed for gear extension. It is the same with flaps, spoilers and lift dumpers: any of these vital flying mechanisms can simply break off if suddenly blowtorched by an unacceptably powerful air flow.

So a jet jockey can't show off to his girlfriend how fast he can fly - even though no sky police will ever pull him over to book him, but he might easily embarrass himself and ruin his whole afternoon should he exceed the intractable laws of aeronautical science and come tumbling down from the sky.

'Curse it,' Tom mumbled: there always seems to be laws everywhere to prevent us from ever having fun!

Now that Tom's head had cleared sufficiently, he carefully trimmed the plane and levelled it out to a modest 240 knots, a suitable speed for two-engined operations at this altitude. Glancing out, it was a dull morning with scattered rain showers falling from castles of alto-cumulus clouds, and with several strato-cumulus cloud layers hovering over the sea below them. But where on earth was that headland the little girl had pointed out? God forbid that he'd lost sight of it . . .

No, there it was again. A distant headland jutting towards them with two steep pinnacles rising straight out of the water and shouting "Welcome back to the world!"

Enormous relief washed over the young pilot as he rejoiced in gazing down at the only sight of land they had seen in more than fourteen hours – apart from those eerie midnight lights on Kiribati. But he quickly recalled that this thing must be flown by three pilots and not one, and he was no junior super hero or space cadet. His minimal flying experience at the age of twenty-three was really nothing compared to the captain's twenty thousand hours or Roslyn's three thousand, both of whom he desperately needed to rejoin the A-team right now.

He knelt behind the right seat and held a bottle of water to Ros's mouth; forcing her to drink as he slapped her face. Then he did the same for Ray Cardin. Soon, both of them started waking slowly; groggy and disorientated at first . . .

'Look Boss!' Tom yelled in Cardin's ear. 'Our headland. See? Right there. Straight ahead!'

'What the hell happened here?' Cardin demanded in his usual crusty manner - with no thanks being offered for services rendered.

'I've got a headache,' mumbled Roslyn. 'God, what am I doing on the floor?'

Tom enthused to them both: 'Look, you two: there it is! Now all we need is to establish just where along the whole east coast of Australia we actually are. What do you think, Boss?'

Cardin was alert and said, 'Are we at eight thousand already? I don't remember descending. Anyway, young Thomas, that is not a headland: it is an island!'

And it was too. Tom stared down in awe at the twin volcanic upthrusts and surrounding lush vegetation that was itself surrounded by water on all sides. Yes it was, without doubt, an island.

'Wow!' exalted Tom. 'It's beautiful, but then . . . where the heck are we? Vanuatu? Fiji?'

Tom searched his mind as Roslyn stared from a side window. The beautiful island approached from below, then began to pass underneath. Tom suddenly realised that he'd seen this island before - not from eight thousand feet but from lower down when approaching to land.

'I know it!' he rejoiced and screamed. 'It's Lord Howe Island and we're almost exactly on track to Sydney after an eternity of flying blind in the dark! Yeehaw! How about that?'

'Oh my god, it is too!' Roslyn and Tom yeehawed in unison.

'Of course it is,' concurred their captain. 'I've flown here too.'

Tom cheered in sheer delight. 'I flew out here once from Bankstown in a Cessna-182. Plain crazy I was. A single-engine plane over water for 330 nautical miles, but they made me accept the charter or I could say goodbye to them. So I sat there for three painful hours listening to every revolution of that engine. *Auto-rough* is the mode they say engines adopt as soon as they're over any body of water. Anyway, we made it there and back, and how wonderful was that little three-day freebie holiday for me? It's a gorgeous island and the most southerly coral island in the world, even though it's far to the south of the Barrier Reef islands . . . '

Cardin held up his hand. 'Whoa! Tom, are you a travel guide now? Are you forgetting our slight predicament? But hey, you've done a real hero's job here today, especially when we blacked out. And I still can't believe that our hit-and-miss navigation all night guided us almost spot-on to our final track for home.' After checking with the purser that all the crew and passengers had revived, he leaned over and shook Roslyn's hand, 'and a huge thanks to our other hero, Miss Roslyn, for steering this thing on ded -reckoning for endless hours. Anyway team, we still have much work to do. So, the most important item on our agenda now is this: how much fuel do we have left?'

Without functioning gauges or hardly any data input to the flight management system, this was still a depressing guess as the two faithful RB211's continued to turn over, but for how long? Obviously, their total fuel consumption rates were only about half when running on two as opposed to four, but unforeseen headwinds at different levels can mercilessly attack the ground-speed while many other variables can also leap into play. But generally, if you're running low on fuel you should expect things to get really nasty very quickly. And it was out of the question to even think about plonking this 747 down on Lord Howe's tiny landing strip of less than 1,000 metres in length. Even if a foolhardy or desperate pilot attempted it, water lay at both ends of the strip so that a jumbo could plough off either end and write itself off just as badly as if it had ditched into the open ocean.

Way below, the sight-starved crew spotted little yachts bobbing lazily on Lord Howe's picture-postcard lagoon, while surfboard riders could be seen riding the sparkling waves of Ned's Beach at the runway's western end. Tom undoubtedly and eagerly wished he was one of those.

Now they only had to fly to Sydney or some nearby airport and it would take just half an hour. And what was a mere thirty minutes compared to the lengthy and terrifying trauma they had all undergone so far?

Roslyn asked for her seat back, so she and Tom played musical chairs once again, then Tom spread out his plotting charts across the floor. Pointing to his scribble, he held them up in triumph and grinned, 'I hereby nominate myself as the greatest navigator of all time!'

'Yay! I'll second that,' clapped Roslyn. 'But I was the helmsman. The driver!'

'And I was the commander,' boasted Ray Cardin. Now that they were all self-declared heroes of modern aviation history, Roslyn suddenly remembered their wonderful cabin crew down the back; headed by that peerless purser, Haneed Zaresh. They'd better relate the fantastic news to him instantly.

They called his station but had no reply. 'Try him again,' ordered Cardin. 'They've all got to get with it right now anyway because we should be landing in half an hour. Wake 'em all up with a few loud gongs, Ros.'

'Ding Dong!' the chimes peeled several times through all the cabins. 'Wakey wakey, folks! This is your captain speaking, not only to say sorry that the big party is over, but also the best news by far is that we have finally established our exact position over lovely Lord Howe Island, only about half an hour's flight away from Sydney and home. Now I'd just like to say - without boasting of course, that this was no mean feat of navigation as we've just circumnavigated most of the vast Pacific Ocean with hardly any equipment to assist us. Since we left Sydney last night, we've had just *one* navigational fix to steer by, and that was from a tiny GPS unit which gave intermittent readings . . . then it died. Anyway, it's all part of the service here on Air Australia and on behalf of your friendly crew we welcome you all back home. You will, of course,

212

all be given free tickets to undertake this flight to the USA again at a later time of your choosing. Thank you.'

Listening to Cardin's boasting, Roslyn was resentful that he was unashamedly advertising that this was mostly his own personal success, however if the captain must always take the blame for disasters then she supposed it was only fair and reasonable that he could also claim the fame for any successes.

'Okay, let's get down to three thousand,' Cardin ordered. 'Ros, just weave around those low strato-cu patches over there. As I stated repeatedly, we don't want to be going into any cloud at all.'

Cardin rubbed his blood-red eyes as he exalted in imminent triumph. 'Now listen-up you lot, we all realise what happens if we stray into any cloud, don't we?' The other two nodded seriously as he continued. 'Well, normally we would instantly climb up to the lowest safe altitude, wouldn't we? But we don't know what that is - only out here over the sea of course - but once we're near that coastline . . . kaboom! So, if we sight any land while we're in VMC then we damn-well *stay* in VMC! Is everyone crystal clear on that? We are just as restricted as a little lightie on VFR procedures. It is irrelevant if we are operating RPT on an IFR flight plan; we are, for all intents and purposes, VFR . . . Visual Flight Rules. Okay?'

Tom interrupted, 'So Boss, I suppose we should say that whatever happens in VMC *stays* in VMC, right?'

Roslyn burst out laughing as Cardin persisted; deadpan: 'So, once found, we do not lose sight of any land and we *do not* enter any cloud. Then we go for any airport with a runway of even half-decent length. Approaching their traffic pattern, Ros and Tom will have all eyes peeled for other air traffic, right? But we do not give way to them because, as you know, we only have two engines turning and we are out of fuel so I won't be practicing my two-engined go-rounds today, thank you very much. Other aircraft will just have to avoid us and if they can't spot a bloody great 747 coming straight at them then they need their damn eyes tested!'

'So, I will fly the plane while Tom will call out if he sees any green lights from the tower. If there is no tower, then it's back to our old days when we learnt to fly at uncontrolled country airports using the see-and-be-seen method.'

'In such a case, any crop dusters or light planes flying circuits simply *must* see something our size in their circuit. If they haven't heard our inbound radio calls and can't believe their eyes - or simply won't accept that we're landing, then it's *get real brother* because we *are* landing! I will sort out any relevant paperwork afterwards. Any questions?'

Tom said, 'Boss: I say we get the flaps down fully and the config just right well before final approach. And we must aim to touch down exactly on the piano keys and not a centimetre after them because we won't know what is the runway length. We just can't go screaming off the other end because there might be houses there – or schools. Or a river. Anything.'

'Yep, agreed. What about you, Ros?'

'Well, what if a tower flashes red lights at us?'

Cardin snapped at her. 'We bloody-well land anyway, Roslyn! That's what we do. What the hell else *can* we do? Go and enter a damned holding pattern in case they email us nasty reprimands later? We will be out of fuel, Ros. In half an hour there'll probably be about one teaspoon of Jet-A1 remaining, then that's it! Now, you just let me face all the difficult questions later because I'll probably be spending the next ten friggin' years attending official inquiries anyway . . . '

Tom asked, 'And if we don't find any airport?'

'There are little airports all up and down the east coast, as both of you well know. Maybe some are just for small commuter flights and training, but if we can find say, 1,500 to 2,000 metres of sealed runway, then we're in luck – bearing in mind our reduced braking performance when only two engines are in reverse thrust. But, without any proper runway, and if the worst comes to the very worst then it's gonna be some long flat paddocks where I hope the cows are bloody fast runners!'

Tom chuckled, 'Hey guys, just imagine if we ever had some *real* problems!'

Roslyn smiled, 'Yes, then we could really worry.'

Ray Cardin assured them, 'Hey, we'll make it. This is the A-team here on the flight deck today, is it not? And, ah, I'd just like to say another huge thanks to you two. I know we've had some big disagreements on this flight but we've also had one hell of a damned ride and I don't think we'd be human if we hadn't tossed the ball around a bit, eh? And finally, if, ah, anything happens to us – well, you know, there are always the CVR voice recorders which tape our last conversations. They'll tell the world how we did every damn thing possible to keep this ship afloat . . . '

215

Tom laughed, 'The good ship *Lollipop*, eh Boss?'

Cardin laughed. 'Yes, that ship. You're a nice guy, Tom. And Ros, I like you too . . . believe it or not. I hope we can remain friends after this, ah, little adventure because I realise I'm not the world's friendliest captain. Nevertheless, it's a job that is sometimes not easy . . . especially this damned trip!'

Roslyn smiled, 'Let's just concentrate on the job in hand now, please. And Ray, I will personally buy you and Tom a drink in the nearest bar we can find after landing.'

Cardin was a non-drinker but spoke to her nicely, 'Now Ros, please tell me you won't give up flying like you said.'

'No, I am getting out of it. I want to live. I'm going teaching. This next landing will be for me like that old Rolling Stones' song: *This will be the last time.*'

Cardin sighed, 'I bet you change your mind. And you, Tom?'

Tom fired back his usual witty riposte and laughed: 'Ah, I'll probably keep flying while singing another song: *Most people I know think that I'm crazy!*'

Their optimistic smiles evaporated instantly as none of them could have envisaged – not even in their wildest dreams, what happened next . . .

17.

'Shee . . . eet!' exclaimed Ray Cardin as he desperately hauled back on the control wheel. They all gawked in horror as another aircraft flashed right past them at an angle. It had a strange shape - then it turned back towards them . . .

'Wow!' whistled Roslyn. 'That was close! Oh, now it's coming back . . . '

Cardin's recent affable charm instantly vaporised. 'See, that is exactly what I was just saying! I told you two to be on a sharp lookout for any other traffic! Well, didn't I? I'm trying my damndest to fly this old bucket of bolts on two friggin' engines while on VFR procedures, and also while searching for a place called *Where the flamin' hell are we*. So I was expecting my two overpaid assistants to be my eyes and ears - but now see what happened! We just about scraped the paint off his side!'

Thinking ahead, Roslyn was excited. 'But at least it's a human contact at last. Now he'll report us on his radio, won't he? That's just what we want. People will finally know that we're still alive because right now he'll be radioing something like "Hey guys, guess what: I nearly ran into a 747 heading inbound. And his tower will say: 'A 747? What 747? And the pilot will reply, 'Well, it was an Air Australia 747. They're easy to identify with those massive letters and our flag painted down each side. Then the tower will declare: There's no AA that flies in here, so it must be that missing one.

Incredible! Let's hit all our red buttons and call out the emergency services because they are undoubtedly in some kind of trouble.'

But no such radio conversation took place at all; Roslyn had simply hoped that it would have transpired like that. What actually occurred was that the strange-shaped rotor-winged craft that flashed past the giant Boeing automatically signalled a coded flow of data back to a control centre which urgently warned "Intruder! Intruder! Code Zulu Red!'

On the ground, an alerted computer reacted with the command: 'Scramble the Zee-Dee's! Shut down airspace. Zone enforcement now in place!'

Within minutes the 747 was surrounded by five or six whirring drone-type machines; swarming like bees around a hive. Cardin and Steinhouse gawked in sheer astonishment as Tom whistled, 'Holy macaroni, where did they come from? Are they airforce? Must be from Williamtown - I suppose.'

'No, they're damned drones!' cursed Cardin, glaring out his window while angrily trying to wave them away with his hands. 'Looks like those four-rotor types. They're just stupid little toys!'

'We've got one at home like that and they are not toys,' said Roslyn. 'My Dad flies one near Mangalore because he's not allowed to fly planes anymore.'

Ignoring her, the captain's ire was rising. 'Actually, they're not little things at all; they're the size of bloody Cessnas! Damned dangerous too! We must not hit one of them. Hang on; this one is flying up to my port side here. I don't think they're manned . . . let me see . . . Look out my side, Tom. What the hell are they doing?'

Tom gawked from the seat behind the captain and peered from his window. 'I think they're actually larger than Cessnas, and they're doing 250 knots like us. Wait, let me see . . . '

There was a pause, then Tom gasped, 'Unreal, banana peel! They're flashing a red sign at us from their solar panel saying . . . '

Cardin barked furiously, 'I can damn-well see what the flying be-Jesus it says for my friggin self! It says: *YOU ARE AN INTRUDER INTO THIS WAR ZONE AIRSPACE. FOLLOW WHITE ZEE-DEE LEADER. UHF 253.75Mhz*

'Whaat?' screeched Roslyn. 'Intruder? And what on earth is a Zee-Dee? We're in a most desperate emergency and here they are telling *us* what to do! Ray, tell them that emergency air traffic always has priority over all others . . . *Ray!*'

But Cardin was beside himself with anger because a white-painted drone had now zapped across to fly just meters in front of the 747's bulbous nose. Cardin screamed at it as he waved his arms in fury. He had never seen anything fly so close to his giant planes, and certainly not right in front of the windscreen - a frightening spectre for any pilot at any time.

He screamed over the radio, 'War zone be damned! Get the hell away from my goddamned aeroplane you insane idiots! Jesus Christ on a skateboard, throttle back Roslyn before we run right up its . . . '

Roslyn hauled the throttles rearwards as Tom decided 'It must be some kind of air show or display. There'll be a crowd down there somewhere with a few amateur locals controlling these things. Boss, I hope we get to the bottom of this and you tear strips off them when we land.'

'Tear strips?' screeched Cardin. 'In their friggin' dreams! I'll tear their bloody *heads* off! Half of these drone morons don't even have a drone licence, let alone proper pilot's licences or registration for these cruddy things.'

Roslyn urged, 'Ray, it said go to UHF 253.75. Can we do that?'

Cardin grunted, 'Alright then. Try it. Maybe we've got our radios back again. So talk to these amateur clowns and tell them clearly to *piss right off* out of our damned way right now!' The plane's nose pitched down again from another thrust reduction as Cardin hurriedly disengaged the autopilot in an effort to avoid ramming the threatening object just metres in front of them.

Adjusting her microphone, Roslyn was almost as angry as Cardin to be confronted with this horrific impediment to salvation in their very last minutes of flight. She switched on the rarely-used UHF radio and selected the given frequency.

'To the drone aircraft operators: this is Air Australia flight two-zero-zero. We are the Boeing-747 approaching the New South Wales east coast on descent from three thousand feet. Do you read?'

An illuminated sign from a nearby drone instantly flashed a reply: 'Affirm. Go ahead.'

Roslyn transmitted, 'Now, we're not sure what kind of crazy and dangerous air show or flying circus you people are running up here, but let me be quite clear about this . . . '

Cardin simply could not help himself and angrily overrode her PTT button; seething with a white-hot fury. 'And this is the Boeing captain speaking! Now you listen to me really carefully, you hear? You are impeding this aircraft's legal progress and safety by committing an act of terrorism here! Yes, it is *terrorism* so get your friggin' plastic toys the hell away from my plane right now and clear our flight path or I'll see you toy-boys spend the next few thousand years in jail! Got it? We are a commercial RPT passenger transport flight and demand our rite of passage. We haven't been flying around the entire Pacific Ocean for this whole rotten night just to have our last chance at making a safe landing destroyed by your crappy, cruddy little air show! We have been crippled by multiple system failures all night and won't let your amateur-hour pranks get in our way under any circumstances whatsoever! We are emergency traffic and therefore have top priority! Got it? And don't try to claim that you haven't heard about this missing flight!'

In an instant reply, the drone to their left flashed a new sign saying: *'INTRUDER, YOU ARE UNDER ARREST. FOLLOW WHITE LEADER.*

Cardin shook his fist violently at the window as he transmitted: 'Under bloody arrest? You mean I'm the world's first 747 captain to be placed under arrest? I'll give you plastic criminals under arrest, alright! You are just goddamned schoolboy hooligans!' He was still yelling as he turned to Roslyn. 'They're just kids being damned smart-arses! Oh yes, this will be great fun for them back at their club house. And when they turn thirteen one day they can write about this exciting day in their stupid magazine – if they can write.'

Roslyn urged him, 'Look! The white one has moved further away.' The white drone had zoomed away in an instant to maintain a steady position about two thousand metres ahead of them. It kept flashing a blinding white strobe back at them, plus a steady sign saying *FOLLOW*. But two thousand metres wasn't nearly enough separation for the volcanic Captain Cardin. Possibly two thousand nautical *miles* may have placated him, but it seemed he had no choice.

And then, from within low and gray cloud banks ahead - and approaching two thousand feet on descent, a miracle emerged: a long and sandy beach appeared through light rain. Adjacent to the beach was an endless stretch of urban houses, buildings and roads. They were home! A cheer went up and handshakes flew all around as Captain Ray Cardin grinned wickedly, 'Now all we need is to use their cruddy little airport. Ah, I don't suppose I was rude to them, was I?'

Behind him, Cardin heard Tom quip, 'Boss, should we call them and say *Take me to your white leader?*'

The captain, reasonably polite for once, moaned, 'Not now Tom, please.'

18.

Near the rear of the plane, Purser Haneed Zaresh was making a monumental announcement; beating the flight deck crew with an astonishing piece of news.

'Ladies and gentlemen and kids, if you look out your windows now you should be delighted to see . . . land! Yes, real dry land! We have finally made it back!'

The cabin erupted into wild jubilation; almost drowning out the joyful purser. Zaresh continued: 'Yes, we have been roaming the entire Pacific Ocean for about fifteen hours with hardly a thing to guide us, but our dedicated flight crew has returned us home safely. Mind you, we achieved this through none other than professional perseverance of the highest order plus a tireless determination to navigate through our darkest hours. Now, I'm not exactly sure just what city we are over right now, but our hero Captain Cardin should inform us very soon. Meantime, I'm sure everyone will agree that we've enjoyed the greatest party of all. Thank you.'

In economy class, Annie Slade gripped Allan Henner's hand in elation. 'I just knew we'd make it somehow!' She kissed his cheek and they shouted cheers with everyone else. Nearby, the Kennard couple both blew breath like surfacing whales while jointly declaring that they would never fly again - *ever!*

In the Business-class cabin, eighty-year-old Cheng Xingu grabbed at people's sleeves and asked repeatedly: 'What happen? What happen?' A man excitedly pointed out the window at the town below and her gaze followed his finger.

She wrinkled her nose and asked: 'This America?' Some joker answered *yes* so she sat back and wondered what on earth all that fuss and raucous noise had been about last night.

Another gong chimed and a stewardess's voice announced, 'Ladies and gents, welcome back home. It seems that we'll be landing very soon and we're just waiting for our captain's announcement. We hope you all enjoyed the big party but we really do need all this rubbish cleaned up, thank you. Could everyone please collect their rubbish and put it in sick bags and our trolleys will be around to collect them very soon.'

Richard Rendy, alias Dirty Dick, blinked his eyes open and gazed out a window at the extraordinary vista of buildings below. 'So, all my brilliant end-of-the-world songs were for nothing! I should sue this shoddy airline . . . '

From across the aisle, an elderly couple smiled at him, 'See, Mr Rendy, we warned you it would be up to the will of God.'

'Yes, you did too! So all my sins are now forgiven, are they?'

They giggled, 'Ah, we don't quite think he'd have the time to forgive all of yours.'

Rendy laughed then turned to the man on his other side. "Jee-zuss Andy, did you ever think we would get out of that? I thought we were going to be the main item on last night's dinner menu for the sharks!'

His companion grinned and wiped his sweating brow yet again, recalling how many times he'd caught sharks from their Gulf of Carpentaria trawlers years ago. Most times they'd casually laughed as they hauled them up, sliced their fins off then callously threw them back to drown and bleed to death. 'Sorry guys,' he apologised silently.

Stewardess Suzy Tayne shook young Corrie Newnes tenderly. The girl stirred then woke her little brother as Suzy handed them orange juices - the last two bottles remaining after the stock had been voraciously pillaged to flavour numerous shots of Vodka.

Corrie rubbed her eyes and said, 'Thank you. I didn't get much sleep last night because everyone was having so much fun and making all that crazy noise. But I hope our Aunty and our new family will be here to meet us when we land. I'm just so excited!' The stewardess gave her a little kiss and assured her that everything would be explained to them by their chaperone, Mrs Grayling, after landing.

Jane Grayling seemed relieved to be approaching home again, but wondered how to explain to her agency how an entire flight that went nowhere was basically back to where it started and she hadn't delivered her two young charges anywhere. Many other people were obviously pondering similar questions, while high school maths teacher Mark Dekanic, sitting nearby, had overheard the heartbreaking tale of the two orphaned children and pined for their future happiness. Impulsively, he rose and took two thousand US dollars from his wallet, went over to Jane Grayling and handed it all to her.

'Please convey this to their new step-mother to take them to Disneyland - when and if they ever get there. And to buy them some clothes or presents. It will be my pleasure.' Grayling was shocked but thanked him profusely as Dekanic smiled, 'I'd only blow it in Vegas, anyway.'

First-class celebrations were being enjoyed in the First Class lounge by Rod Appleby, Stuart Rhys and the ailing Maggie Silverstone. 'A toast all round!' cheered the scientist Rhys as they clinked glasses of mineral water together. 'Looks like someone has quaffed all the champagne - probably us – but who cares!'

Rod Appleby's feelings of relief soon retreated to worldly matters as he reconsidered how to recover almost half a million dollars from his so-called friend who had apparently turned embezzler. He grinned wickedly, 'Oh how quickly we can forget our own imminent mortality and return to Earth with its daily greed and grind.'

Gazing from her window, Maggie Silverstone was unsure whether to laugh or cry. So now she wouldn't be dying in a plane crash that plunged into the deep blue ocean, but would still be facing her own highly uncertain future. She wasn't sure which alternative would be worse, or if either of them were an option at all. Rod Appleby gave her a hug then said 'Keep in touch, Maggie.'

In the cramped Purser's station, Haneed Zaresh felt great surges of relief wash over him. The pilots may have fought several heated debates over what to do and how to proceed, but they'd managed to achieve triumph somehow. No matter that Ray Cardin was a somewhat gruff aircraft commander who Zaresh hardly knew, or that he'd never met Roslyn Steinhouse and Tom Tyson before, but between the three of them they had mastered an historical navigation crisis beyond comparison to save not only their own bacon, but the entire load of passengers.

Zaresh thought of his loving wife Sulu and their three teenage sons growing up in Melbourne. In one way he was much like Ray Cardin in that he'd elected to remain on the international long-haul roster despite frequent opportunities to switch to domestic flights, so he was now puzzling why he'd persisted for so long while his family had grown up mostly without him. Now he'd learned a real kick-in-the-pants lesson from this trip; that was certain. Shaking his head, he wondered why anyone would prefer being nice to hundreds of strangers instead of being nice to his own family at home? Why did he elect to sleep alone in different hotel beds around the world instead of his own loving marital bed back home? And why was he rushing around cramped aisles, soothing old ladies and crying babies, or supervising smelly galleys in preference to the quiet enjoyment of pottering around his relaxing fruit and vegetable gardens in his own back yard?

He had just spoken to Roslyn Steinhouse on the intercom and she'd told him firmly that 'after this landing they won't see me for dust!' Zaresh lamented it would be quite a pity for a smart young lady like her to throw away her entire flying career, but he could easily sympathise with her line of thought. Yes, they'd all been badly scared all the way to Hell and back; and yes, this was a real bone shaker and game changer, but now a refreshing clarity of common sense glared at him, forcing him to reconsider all his life's options and priorities. Thinking of the First Officer, Zaresh could easily picture pleasant Roslyn Steinhouse teaching a class at school. She should make a lovely teacher, he thought; but then he gulped with shame that he didn't know the names of any of his own boys' school teachers because of his frequent absences.

Meanwhile, the local aviation control directors were stunned by the incoming data. A Boeing-747, for heaven's sake? No, it can't be one of those old lumbering gas guzzlers? Those giants of the air used to take up to 4,000 metres just to get off the ground, so how could it ever land here? And who still operates one of those anyway? Who can even afford to own one of those things? Is this a stunt . . . or could they be enemies?

An anxious supervisor asked a controller, 'Is it manned?'

'Yes, and the radio person is highly belligerent and volatile. So beware!'

Approaching the coastline, Cardin gawked at another flashed message: *CALL TOWER NOW - 289.755 – YOU HAVE NO OPTION.*

'Okay, I'll play their silly no-options game,' sneered Ray Cardin. 'I'll call them - if I can.'

So he called them. 'Ah, whatever tower you are called, this is Australia two-zero-zero, we are calling Mayday and are out of fuel!'

The reply came back, 'The station calling New State Flight Director, say again that callsign.' Cardin repeated it. There was a silence then a few clicks were heard.

Cardin was suddenly astounded that their radios seemed to be finally working again; he barked: 'Are we still playing cat-and-mouse games with you and your plastic toys, because we are out of fuel and in no mood for your stupid antics . . . '

The Director answered, 'Air Australia? How can you possibly be Air Australia? You face prosecution and exile if you are posing as a scheduled air transport flight.'

At full volume, the sarcastic reply screamed back. 'We are calling ourselves Air *bloody* Australia because we have the words *AIR AUSTRALIA* painted down both sides of this plane in letters as high as friggin' barn doors. Or do you think I painted those words myself with goddamned crayons and your boy scouts are too young to read writing that size yet?'

Despite his volcanic raging, the three crew were simply astonished and delighted that their radios were working again. There was a long pause so Cardin continued to vent his entire vocabulary on these, as yet unseen, enemies. Running out of breath, he asked, 'Well? Can those jerks read our company name and emblems or not?'

A reply came. 'They are not humans; you should know that. They are Zee-Dee patrol robodrones for this restricted war zone. Central has already processed images of your antique plane and cannot understand what your intentions are in conducting this phoney flight, or why you have not transmitted any secure transponder I.D.'

Cardin snarled back at them. 'It's because most of our gear is not working, and, for the third time, we are out of bloody fuel! So is there any part of that short and simple sentence that you do not understand? OUT OF FUEL means we are gonna crash all over your shiny little airport into a million pieces within the next sixty seconds or so. And since when has any controlling authority anywhere in the world ever denied a landing clearance to an aircraft in extreme distress by harassing the living christ out of it, huh? I will remind you that your duty is to provide all help and assistance to any aircraft in distress; not to conduct an entire inquisition over the goddamned air/ground channels! Do you get my drift?'

Cardin was an active volcano that had blown its top, but now he himself was being blasted with blaring 'FUEL WARN' claxons and lights. As Tom gulped in horror and primed the fuel cocks to squeeze out a few more litres of Jet-A1, Cardin yelled on the radio again. 'Okay. So, now I can see your runway and am following that Boy Scout thing in front of us. For your info, this plane has a total range of 13,500 kilometres and I reckon we've already flown 13,499 of them, so our system is now telling us, loud and bloody clear, that we have run right out of fuel and are landing now whether you and your plastic soldiers like it or not; and even if they flash a million signs at us or not. So don't bother to say "clear to land" because we are gonna land anyway. Now!'

Regardless, a huge strobe sign leapt up from near the runway threshold and flashed a sign, 'Intruder, Runway 02, clear to land.'

'See, that told the bastards!' grinned Cardin, as he gripped the controls for their final approach. 'You just need to be firm with some of these morons. Friggin' weekend cowboys! Now Roslyn, gear down, flaps thirty, speed brakes armed, auto brakes to max . .

230

. Boy, am I gonna relish racing up those tower steps and taking that bastard's head off . . . '

Roslyn glanced outside and was terrified. She warned, 'Ray, don't you see what's going on?'

'Of course I do!' boasted the Boss-man. 'It just needed a man of my experience. Ah, sorry, nothing against you women pilots of course, but some smart-arse public servants down there needed me to put them in their places.'

Tom Tyson sucked in a huge breath and interrupted. 'But Boss, you're not really getting the picture. You seem to have missed the point!'

Cardin exploded again. 'The point? What friggin' point, Mister Einstein? I am on short finals for a landing when we haven't even got a squirt of fuel left in the tanks, and my back-seat driver tells me that I've missed the point! So just what in the flying hell could possibly be the damn point?'

Tom told him, but the captain was too busy listening to the GPWS intoning *Five hundred! Two-hundred! One hundred! Fifty! Twenty! Ten!* . .

Bang! The eighteen huge wheels screeched onto the tarmac among curtains of blue smoke. The landing was fast and furious and, with just two engines thrusting, they had only half the usual reverse-thrust power available, giving them a nil margin for error. 'Seventy knots,' Roslyn reported eagerly. 'Close reverse thrust. Throttles to idle.' They slowed down under seventy knots then knew they had made it. Near the piano keys at the runway's far end, Cardin trod on the foot brakes and halted the giant plane on the runway as loud cheering and whistling could be heard from behind the flight deck.

Roslyn sighed with undeniable relief. 'Phew! Thank God! But what airport is this? What city is this? I've never seen this place before.'

'Me neither,' agreed Tom. 'Hey Boss, we might be still alive but we've got huge problems here.'

'What?' barked Cardin. 'Could you have done a better job, Mister Whiz Kid? And what about you, Roslyn? Anyway, it's no thanks to you guys for playing stupid quiz shows while I'm on short finals and nagging me that I've missed some damn point.'

Roslyn replied, 'But look at all these strange vehicles racing out to us. They look like Batmobiles. You've been antagonising these total strangers when it's time you faced up to the real facts, Ray.'

'Yes, you two keep rabbiting on about the damn truth. What bloody facts?'

Tom said, 'Boss, this is why all our gear failed last night. And why all the latest GPS's on board wouldn't work either. It's why no-one could hear our transmissions and why no satellites picked up our transponders. It's why . . . '

'Get to the bloody point, Tom! That's what you told me to do.'

Roslyn interrupted: 'Ray, nothing worked for us because it was all way out of date.'

'Out of date? Our gear is the finest available and is approved by ASA and the FAA - and probably even by God himself. Our data link gear was only installed on this plane six months ago.'

Ros said quietly, 'I know, but remember that huge lighted area on Kiribas. It was five times larger than earlier this year. And did you notice the endless suburbia here, stretching far into the distance up and down this coast? Then, our data systems failed but our old analogue dials all functioned perfectly because they needed no electronic or digital input. Remember all those GPS's saying their software was out of date? Remember that giant flash in the sky? Remember how the tower called us an *antique plane?*'

'Yeah, yeah, yeah! So bloody what, little Miss Muffet?'

She seethed at his insolence. 'It's because we *are* antique, Ray. And all our stuff *is* out of date and so are we ourselves. They've probably never seen a 747 flying in their lives. We might even pose a huge threat . . . '

Cardin was unamused, to say the least. 'What is this? Kindergarten playtime? Guess who's hidden the missing Barbie doll?'

Tom took a daring leap. 'Time to face up to it, Boss. We have somehow travelled out of our world and into another, ah . . . time zone or dimension.'

Cardin roared laughing and slapped his knee as he taxied the plane off the runway and onto a narrow taxiway. 'What absolute crap! If you told that to a donkey it'd kick you to death!'

'But it's true, Boss.'

Cardin derided them both. 'Jesus Christ in leotards! So I've just pulled off the landing of the century but it's on the wrong damned planet! Oh well, if this is another world then I always wanted to fly to the stars and have a look around.'

In fright, Roslyn gawked out Tom's window and hissed, 'Sssh! I think they're coming up the stairs. Please be careful, Ray. Try not to be abusive and confrontational towards them. We don't know who they are or how we stand – except that we're under arrest and we have probably violated their airspace.'

'*Their* bloody airspace!' shrieked Cardin. 'This damn place is called Australia - believe it or not, Miss Roslyn. We positively identified Lord Howe Island just half an hour ago, did we not? Lord Howe is only 313 nautical miles east of the Aussie coast – is it not? It is a territory of the state of New South Wales so we are not on the planet Zyrgon or anywhere else because this is *our* home and *our* country - is it bloody not?'

'Yes, but you should convey all that to them *politely* Ray, because they're banging on our door right now to get in. I'm pleading that you use some restraint and don't antagonise them.'

Cardin smirked like an executioner who secretly relished his work. 'My name is Mother Theresa. Or maybe the Virgin Mary herself. Yes, I'll be the very essence of restraint and civility itself. Tom, please go downstairs and open door number-one to welcome our distinguished but uninvited guests, then invite them aboard my ship. But if they've got three heads I'll only allow one head in at a time, thank you.'

Tom stood up and gasped, 'Now this *will* be somewhat interesting – to say the least.'

Cardin laughed. 'Bah! What could possibly go wrong?'

Roslyn warned again, 'Just don't provoke them, you guys. We don't know what's going to happen . . . and they might be armed!'

Cardin said to Roslyn, 'After we disembark you can't give me any more advice young lady, because you informed me that you would be quitting flying as soon as we've landed.'

Just then, the two remaining engines flamed out on the exit taxiway - obviously after consuming their final dregs of fuel following an unparalleled marathon flight. Cardin beamed with pleasure as he watched both inboard engine dials spool down towards zero. He dramatically saluted the dials. 'And for service above and beyond the call of duty, they should be preserved in an aviation museum's Hall of Fame forever!'

'The whole plane might be,' whispered Ros.

Before leaving the flight deck, Tom pinched his nose and mimicked a robot's electronic voice. 'Welcome Aliens. What is the name of your planet?'

Cardin glared at him while wagging a warning finger at Roslyn. 'Just repeating, you haven't finished employment with AA till we've disembarked, Miss Roslyn. Until then, you are to stand behind everything I say and you will back me up all the way. Get it?'

The First Officer was almost too terrified to answer him, but mumbled, 'If they don't shoot me first . . . '

19.

The flight deck door was opened by Tom Tyson first, then followed the purser. Behind them came two tall men of Scandinavian appearance with pale skin, blond crew-cut hair and piercing blue eyes.

In barely-disguised anger, Ray Cardin rose from his seat and turned to face them. While his face momentarily flickered an uncomfortable fear of the unknown, he maintained his facade of bravado.

'Gentlemen: welcome to my unarmed *antique* aircraft, which is not antique at all but was actually built just seven years ago in 2010. Now please let me guess: you are from the local Sunday afternoon drone club and your latest trick is committing acts of terrorism against an innocent passenger transport aircraft by impeding its landing approach when it is out of fuel.'

The two visitors did not answer, but gazed around the flight deck in awe like many visitors do on their first visit to an airliner's cockpit. One said to the other, 'I didn't know there were any of these still flying in the world.'

The other said, 'And four engines! Who could ever afford the fuel bills?'

Eventually, the first man stared at Cardin as he stated firmly: 'Well Captain, you most certainly have a sharp tongue on you, don't you?'

The irate captain retorted, 'And you ain't heard nothin' yet, buster! So just what exactly are you two, anyway: robots or something?'

Ignoring him, the first man persisted. 'It is my duty to inform you that your type of language and behaviour is not permitted anywhere within our society – especially not over our official aviation air/ground channels. Further, you should know that we are at war and you should be aware that we could have easily lasered this big thing out of existence with the mere flick of a switch.'

Cardin responded with all the subtlety of a Molotov cocktail: 'Pigs flying arse, will you! And war? What bloody war? Australia wasn't in any damn war when we left it yesterday, Mr Robot Man, so I will therefore advise *you* now that if you or anyone else threatens to obstruct or endanger my aircraft again in any way whatsoever – imaginary war or real - then I will use whichever sharp words that I damn-well choose because I am responsible for more than four hundred peoples' lives including my own.'

The man nodded. 'Captain, we are people just like you. But let me first ask: you just stated that this plane was built in the year 2010. Is that correct?

'Yes, it was,' said Cardin, folding his arms in defiance.

'And you also stated that it is now seven years old.'

'Yep.'

'So just what year do you think this is now?'

Cardin snapped, 'Ten plus seven is seventeen. This is two thousand and seventeen - of course.'

237

Both Roslyn and Tom sucked in huge breaths while Cardin glanced nervously at them and probably knew deep down that something acutely uncomfortable was about to occur. Roslyn glanced away to stare out her side window. She had already guessed the horrible answer and had suggested it to the captain.

Tom addressed the two men. 'I know what you are going to say – whoever you are. This is in the future, isn't it? I mean the future for us.'

The first man stated, 'We have names. My name is Thor. I am the Area Director of Civil Order and Aviation procedures and this is the year two thousand and ninety.'

Cardin glared; his face sparking cynicism into Thor's face. 'Twenty-ninety, eh? Oh, is that bloody right? So I just flew this plane non-stop around the skies for seventy three bloody years and it's only just now run out of fuel! Well that's got to be a ripper of a world endurance record, hasn't it? Ha! Talk about long-range fuel tanks! And ah, I don't suppose you are going to tell us just where the hell this is? You see, we have 411 people on board who may be slightly interested in your answer.'

Thor almost whispered, 'We observed you pass over the island. You tracked due west from there. As you should know, this area used to be called the Port Macquarie district of New South Wales but is now part of one vast metropolis that runs from Melbourne right up to Cairns. This is airport number #2492 in division #119. It has no other name. I repeat: this year is two thousand and ninety.'

Roslyn had tears on her face as she calculated: 'Twenty-ninety? So I am 104 years old! Oh my God . . . '

Tom grinned, 'And that makes me ninety six and I *still* haven't got a regular girlfriend! That's gotta be some sort of record . . . '

No-one laughed as Roslyn almost wept, 'But what about our families? Our friends? Our society? Our whole world? And what on earth are your Zee-Dees?'

'Zone Defence drones.'

Meanwhile, Cardin's face exhibited some raw fear while his mind was obviously juggling if this entire nightmare could in fact be true. He attempted to calculate his own current age, but gave up. But even if this was remotely correct his little son would now be seventy-five years old and that certainly made no sense at all.

He asked, 'Twenty-ninety? Okay, so why are we still here then? According to this whacky game we're playing, I'm way over a hundred years old and even my first officer is 104. In that case, why haven't we already died? And how come we're still able to fly a thing like this?'

Thor shrugged. 'I really have no answers for you, sir. It is you and your intruder aircraft that burst upon our airspace and society without authority. We did not intrude into yours . . . although we are just as astonished as you.'

Tom had an idea. 'Mr Thor, why don't you just Google our missing flight and see what it says.'

'Do *what*?'

'Just look it up on your internet – or whatever you call it these days.' Obligingly, the man pressed a few buttons on his black tablet and stared at it. After whispering with his assistant, he turned to Ray Cardin.

239

'Captain, your plane went missing and was feared crashed in 2017. Therefore, you are no longer under arrest but subject to detention, nonetheless. All your crew and passengers will be held until this entire mysterious matter is resolved. Meanwhile, I can read here the intense media coverage of your disappearance seventy-three years ago. We now believe your story and will try to accept the even-greater mystery of your flight's re-appearance. The event was huge headlines in those days and will surely ignite more controversy when this sudden re-appearance is revealed.'

Ray Cardin was still not satisfied. 'I just figured it out: I am now one hundred and twenty two years old and easily the world's oldest pilot. So why did we zoom off into Fairyland then return after seventy three years into this crummy carnival? And why seventy-three years at all? Why not three hundred years - or a thousand?'

The man called Thor assured Cardin that they could not be expected to know any appropriate answers, while Tom the young second officer lamented to himself, 'Now I'll never get a girl if they find out I'm ninety-six . . . '

By now the three flight crew plus the purser standing nearby had realised with sinking hearts that everyone they'd ever known, and all their families and friends, were probably deceased many decades ago. They had unwittingly arrived in a very old aeroplane into a totally foreign society bringing their (naturally) old-fashioned ideas, educations and beliefs in which no-one of this new and strange era - except for curiosity value - would be likely to show the slightest interest. Besides, it certainly looked like they'd arrived into a grossly over-populated Australia of the future that was in some kind of war state; a society which might be unwilling or unable to feed and house over four hundred instant new visitors.

Roslyn Steinhouse was deeply distressed that her wonderful parents were apparently now long deceased. But when this happened, she realised they would have endured the loss of their only daughter, in whom they were intensely proud, in Australia's greatest air mystery. Never knowing where their daughter's body may lie and never having any closure, they had most likely died of broken hearts.

Ray Cardin was slowly and unwillingly accepting the stark reality of it all. Hell, married for just four years and already he'd lost his wife and only son! He tried to envisage the ridiculous impossibility of a new life at the age of 122? And imagine seeking another wife here - or even advertising for one: "Wanted: loving wife for former airline pilot only 122 years old. Likes movies and flying kites." Maybe he should have just kept flying over the endless sea until all those wonderful engines gave up the ghost and stopped forever?

As everyone started disembarking down the portable stairway, Tom smiled at Roslyn, 'Hey Ros, it's my birthday next week. Would you like to come to my ninety-seventh?'

She berated him. 'This is not funny, Tom! It's an unbearable tragedy. I've lost everything. Don't you get it? And surely you must have some family like the rest of us . . . '

Tom told her that his parents had gone their own ways long ago and he only had a young sister who was aged fifteen. He hoped she wouldn't be thinking that her big hero pilot brother had been responsible for their disappearance. Then again, his sister might not even be alive now, but if she was then she'd be eighty-eight years old. He shuddered.

They crowded into one of the Batmobile-type vehicles and, followed by a fleet of army trucks driven by men in purple overalls, were driven away to a highly uncertain destiny in a completely unknown realm. Inside, Purser Haneed Zaresh remarked, 'Actually, we've already had our future, haven't we?'

'Or is this just beginning?' asked a passenger.

Another was cautiously excited. 'I just can't wait to see what marvellous progress we've made over seventy years or more.'

Six-year-old Corrie Newnes squeezed in next to her favourite captain and insisted on holding his hand. 'Are we in America now, Captain? And where is Disneyland?'

Cardin gripped her hand and thought about it. 'Well, you just never know, Corrie. There might be something down this road here that is even better than that.' Her little brother sucked his thumb and, bewildered, gazed out a window.

Gaining his attention, Purser Zaresh leant over to Cardin and whispered: 'Well Captain, I am sure we are all most grateful to you for getting us back onto dry land, and I fully acknowledge the terrible strains you have endured on this flight, but I must officially state here and now that your machine-gun diplomacy was an absolute disgrace!'

'Oh, so you don't approve of my Shakespearean eloquence?'

'No.'

It was water off a duck's back as Cardin just shrugged. 'This is not a popularity contest and I am not popular anyway. Neither is this a beauty contest because I am not beautiful. However, I am not a career diplomat, I am an airline pilot.'

They were delivered to a drab and dreary settlement of hostels that may have been constructed as army barracks. Inside were wall-mounted buttons where bunk beds slid out from the walls. A detention camp? Everyone looked around with great unease and someone called out to Cardin: 'Captain, what's going on? Where are we?'

Cardin took off his pilot's hat and jacket. 'Sorry folks, but I just can't explain any of this, except to say that this is surely some type of real live nightmare. Anyway, I am not your captain anymore. My duty was to get us back down onto the ground and, having achieved that, I haven't a clue what the hell is going on here. And I still don't believe, by the way, in any of this time-warp/time-zone/sci-fi mumbo-jumbo. So, at my apparent new age of 122 - and if we are all going to be held here, then I suggest that you create your own governing committee and elect leaders to represent us because I am no community leader, I was just a pilot. Meanwhile, I feel absolutely exhausted and must lie down. Actually, I feel like I could sleep for a hundred years. Oops! I suppose I shouldn't have said that . . . '

A few passengers giggled, then their faces quickly dropped as reality struck with a blunt force. They had *all* lost their families and their whole way of life. Plus their businesses, their wealth and probably their entire life's aspirations and dreams. Many people were either thoroughly bewildered or very angry – especially those who had always been non-believers in the mystical space/time-zone theories of science fiction, but were now confronted with some highly unpalatable facts of reality.

It is often impossible for people to concede that something they've implicitly believed in all their lives was actually wrong, while other values that they'd always refused to accept had been essentially right all along. But whatever their former beliefs, this was no dream.

Very soon, the flight and cabin crew had chosen bunks in a corner of a huge room then flaked out for well-deserved rests that were sure to be quite lengthy. Many passengers did likewise, while others were still too stunned to simply drift off into contented sleep when they felt they'd been suddenly incarcerated in a prison-type of *other world.* But looking out the windows they saw no more troops in purple jumpsuits or forbiddingly high walls. Neither could they spy any barbed wiring or guard towers - just rows of plain buildings of warehouse appearance.

It was pleasing to see no weapons anywhere, while the few bedraggled locals who ambled past seemed to show little interest in peering into the new arrivals' compound. This was hard to reconcile against a similar scenario back "in real time" if strange people had suddenly emerged from other time zones: either earlier or later. Dick Rendy remarked that if such an event as today had occurred back *at home* - as it was now being called, there would have been more TV cameras poking through these compound windows than there are cane toads hopping around northern Queensland!

In the far distance they could see their airport of arrival, yet no planes were sitting on the aprons – apart from the huge hulk of their 747 which was blocking a taxiway - and rarely were any to be seen or heard in the air. The bat-winged vehicles and military trucks in which they'd arrived had now disappeared, while not many sounds of traffic or industry or crowds could be heard. Yet the whole district, as they'd briefly seen from the air, was simply enormous and indicated that maybe several million people lived in this local region.

So, just what did they all do with their lives in an era seven decades hence? Did people still work? If so, perhaps it was all work from home these days? And was life any better in this year 2090, or was it worse? Many people suspected the grim answer was the latter.

But the inquisitive scientist Stuart Rhys was simply fascinated beyond measure and remained determined not to sleep just yet. He'd often fantasised about exploring the stars but had never in his wildest dreams imagined that he would travel forward or back in time to other dimensions. Although he'd studied and understood Einstein's revolutionary theories about time warping and relativity, he seemed to be the only passenger who had instantly and enthusiastically adapted to this unique predicament - this whole new world; a new dimension. He snatched an old school exercise book from his briefcase and began scribbling notes furiously, unable to make his hand race at the speed of his galloping mind.

Unlike Rhys, others just wanted to smash out at everything in sight in the futile belief that clenched fists would somehow neutralise this horror movie - this new existence. A man stupidly punched a small cupboard and was watched with alarm by one of the local escorts who had brought them here. Some passengers dragged him away while he argued furiously with whoever would listen. Later he was seen crying for his beloved Polly; presumably his wife, but later turning out to be his pet parrot.

Six-year-old Corrie Newnes no longer had pets. She told a sympathetic couple that her cat had been lost in their house fire - along with her two parents. 'But my lovely little fluffy dog Destiny escaped and ran from the fire - only now I can't take her to America with us. But she has a new home now and they're going to send us photos of her all the time.' Such an ebullient and positive young girl in this bizarre new life that had enveloped her and her brother, she grabbed Slater's little hand and they skipped outside the hostel to play exploration games. Their chaperone, Jane Grayling, ran after them but soon fell behind. Puffing, Grayling feared that she was breaking apart from the shock of their situation and had never imagined that she would still be these kids' chaperone long after their advertised arrival time in America. So who would look after them now? Who would feed them? And who would feed *her*?

'On the subject of food,' asked Mark Dekanic. 'Do we ever get fed? Does anyone know? Do they even *eat* food here?' Everyone glanced around but saw nothing resembling kitchens. A man suggested they probably eat plastic these days, and another said: 'Air. They have a machine that turns air into food. I saw it on TV.' He seemed quite serious.

'Rubbish!' a woman hurled a pillow at him.

246

Another woman chimed in, 'Yes, rubbish. They can turn rubbish into food. They were planning to do that on Mars, you know. It was on The Late Show.'

Stuart Rhys held his hand up. 'Please, everyone, let's not be sidetracked and just do as the captain suggested. We need to elect community leaders and spokespersons now. So firstly I volunteer myself, but there are plenty of you here that must be committee members or community captains or elected officials somewhere. Or maybe school principals or business managers or Rotarians? Come on, people – speak up. We need to get organised now. We mustn't end up like Orwell's *Animal Farm* or *Lord of the Flies.* We need a delegation right now to front up to those in charge of us and to negotiate our first basic necessities . . . like food. '

'And if they're going to shoot us or not!' yelled a voice that was quickly howled down.

Rhys scowled at the speaker. 'We don't need to inflame matters with comments like that,'

Soon, Allan Henner stood up with his lady friend, Julie Page. 'I'm not a business owner or manager, just a chartered accountant and a Rotarian. But I'll volunteer to be on the committee. I can run the financial side of it – if we ever get that far down the track.'

Financial?' someone queried.

'Yes, we will need to purchase food and supplies, so obviously funding will be required for that. You don't honestly think they're going to feed four hundred of us for nothing, do you?'

'Well they're the ones who forced us to land here . . . '

'No, we are the ones who barged our way into here.'

A woman spoke up. 'Please, everyone. No arguing. I am a high school teacher and I was Deputy-Mayor of our town for five years, so I could help. I know all the local government procedures.'

Another voice called, 'My name is Kim Beniton and I am a police sergeant and a Mason. I can run the law and order side of it - if you need me.'

Rhys smiled with relief. 'Excellent, and thank you volunteers. Okay, only one more, then that's it. We only need five leaders to represent us because this is not Parliament House.'

The committee was quickly finalised with the addition of Rod Appleby, a millionaire marine businessman, while the chairman would be Stuart Rhys himself, a scientist. All in all, this was quite some experience and talent just to go begging for food and a few basic necessities.

It was soon discovered that the facility had toilets and showers in the building next door. Stuart Rhys remarked, 'Well, of course it has. They've only moved ahead seventy-three years. People still do the same things now as always. We're not light years from home. We aren't on another planet.'

The two missing children were found around the corner, playing in some kind of sand pit and enjoying their new world. Kids have played in sand for thousands of years, Jane Grayling told herself as she breathed a sigh of relief, but what might happen next; both to her and the children? She had no-one in this crazy time warp - as they were now calling it, except these two children who she had known for only two weeks. She, like almost all passengers on the ghost flight, had lost virtually everyone she knew.

What was quite noticeable, however, was the absence of their captors - or more correctly, their new hosts. It could be quite unreasonable to refer to them as captors when it was the Air Australia plane and those on board who had somehow blundered, or intruded, into this new territory. In fact, their new hosts had hardly been seen at all since the mass arrival at the compound.

Outside there were no workers milling around, no guards and few local civilians.

The committee addressed everyone present. 'Perhaps they are afraid of us,' suggested the self-appointed chairman of the people's council, Stuart Rhys. No-one had thought of this concept, but it was certainly a notion of merit. Most of the four hundred people had gathered around to observe the new council's inaugural meeting, and now, with true democratic process, they allowed their leader to hold the floor.

'Firstly, I'll ask the panel to discuss my theory that these people could be wary of us,' declared Rhys, 'then call for anyone else who wishes to comment.'

Rhys explained said that the local people would certainly be very wary right now, and might be arming themselves as a precaution. After all, 411 newcomers is no small force to tackle and might need to be resisted with more than a few stern words.

'Look at it from their point of view,' Rhys addressed them all. 'They may well live here in relative peace and harmony – a refuge away from their wars - then, all of a sudden, a very old and large plane barges into their airspace and loudly demands to land!' Everyone grinned as they recalled Captain Cardin's vociferous outbursts over the radio which someone had relayed over the loudspeakers throughout the plane. Cardin had certainly expressed his fiery opinions in no uncertain terms about their captors' plastic toys, their cowboy antics and Boy Scout threats . . . and also labelled them terrorists.

Rod Appleby declared, 'Hmm, not exactly an endearing maiden speech from a blundering group of unknown people from the ghostly past, was it?' Everyone turned around towards Ray Cardin's bunk where the commander appeared to be fast asleep. This was the man who may have once been detested but was certainly now respected by so many.

Appleby continued, 'I organise fishing charters out to many Barrier Reef islands. Now, if some strange boat turned up one day and its occupants started abusing the hell out of me and my people, I would instantly be on the defensive . . . wouldn't you? And if they were calling me a terrorist before they'd even dropped anchor. . . '

'Yeah!' cheered many people in agreement, while others yelled that Cardin was only doing his job.

'That's right. He couldn't possibly have known that we'd flown into this crazy time warp - or whatever the heck it is,' yelled another.

'He was paid to defend us and that's what he did,' a man added. 'He's a hero!'

Stuart Rhys spoke up. 'Okay people, settle down please. Everyone will get their say eventually. Now, what is the most pressing item on our agenda? I have suggested that these people may be afraid of us, even though they have generously given us sanctuary so far. It has also been alleged that we barged into their world in a quite belligerent manner . . . '

'Like a sledge hammer!' someone called.

'Or a runaway D9 bulldozer. So okay, we may have made a bad start while under extremely harrowing circumstances, but let us now move on. We need to approach their community leaders to firstly offer our apologies for our initial behaviour, then enquire politely about our highly uncertain future: particularly the immediate and pressing necessity for food, water and the usual items of life. Then, maybe another day we'll ask about our freedom – if we can indeed expect any at all.'

Many people commenced mumbled conversations, but Rhys told them all to *shoosh!* 'There are sound reasons why they are staying clear of us just now. Those reasons are tribal and go right back to the caves. Tribes always exhibit initial distrust at the sudden appearance of other unknown tribes. Often this doubt and fear quickly degenerates into violence. As Mr Appleby suggested, you should all try to imagine what you would do if a very large group of strangers suddenly knocked on your door back home and claimed they were from a past era.' A majority in the hall showed uncertainty then noisy discussions erupted on how they might react.

'I'd invite 'em in for a barbecue!' yelled the jovial Richard Rendy - also known as Dirty Dick - from down the back. Then he added, 'So long as they've brought their own grog!'

For the first time since their arrival, everyone laughed as one.

20.

Most of the Air Australia crew slept for about eight hours then woke to discover that none of them had been invited to participate in the ruling council that the passengers had created amongst themselves. So now the crew's salaried duties had ceased, their authority had gone, and even their fashionable uniforms were discarded as irrelevant. An atmosphere of depression soon overtook the eighteen crew members as they discussed this unique and unworldly realm in which they now found themselves. Used to living the high life of the jet-set, they were now nothing but a small group of superfluous mouths to feed amongst so many others in an unknown and frightening new world.

Meanwhile, on the outskirts of the largest compound a pioneering contingent from the council of representatives were bravely walking the perimeter roads; looking for a sign indicating an official office of administration - or a police station of some sort. But these dusty roads simply encircled the whole complex and the committee could easily cross over main roads into adjacent suburbia if they wished. They were not imprisoned and faced no obvious impediments to escaping the whole area – but to where?

Gazing upon dreary housing and buildings all around them, scientist Stuart Rhys made copious notes of his observations. 'Amazing; many of them seem to be empty,' he wrote. 'I see endless houses and other buildings almost in disrepair, with only the occasional strange-looking motor vehicle going past. I have not seen one person walking anywhere and only a few patrol drones have floated lazily overhead. Are we the only people around here?'

Rhys decided that they'd been encamped at the outskirts of a barracks or factory area that had ceased to function. Fine, but from where would their food supply come?

Rod Appleby remarked that it reminded him of Eastern Europe towards the end of the Communist era. 'I went through East Germany a few times and it all looked so very drab; just like this. Many empty gray buildings, gray streets and gray-faced people in gray clothes. Even the sky was gray most days.'

'A communist sky?' smiled Rhys.

'Maybe, but the people all had that hang-dog look on their faces. You know: the look of defeat. Their clothes were decades out of fashion and some shop windows had maybe three old sausages hanging from a hook, plus one tattered rag doll for sale. It was Despair City where they all gawked in great envy at our modern denim jeans and Seiko watches and Reeboks; knowing they could never afford such luxuries.'

Police officer Kim Beniton interrupted. 'Listen up everyone. There's no-one around here at all. If I was on a police recon operation right now, I would radio back that it was all just too suspicious and to please send reinforcements.'

'So, could they be hiding from us? Waiting to strike, perhaps?' asked high school teacher Barbara Hayes warily.

'Sure could,' answered Beniton from experience.

Allan Henner said, 'Well, word would have quickly spread that we've come from some other time zone, and many of them would have seen our huge plane approaching to land. You can understand their concern if they've never heard of time zones - just as we'd never heard of them either. Imagine if our news back home announced one day that a huge plane had landed in Sydney or Melbourne and it was full of people from a past era.'

Stuart Rhys said, 'Yes, this scenario has already been bandied about like a football at the MCG, so let us please move on. We will continue walking until we find something of interest. If we stumble across any people we will instantly befriend them. There will be no scuffles and no showing of any weapons of any sort. I hope none of us are carrying sticks, knives or other concealed weapons. How about you, Kim?'

'Hell no, I'm on holidays,' assured Kim Beniton the cop. 'I was going to meet a lady at Yellowstone National Park and we planned to walk the trails. I'm having a break from crime and weapons.'

'Good,' smiled Rhys, 'because we all know what happened upon Captain Cook's arrival in Botany Bay in 1770. The local natives stumbled upon them and immediately brandished spears - because that is what they normally do every day - so Cook had his men shoot towards them. Unfortunately one was accidentally killed by this previously unknown *fire stick,* and so it was war from then on. A total misunderstanding from the word *GO,* but impossible to ever rectify. So I won't allow that to happen here?'

They all agreed to raise their hands in surrender should anyone suddenly appear; and if fired upon, dive for cover. After that, tactful diplomacy might hopefully smooth the waters between these time travellers from another era and the locals, who might be justifiably unfriendly.

'So, are they Australians?' asked Barbara Hayes as they walked past more suburban dwellings. Timid about peering into windows, they occasionally sighted the outlines of people sitting inside. But no kids were seen playing, no TV screens flickering, no music was heard and not even a dog barked while no birds flew in the sky.

'Of course they're Australians,' asserted Allan Henner. 'This was the Port Macquarie district in northern New South Wales. We used to come here for Christmas holidays when I was a kid. I recognise a few things here and there . . . '

'But where has the beautiful Hastings River gone?' asked Rhys. Henner was unsure. He hadn't spied it from the air and had no idea where it might lie now. He hoped the lovely river hadn't been covered over.

'All I saw from our plane was ugly concrete everywhere,' rued Henner. 'It's a bit like my visit to Japan a few years ago. We were racing along in one of their famous Bullet trains, waiting to see the beautiful Japanese countryside once we'd escaped Tokyo and the cities; but we never seemed to get out of the built-up areas. We saw no forests or farms, or seaside scenes or natural parklands. It was just an endless expanse of concrete all day. Later we heard that the Japanese sometimes concrete over their sandy beaches to build more resorts and housing developments.'

'That probably happened here too . . . by the looks of it,' said Stuart Rhys. 'That small hill we just climbed revealed nothing but development to the indefinite horizon in all directions. Remember, we were told that this metropolis extends from Melbourne right up to Cairns – four thousand kilometres of humanity's contribution to destroying nature with that great eyesore called "development." I wonder if every other country is now the same?' This was certainly disheartening, especially when nothing appeared likely to challenge this grim outlook for their immediate future.

The group of five wandered on, gazing at endless rows of drab warehouses and abandoned factories, then past hundreds more homes with unmown lawns and depressingly overgrown and tangled gardens. Then someone moaned, 'I'm hungry' and they all felt instant pangs.

Beniton said, 'Well Stuart, you're the boss so what do you say about us knocking on someone's door to enquire about food? It has to be done eventually . . . '

Rhys thought about it. 'Yes, but it would be quite intimidating if five people knocked on anyone's door and begged for food. And what home would have enough spare food for five adults anyway? Imagine if the home owner asked how many of us there were in total, and we replied "over four hundred" then it would be big trouble; would it not?'

Barbara Hayes insisted they only send one person to knock. 'Just to inquire about where we can buy food . . . not to *ask* for food.'

'And how do we pay for it?' asked Rod Appleby. 'Our currency might be long out of date – like our plane's equipment and all those GPS's. Even if they still recognise our old dollars, one dollar these days might not buy a single clothes peg or even a grain of sand. Inflation marches on - especially after seventy-odd years.'

'Well, we might have to just *take* some food eventually,' declared Beniton. 'Otherwise, we starve to death real soon. Hey guys, don't argue: it's called reality.'

Rhys was angered by his audacity. 'Just steal it? You're a police officer and we've been here in this new land for only half a day and already we want to become a militia to forcibly steal enough food to feed over four hundred of our people every day – indefinitely. We would need a highly-trained and armed force to even contemplate such foolishness, and anyway that's a blatant declaration of war if ever I've heard one. And what if they fire weapons back at us? Weapons that we don't even know have been invented yet . . . '

Kim Beniton put a rough slant on the matters in hand. 'Survival of the fittest, I suppose. Been going on for millennia – otherwise

256

we'll be as desperate as rats in a sewer. So we'll just have to find some weapons. The only tribes who won in the end possessed the better weapons and went out to kill everyone and just take what they needed. Nobody ever remembers the losers.'

'Well I do,' countered Rhys. 'I remember our dispossessed Aborigines – even if most Aussies don't care. And I still sympathise with the North American Indians and all those other indigenous civilisations around the world that were trampled on then unjustly labelled as losers. I care.'

Barbara Hayes was angered. 'Oh, you men! This stupid debating could go on all day. Meanwhile, we're all getting hungrier by the minute – and so will all our people back at the . . . whatever it's called where we are now . . . '

'Home sweet home,' smiled Allan Henner. 'Well, we can either lie down and die or we go and politely ask someone now about where we might obtain food. Okay Stuart?'

Fortunately Rhys and the group soon turned a corner and spied a plain and dusty sign that said *Barracks #922.* 'Okay,' Rhys was bravely resolute. 'You lot wait back here while I go in and test the waters. Wish me luck.'

Never in his life had he envisioned himself in such a bizarre position: fronting for a committee that needed food and provisions for hundreds of people in some kind of *other* world. He decided that his chances of a friendly local saying: "Oh sure, here's the keys to our food warehouse. Just go and help yourselves," were probably zero, and his risky mission might easily result in a one-way mission impossible. Gingerly, he climbed a few rickety steps, turned to make sure the others were out of sight, then knocked on the door of *Barracks #922.*

Rhys heard a gruff voice from inside and assumed it was an invitation to enter. Inside, he saw an old man with a dour face and a white beard flowing over his chest. The man seemed to hold little interest in who was approaching his enquiries counter and continued gazing at sheets of dusty paperwork while ignoring him.

'Excuse me sir,' Rhys began nervously. 'Ah, I represent a group of people who have recently arrived here. We were wondering . . . '

The untidy man turned his back while interrupting: 'You are not wanted here.'

This was a disappointing start and Rhys spun his mind to seek another approach. 'Ah, yes sir, I appreciate that. But you see, I am a scientist. I am not the pilot who was flying that plane. And anyway, we . . . '

'Scientist!' the man spun around. 'It was your type who started all our troubles. Invented everything including our own certain destruction! And anyway, why are your accomplices hiding around the corner?'

'Ah . . . '

'Do you think that we don't have camera surveillance in this day and age?'

Damn, cursed Rhys silently. He should have sent in the friendly school teacher – but certainly not the police officer who might have burst in like Clint Eastwood with both guns firing from the hips, or Rod Appleby who would probably try to sell him a boat. Too late, this scientist would just have to suffice - take it or leave it.

Rhys started again. 'Okay sir, I agree with you. But I am merely a representative of our people who quite mysteriously arrived here from our own era in the past. We have no idea how this could have occurred and are extremely sorry if we've disturbed any of your people. We would like to leave right now if we could, but have even less idea how to return. In the interim, we are naturally asking where there might be any spare food and provisions for us. We will try to pay for it . . . of course. '

The man, who still hadn't introduced himself, looked up from his papers. His face was worn and craggy; lined with years of worry or trauma. 'I have already told you that you are not welcome here.'

Rhys was exasperated. 'But what can we possibly *do* about this? We did not set out to intrude into your territory. We had our own lives back then. Our own food. Our homes and money. And a future – which did not include being here in this . . . ah, just what is this place?'

'One of many military barracks supporting the endless wars which come and go.'

Rhys sighed in despair. 'Endless wars? Yes, humanity has disgraced itself with wars throughout its entire history, and now it seems that nothing has changed. We were rather hoping that the world had improved, not worsened. So you've seen many wars, have you, over the last seventy-odd years?'

'Endless, as I said. Some nuclear. Many were religious. Others for any excuse or for who-knows-why? The Australian wars started out to sea east of here. Some long-forgotten naval battle that became nuclear. Then it moved up to China. Across to Russia. Then a few years of peace, then more years of wars again. We are all so sick and tired of it . . . '

'Yes, I completely understand and sympathise. So, may I ask where all your people are? We've hardly seen anyone.'

'They come and go. The population ebbs and flows. Just now, many are away in the African conflict, while others returned to the European fronts. Even more are fighting in the Antarctic wars over the below-ice minerals bonanza, while others are skirmishing up at the North Pole. Sadly, it extends from pole to pole; from sea to shining sea . . . '

'Anyway, during each lull they return to occupy these compounds and barracks. At the moment we have a stockpiled a hoard of food that is kept somewhere, but it will soon diminish when they return again and not a scrap will remain for your unwelcome community. This is why I repeat that you and your time travellers are not wanted here. Or do you think it would it be fair if our people returned to their homes only to find no provisions remaining because their trusted guardians simply gave away it away to you gate-crashers from the past?'

Rhys was shocked. 'Gate-crashers!'

The surly old man glared up at him. 'Well, just how do you perceive yourselves, then?'

'Ah, accidental arrivals, I suppose. Like sailors shipwrecked on an island. None of us ever wanted to be here, but while it was wonderful to be saved from plunging into the ocean, we still need housing and food every day.'

The man turned his back to Rhys. 'In that case, where shall our own brave warriors and defenders stay when they return once again from the wars? And what should *they* eat?'

'I just don't know,' confessed Rhys, thoroughly embarrassed and confused.

The man turned his back again to gaze forlornly out a dusty window and mumbled, 'You should search for someone else who may wish to help you and your people; but I don't know where you could look. We are just the skeleton staff here at the moment. However, if you can find someone who might want to buy your old antique plane to display in our museum, then that might give you some cash to buy some food.'

Rhys was amazed. 'Sell the jumbo? Ah, that never occurred to me. But we don't even own the thing; an airline company owns it.'

'And, seventy-three years later, where is this company now?'

'I have no idea.'

The man said, 'I believe I heard that they went broke about sixty years ago. But assuming they still exist, would they ever want an old plane back that was over seventy years old?'

'Well, they certainly wouldn't want all that outdated electronics inside it. But it's just a preposterous notion. Anyway, how much would your museum be prepared to pay for the thing - assuming that we could ever sell it?'

The old man mumbled at the window. 'Don't know. Maybe five hundred . . . or a thousand . . . '

'Five hundred thousand for a whole jumbo jet that size?'

'Not thousand - five hundred *dollars*!'

Rhys' mouth dropped open as the man lectured, 'Well, you either need the food or you don't.'

Stuart Rhys stammered. 'But . . . five hundred *dollars?*'

Outside, Rhys explained to the waiting four, 'It's worse than I thought; much worse. There are wars everywhere. Most of the local people are away fighting them. But they'll be back from time to time and they'll fill those big dormitories and will need all their stored food stocks. However, he suggests we can hopefully buy some in the meantime . . . '

Barbara Hayes asked, 'From who? Where?'

Rhys balked at the question. 'Ah, obviously we would have to sell them something first.'

Barbara agreed. 'Of course. We don't ask or expect anything for free.'

Allan Henner offered some ideas. 'Alright, I can organise a whip-around and raise whatever funds we can. Maybe we can throw in some jewellery or somesuch. We could sell our luggage, I suppose, but I can't think of much else we have to offer them. Can anyone?'

Kim Beniton grinned, 'Well, we once had plenty of expensive grog down in the cargo hold, but certain persons of interest happened to consume it all!'

Everyone smiled except Rhys, whose mind was further down the track. He gulped and said, 'The old man in there suggested we might want to sell them the . . . ah . . . '

'The what?'

'Well, promise you won't laugh . . . but he suggested we try to sell the, ah, plane to their museum.'

Everyone's eyebrows shot up as one of them asked: 'The plane? You mean *our* plane? The Boeing-747 jumbo jet? Firstly, we don't even own that plane so how could we possibly sell it?'

Allan Henner employed his accountant's mind to estimate the approximate value of a used Boeing-747. 'Let's see, what was it worth before we left . . . maybe $250 million or so? But now it's quite obsolete, isn't it, so it's almost impossible to value the thing in this strange new world we are in now. Did he give you any indication of what they might pay for it?'

Rhys gulped and turned his face the other way. 'I'd rather not say.'

'Why not?' demanded Sergeant Kim Beniton.

'Five million at least,' guessed Barbara Hayes. 'That would buy us a lot of food – hopefully.'

Rhys was too embarrassed to answer and remained silent.

'Okay, one million then?' estimated Rod Appleby. 'And that's gotta be a bargain! That thing is the size of a football field. It's ready to fly and just needs refuelling. Actually, it should look quite grand sitting in their museum - if the museum is big enough to house the thing.'

'So how much did he say, Stuart?'

Rhys said sombrely, 'I'll announce it at the meeting I will call when we get back to the barracks. Meanwhile I'm hungry – like all of us. But first we'll have to walk to the plane at the airport and raid whatever's left in its galleys and cargo holds in case we find nothing out here. I'm not sure that we'll find adequate nourishment for over four hundred people, though.'

On the way they located several deserted Army trucks with keys in them. They took one and no-one stopped or questioned them. Driving along, it certainly was quite eerie: empty streets and dust-blown roads where all the traffic lights were disturbingly blacked-out.

At the nearly-deserted airport the mighty Boeing-747 stood abandoned where it had stopped on a taxiway leading off the northern end of the main runway. No-one had towed it clear and, it seemed, there was no urgency to move its bulk anyway.

They had arranged to meet up with Purser Haneed Zaresh who showed them how to enter the plane by tapping codes into a security keyboard under the plane's belly.

A huge cargo door creaked and swung open, then several hydraulic ladders whined down. Eagerly, the committee climbed into the lower cargo deck and went to work, frantically scouring every box and crate for food. Instantly some unpleasant smells wafted around them and Zaresh remembered that they were carrying, amongst many other things, several pallets of prawns and a variety of other seafood.

Destined for gourmet plates in Canada, these consignments had nevertheless ended up back where they started: in Australia. But now without refrigeration, they were starting to decay and odours wafted among the searchers. This, however, doesn't greatly matter when people are nearly starving, so each crate was hurriedly wheeled down ramps and lugged onto the truck. Then they found a few dozen cold airline meals that had not been wanted or remained unserved for whatever reasons, plus several dozen packets of biscuits and other assorted packages that may have contained food. There was no time to inspect every item.

With the truck loaded, they raced back to divide the spoils among their four hundred very hungry people. There, no-one complained about eating a few smelly prawns followed by a biscuit. Fortunately, they had running water from the basins in the adjacent shower amenities building, but apart from that, if you were a coffee lover or a smoking addict or a connoisseur of fine banquets, then it was highly likely you were facing one of those nights that really could last forever.

21.

Over the following day the steering committee, headed by the popular and likeable Stuart Rhys, repeatedly discussed their ominous predicament. Most of the passengers admired Rhys for his intelligent and insightful leadership, while the plane's captain, Ray Cardin, was occasionally consulted for opinions but mostly remained silent and withdrawn . . . for a change. Now dressed in jeans and a t-shirt, he looked like any other thin man his age with a greying, balding head and weary eyes. Incredibly, only one passenger had walked up and shaken his hand for saving them all.

When Rhys revealed that they might only receive the preposterous price of five hundred to a thousand dollars for selling the 747, widespread despair broke out. Many had been expecting the sum to be at least a million dollars or so, which should buy enough food for perhaps a month – depending on the price of food, of course. However, this paltry and insulting amount probably wouldn't feed them for even a single day.

'This must be a joke!' an angry voice shouted. 'They're just playing with us!' shouted another.

Accounting auditor Allan Henner explained. 'It is simply a case of supply and demand and there's just no demand for what we're flogging. Look, *we* aren't wanted here . . . let alone our plane. That was made very plain to Stuart. In any case, how can we sell something that we don't own? Captain Cardin?'

Cardin sat on his bunk and replied reluctantly. 'Hell, just imagine if I signed it away for peanuts and then this all turned out to be a crazy dream! Anyway, the suggestion is quite untenable as I am not an AA director who is authorised to sell off any company assets, I am just an employee - or was.'

'The captain is right,' spoke a voice from the back. 'We have to think of something radically different which might feed us over the long term.'

A voice spoke up. 'But they told Mr Rhys that we are not wanted here. What happens if many of these people arrive home from their wars tomorrow and need to re-occupy their accommodation?'

'Violence will erupt,' Beniton assured them. 'People will automatically defend their homes and food supplies without even blinking.'

Stuart Rhys added, 'And we would have to get the hell out of here – fast! Don't ask me where . . . just anywhere.'

Someone shouted, 'How are we going to transport over four hundred people away from here? Steal twenty of their trucks? Or thirty? Or maybe we just heist eight or nine tour buses from somewhere, eh?'

Rhys spoke loudly. 'We'll simply fly away in our four-hundred-seat aircraft, of course. But first, we will all walk back to the airport if we have to. In the meantime this panel will go out on a scouting mission, then report back on our next step – *if* there is one to be had.'

'I won't stoop to stealing food from people's homes and properties,' a despondent Barbara Hayes declared to the crowd. 'I could never descend that low. That's not how I was brought up.'

Police Sergeant Kim Beniton stated, 'In that case you'll starve to death. Barb, you'd be very surprised how low people can go when their food runs out. We were caught in sudden food riots in starving Bangladesh where people were clawing at each other with knives. We'd been out shopping at the local markets and had to run for our lives!'

An elderly man added that his grandfather had been imprisoned in Singapore's Changi jail during World War Two. They hardly had a thing to eat for over three years, but some of them managed to survive.

'Three *years*!' many people groaned; their hopes choking in despair.

Voices pleaded. 'So, in the meantime, what else can we do?'

Car salesman Bob Greenly said, 'At least the panel is venturing out on a foraging mission to try to achieve something! But what about the rest of all us defeatists? Are we just going to hang around here and mope?'

From a far corner came a child's voice. Brave Corrie Newnes put her little hand up and spoke, 'I think that if those people here don't like us and if there's nothing to eat, then we should just go back.'

A woman patted her blond hair and smiled, 'Well, thank you, Corrie. But where could we go back to?'

With great confidence the girl replied: 'Back to where we came from – of course!' Several women hugged her then she ran outside to play again with the small group of four young children aged from four to eight - plus one baby.

Soon a small cheer went up as a man announced, 'Guess what, everyone! We just found ten boxes of Australian chocolates that were bound for the USA. Remember all those red boxes we scooped up? Well there are a hundred chocolates in each box, so that's great for energy levels.'

It was a small jackpot to discover these half-melted chocolates because this was wartime and chocolates are always revered like gold in war-torn days – then gobbled with glee. The committee walked towards their truck, taking one small tray of chocolates with them. 'We'll be back in two days maximum,' smiled Stuart Rhys.'

'But where will you go?'

'I suppose we'll head south towards the Sydney area. After all, that's where most of us originated on the flight.'

'What about north?' asked a man called Neil. 'Away from that huge city metropolis. This region is already big enough. If we can ever buy some fuel for the plane we might be able to land somewhere up there. A country airport, a farming area - or at least a friendlier area. Who knows?'

A woman firmly declared, 'I don't care who goes where. I'm never getting back into that jumbo thing.' Many others supported her.

A man sneered at her: 'Then stay here and starve!'

As Stuart Rhys drove the truck along a mostly deserted highway, heading north from the old Port Macquarie district, Allan Henner asked, 'Did you get around to asking that old man about the Hastings River, Stu?'

'Yes, he said it was covered over for development decades ago. It is still there somewhere; it's just underneath everything.'

'No different from the old Tank Stream in Sydney, I suppose.'

'Well, yes. Like so many streams and brooks and fine rivers everywhere.'

'What a shameful environmental sin,' rued Barbara Hayes.

'Most call it progress,' argued Kim Beniton. 'That's why I was going to Yellowstone while it's still untouched.'

Henner recalled something else. 'Stuart, did you remember to tell Captain Cardin that Air Australia went out of business about sixty years ago?'

Rhys grinned, 'I might be brave but I'm not that stupid. Can you imagine what he would say?'

'Um, I can, actually.'

As they motored past unending urban development – much of it abandoned - Rhys took note of the few "Diesel Here" signs along the way. From the odometer, he noted down the exact distance in kilometres from their starting point. It was essential to be vigilant; after all, this was not just a strange new country, but a whole new world they were exploring. It might be called Australia, but could just as easily be some other planet . . .

As they passed another fuel point, Allan Henner asked 'Just how are we going to pay for any Diesel?' They all glanced at each other for wisdom. A very good question, indeed. In fact, it would be prudent to allow for their return journey now by not proceeding past the halfway mark on the fuel gauge. Otherwise they might simply fail to return from their mission to nowhere.

Kim Beniton remarked pointedly, 'No-one will cry for us. If we don't make it back then it will simply mean five less mouths to feed, won't it?'

Rhys pulled over to the side and fumed in frustration. 'So, what exactly are we doing out here in No-Man's-Land? Aimlessly looking for what? Somewhere else to land a jumbo jet? And if we can't find or pay for a tiny bit of diesel fuel for this truck, then how on earth will we ever pay for a whole plane load of jet fuel to get us all out of here?'

Henner asked, 'Anyone know how much it costs to fill up a jumbo?'

Rod Appleby said, 'Ah, yep. I read about it in the seat-back pocket. It said a 747 takes 217,000 litres of fuel. So let's say we manage to buy it for about two bucks a litre, then we can fill 'er up for only about half a million bucks. Yippee, what a bargain!'

Everyone sighed in sheer desperation as Allan Henner the accountant moaned, 'You know what, people? In essence, we are stuffed. We really are stumped and defeated every which way we turn. We don't have the money, the resources or the ability to sustain ourselves in this frightening new world for much more than one week. And when we look at the wider picture, the locals here don't seem to have sufficient resources for themselves, let alone a large planeload of strangers who suddenly and rudely blundered into their world from a past era. And why would they even care about people from the past? Did we ever care about our own past, and would we have fed people who we'd thought were long dead? Anyone like to comment?'

Barbara Hayes spoke up. 'Maybe we should just do what that cute little girl suggested.'

'What was that?'

'She said we should go back to where we came from.'

'Oh that's just bloody great, Barb!' snapped Kim Beniton, angrily. 'Get that Dirty Harry character to fly our plane backwards, you mean? He could announce: "Welcome aboard Backwards Airlines. We will now fly back seventy three years in time on the advice of a six-year-old child. Please fasten your seatbelts and hope for the best. Or, should we just do another grand loop of the Pacific now that we're so good at it?" Hey everyone, get real! We've just agreed that it might take half a million dollars to fill that thing up. Do you happen to have that much cash in your handbag, Barb? What's the limit on your credit card, Allan?'

'Excuse me, Kim,' Stuart Rhys warned. 'We don't need facetious comment like that. What do you mean, Barbara?'

Barbara Hayes said, 'Well, I know she's only six years old but sometimes kids have a clearer vision than adults who are constantly tangled up with the *big picture.* So surely we wouldn't need to fill that monster right up with fuel, we'd just need a little bit - like quarter tanks. Of course I don't know this for sure because I'm no pilot, but if we could fly for just one or two hours then we might make it to Sydney - or heaven knows where. There might be some humans there that are not quite so ravaged as are these destitute people. They might even have food aplenty. We have arrived in a poverty-stricken area where they certainly don't want us for very good reasons. Anyway, we need to at least try.'

The four men considered this then Rhys said, 'That little girl said "back to where we came from." And she meant it: back to our former home.'

Rod Appleby interjected. 'And just exactly how do we travel back in time, Stuart, when we haven't got the faintest or foggiest clue how we travelled *forwards* in the first place?'

Barbara raised her hands. 'Well, we don't know yet, do we? Maybe we fly down to near Sydney somewhere, then start out over the sea on our original flight path. Then we turn around and we might just reverse this whole horrible disaster.'

Kim Beniton was enraged. 'Fly over the bloody sea again? What a great solution that is! What we really should do now is find a gun somewhere and shoot our stupid selves!'

'And just give up?' Barbara glared at the policeman.

Stuart Rhys took over. 'Hold it please, people. I'm going to turn around here and drive back to the compound. I need to ask Captain Cardin a few questions.'

Beniton was incredulous: 'Now just hold on right there! You're not actually taking this crap seriously, are you Stuart? I thought you claimed to be a scientist, but you're going to ask that grumpy old

271

grouch to re-fly the route so we'll be mysteriously swallowed up in yet another crazy time warp – but a friendly one this time? And then we'll be out over that horrible ocean once again and this time with only quarter tanks of fuel? Now, I'm no pilot either, but get real! That's insane!'

'Got a better idea?' asked Allan Henner.

Beniton yelled at him. 'Yes, I just told you: shoot ourselves!'

The despondent committee were back at the barracks, tails between the legs after having found nothing except an extreme plan to an even crazier dilemma.

'Don't be ridiculous, Stuart,' derided Ray Cardin upon hearing their plans. 'We may as well shoot ourselves right now.'

'See? I told ya!' boasted the sergeant, smirking in Rhys' face.

'But Ray,' Rhys implored the captain. 'We came here originally because we somehow passed through warped time. Sometimes they call it a time distortion field. Anyway, why can't we at least try to go back through it? Otherwise we'll all be dead in a week if we don't do something . . . that's for certain.'

Cardin asked, 'You said "sometimes *they* call it a time distortion field." But who are *they*?'

'Well, people who follow this stuff.'

'You're hinting at science fiction buffs, aren't you? But I thought that all you genuine scientists loathed and ridiculed that bunkum as I do? Anyway, half these people here still think this whole disaster was my fault entirely because I pressed some wrong button. Nothing to do with science fiction at all . . . it was me!'

'That's ridiculous,' declared Rhys.

'And so is your whacko idea, Stuart. And you as a scientist – of all people - should know very well that nothing travels into other time zones or travels faster than light.'

Rhys argued, 'Well Ray, that's exactly what we did when we came here, so why can't we do it again? But anyway, I wasn't talking sci-fi, I was referring to real science. And what's your alternative? Apparently they've found a few crates of pineapples and some chocolates in the truck, and then that's it. So we've got maybe two day's food remaining for us all and then we're finished. Kaput! So you could at least consider flying us back towards Sydney and looking around.'

Cardin asked, 'And how will I ever force everyone back onto that hated plane again? Can you answer me that?'

Rhys replied firmly, 'We offer them a stark choice. They either walk up the boarding stairs and take their chances with us, or they stay behind and are dead by the end of this week.'

'But where would you get any fuel, Captain,' asked a passenger who posed the most pertinent question of the day.

Cardin was mildly confident. 'Ah, I saw refuelling trucks out there. They had "Jet A-1" written on the side. We might be able to obtain some and the locals should be quite keen to fill us up if it means getting rid of us.'

Kim Beniton argued, 'Fill us up for free? Unlikely. Who would pay for it? And how? Or would we just steal it?'

Cardin, for once, wasn't sure. 'Now that surely is the million-dollar question, isn't it?'

Listening in, the friendly second officer Tom Tyson offered a miracle solution: 'Hey everyone, I saw a big metal safe in the hold. It had *US Treasury* stamped on it. And it said: *This container is alarmed. Do not attempt to interfere with property of the US Government.'*

'Oh yes,' smiled Allan Henner. 'That would certainly contain cash - and lots of it, too. Our banks collect US currency from

American tourists every day in Australia and regularly transport it back there under international banking exchange laws.'

Tyson grinned. 'Yes, so we simply become bank robbers plus safe crackers so we can illegally fly over populated areas without flight plan approval or airways clearances in order to re-enter a time zone that we should never have left in the first place? Sounds pretty straight forward to me, so let's go!'

The panel nervously watched a few frantic people in a corner voraciously devouring several of the pineapples that had been discovered. This was certainly nutritious fruit but vital provisions that should have been shared among everyone. Watching on, their actions appeared almost feral and quite frightening. It was disturbingly obvious that quite soon there would be hand-to-hand food wars right here in the compound, to be followed by the natural progression that society calls anarchy.

Ray Cardin observed the scene and obviously his mind was whirling, his craggy face looking older by the day. In fact, when unshaven, he possibly resembled a suspect who police Sergeant Kim Beniton might describe on a charge sheet as "a person of interest."

Still unsure, Cardin nevertheless resolved that it would be sheer lunacy to remain here and do nothing for even one more day. Only he and his two other pilots could facilitate their departure for, hopefully, much greener pastures. But he would also need his dedicated cabin crew to maintain some semblance of public order and sanity throughout the passenger cabins.

First Officer Roslyn Steinhouse was sitting on her bunk in a corner. Knees drawn up, she wore a painful look of despair on her usually pretty face. Cardin walked up and sat beside her. 'Now Ros, I know you said that you had quit flying, but you can only bail out after your job is done. However this particular journey has not yet

274

been completed – as you should know. So I need my wonderful F/O to help us get out of here because I can't do every damn thing by myself. Tom's not endorsed for take-offs or landings anyway, so imagine if I happen to collapse at the controls, for example? I'm not a one-man band, you know.' She looked at him in silence.

The captain was getting desperate. 'Anyway Ros, to stay here moping would be suicide, or at least defeatist and unproductive. If your ship is sinking you head for the lifeboats; not sit sobbing in a corner in defeat. Come on, Roslyn. Get up and at it! You're still on the job because I haven't accepted your resignation yet.'

Slowly, she stood and followed him quietly out the door, but not before she made two demands of him.

'And what are they?' asked Cardin.

'That you never call me Little Miss Muffet or *my girl* again.'

'Agreed!' said Cardin, obviously feeling acute embarrassment and regret. Outside, the committee members had organised several trucks to take them and everyone's luggage ten kilometres back to the airport. The rest would have to walk.

At the airport they located a man who was asleep in the refueller's hut. It transpired that he had little to occupy himself these days because most of the current wars were on foreign continents, so he was quite interested in assisting these strange people from the past with their giant plane. When told that he could keep the contents of a safe that was on board and that it most likely contained a wealth of U.S. banknotes, he was suddenly enthused. United States currency was the only note of worth these modern days as continual world instability had seriously eroded the value of all others.

A fast and rough deal was quickly bartered where, no matter what the contents of the safe turned out to be, the refueller could keep the lot in return for about fifty-five thousand litres of jet fuel. This should give the Boeing about one-quarter tanks - much like Barbara Hayes had originally suggested, and Cardin confirmed that one-quarter tanks equated to about four hours of flight to freedom . . . hopefully.

As the old fuel truck dawdled out to the plane, Cardin surveyed the runway. It was probably adequate in length for a 747 take-off with all engines thrusting this time; plus, greatly to their advantage, would be their abnormally light fuel load, and virtually no heavy cargo remaining in the hold. (55,000 litres is an abnormally light load of fuel for a 747).

Each take-off in an airliner is a precisely calculated equation of weight, balance and performance where temperature, ambient air pressure and the prevailing wind all play vital roles. At the moment it looked like they'd be enjoying a favourable ten-knot headwind for their take-off, and this caused Cardin to smile: 'Every single knot will be a blessing.'

Of course, the stronger the headwind the sooner it helps an aircraft to lift off because it means less runway distance under acceleration is needed to reach a pre-determined airflow over the wings. If a hundred-knot headwind is blowing over an aircraft this size before it started its take-off roll, the plane would only need to accelerate for another forty or fifty knots to get airborne. And if the same hundred-knot headwind is blowing over a small Cessna's wings then it would already be flying if it wasn't tied down with chains.

Anyway, ten knots it was going to be as he and Roslyn stood beside the runway and gazed down its length. 'Feeling better, Ros?' Cardin asked kindly.

'Yes thanks. I was just devastated earlier, so I buried myself in self-misery. Not very responsible or mature, was it?'

Cardin whispered. 'No, but don't tell anyone that I also lay down and covered my face so no-one could see me. That wasn't achieving anything, either. Anyway, I think we've made a pretty good team so far, considering the outrageous circumstances we faced that are unknown to everyone in the entire world-wide aviation industry. Now we have to do even better and I can't think of any other co-pilot I know who I'd rather have with me today. So let's get to it. We might be home soon . . . or at least somewhere better than here.'

They discussed at length their "plan of attack" because this certainly was a war against some unknown evil force: a war that somehow *must* be won. Back in the plane, they wrote down their plan and mutually agreed to it. Cynically, it was christened "Plan A" because they both knew that there could be no Plan B and that failure was simply not a viable option. No matter what particular time field they might be in now or tomorrow, they would probably kill everyone on board if they got this wrong.

In the rear galley, the cabin crew discovered several extra-large tins of coffee; a real godsend. But, uselessly, only a few squirts of lukewarm water remained in the taps, plus two cans of lemonade to be shared among kids. Worse, no more food was to be found while several wooden boxes were mysteriously missing from the hold. Whatever they had once contained would forever remain unknown.

On the tarmac, several strong men managed to load the big safe onto a trolley and wheel it to the refueller's hut. Inside the safe, the contents may easily have contained a few million dollars but it was all worthless to everyone except the happy refueller. In parting, he assured them that there were plenty of tools in his works compound to force the safe open and that he had "nothin' else to do, anyway." The crew wished him good luck as he unplugged his fuelling pumps from the wings' undersides and drove away.

After all pre-flight checks and lengthy engine run-ups, everything onboard seemed to be in order so the command was issued to close and secure all the doors. The purser told Cardin that, despite the passengers' previous bravado about "never getting on another plane again" everyone listed on the original passenger manifest elected to come along and trust Captain Cardin once again, while not a single person had chosen to remain behind. After all, who would want to linger in that desert of ghostly time; unwanted, unfed and interred in indefinite solitude?

The giant Boeing roared down runway 20 with all four Rolls Royce engines blasting out their deafening fury. To much relief, and with such a light load this time, it easily cleared the southern perimeter fence and climbed steeply towards the south, while, thankfully, no escorting drones were to be seen. As cheering and applause broke out, a familiar voice sang over the P.A. speakers, accompanied by a guitar.

> *Oh, there once was a grumpy old captain,*
> *In a shiny blue and gold hat.*
> *One day he said that we're all lost*
> *And he didn't know where we're at! Oi!*

The rest of the ditty was rather ribald - as could be expected, so the children were ordered to cover their ears as everyone else laughed.

On the flight deck, Cardin beamed as he took charge of his plane once again. 'Never thought I'd be flying this lovely old girl again. In fact, I never thought I'd be flying *any* damned thing again.'

Roslyn grinned back at him. 'Me neither.'

Cardin became his old serious self. 'Now, it's VFR below five thousand for as far as we can go, right? If we can overfly Newcastle then we turn out over the sea towards Toxar as we did the other night.' Toxar was a fictitious reporting point in the sky, located at one hundred and fifty nautical miles north-east of Sydney. This was where they tried to make their last contact with ATC radar after losing all their electronic equipment.

Cardin repeated. 'So, we fly to where we estimate Toxar is, in the hope that some nice thing happens in our favour for a damn change, then we turn back towards Sydney. We've plenty of fuel – unlike last time. So, then we should be underneath a recognised track, even though it's an outbound one, and hopefully one of our devices just might work this time. In any case, they should eventually receive our primary radar return and can estimate our speed so they'll know it's a jet.'

Tom's exuberant theatrics interrupted. 'So, here's a jet racing towards Sydney, radios not working again, callsign and altitude unknown . . . so who on earth could it be? Santa Claus? No? They watch it intently and are well aware that a jet like ours recently went missing right around here.'

Roslyn said, 'That's if we are back in our old time zone again.'

'Well, yes. So then they contact Williamtown RAAF on the scramble hotline and ask if there's any plane of theirs out there. If not, they can use their special military radar to discern our altitude and other vital details. This is brilliant stuff called stacked beam radar where the radar pulses can beam their layers vertically for computers to estimate altitude, even if none of our SSR signals are operating. Er, sorry, I suppose we don't need to go over all that technical guff, but anyway Willytown should then say, 'Hey, it seems to be a four-engine job!

'Next, using common sense down there they'll all be thrilled – instead of alarmed - that a four-engine jet with no flight plan is inbound to Sydney on the exact same VOR omni radial that AA200 recently flew out on and then vanished. Perhaps they might get some RAAF jets to intercept us, and when they do: Hallelujah! They'll see our giant painted signs down each side: A.I.R. A.U.S.T.R.A.L.I.A.'

'And if they still don't get the picture by then,' Roslyn grinned, 'they should give up their daytime jobs and go fruit picking.'

'For sure!' Cardin grinned. 'So, reading from our agreed flight plan here – and all the while remembering that this is Plan A while there is definitely no Plan B, as we approach Sydney itself we vigilantly scan for other air traffic to determine which runways they're using, then widen out to a very long final fix approach to hopefully squeeze into the traffic pattern without scraping the paint off anyone else. Then we fly as slowly as possible – probably 145 knots with full flaps, to complete finals and land if the crossing runways are both clear. At this stage we should get green lights from the tower, but if not we will proceed anyway if we conclude it is safe. Agreed?'

Tom assured them he'd help in every way, especially watching for flashing tower lights from his side - a distraction neither of the front seat pilots needed.

Cardin asked him, 'So Tom, do you think we might be back in the *real* world by then?'

'We better Boss 'cos there's a cute girl at the surf club who's waiting for me to ask her out.'

"Ha, what better reason,' laughed Roslyn who smiled over at Tom. 'But will you tell her that you're ninety-five years old?'

'Sure - when I'm ninety-five.'

Ray Cardin briefly thought about his lovely wife Alicia and their two-year-old son, Jamie. It was impossible to imagine how they'd react to the news that AA200 had finally landed back at Sydney airport. Or indeed, how the whole *world* would react. But after this, he would take a month off work and stay home, enjoying his little family while thanking the great gods of aeronautics and reality that he was home again. He might even take them out fishing and use his tiny GPS . . . if he can find it.

But it wasn't over yet. The great Boeing overflew more endless suburban development, then turned inland towards Singleton for location identification, then south again towards Sydney. The only navigational difficulty here was that most of this previously familiar rural countryside was now nothing but an dreary landscape of houses and other buildings. Gone were the rolling green hills and fertile Hunter Valley while, glancing eastwards, Newcastle seemed almost the size of Melbourne while the Hunter River seemed tiny. So, they were still in the so-called *Time Distortion Field* and it was still 73 years hence.

'Ah, let's forget about Singleton and turn east now,' ordered Cardin; obviously disappointed. 'We'll cut the corner. Remember, we don't dare overfly Sydney itself while we're still unidentified.'

They passed over the vast Newcastle metropolis and headed out to sea; following a plotted angle to shadow-intercept the 068 degree radial of the Sydney VOR beacon - bearing in mind that they still had no working VOR instrument to confirm this, and that enthusiastic Tom would be down on his hands and knees once again, madly drawing pencil lines on old-fashioned charts.

Upon the estimated radial intercept, they would make a slight left turn then track towards the non-existent place on the RNC nav map called Toxar. Upon reaching it they would then make a sweeping turn to the south west and that should alert the relevant civil air traffic controllers and the military that Air Australia flight two-hundred was finally back in the real world and coming home.

It certainly was a rough plan that was full of holes, guesses, estimations and wishful thinking, but when all your electronic gear has failed then what the hell else is there? . . . as Ray Cardin would undoubtedly curse.

22.

Haneed Zaresh was back on the flight deck again, struggling to comprehend the pilots' puzzling new plan in order to explain it to all the passengers. Sitting together on the floor, Tom endeavoured to clarify once again:

'Okay Haneed, we estimate our last known position out over the ocean – see here where I've put this cross? Then we turn back towards Sydney to fly a reciprocal compass heading beneath our original outbound track. '

Zaresh was bewildered. 'But Tom, my passengers are asking me how will another jaunt out over water like this bring us back to our original time zone and year? They are just as mystified as I am.'

Tom smiled, 'Well it's not a *jaunt*, as you say. I'm not down here on the floor enjoying a Sunday picnic. This was once advanced navigation back in the old days . . . I mean those days even *older* than our real days: back at the dawn of aviation where all the pioneers really had was a compass and a map. Actually, some comedians used to joke that pilots used to hold a cat on a string in front of them, and if the cat swayed to one side then you were turning the wrong way.'

Zaresh's face froze as he looked around nervously. 'Ah, you don't have a cat in here . . . er, do you?'

'We did, but it got drunk downstairs at one of your loud parties. Now Haneed, just tell all your fans that we abandoned that last location because firstly we were unwanted, and secondly it was grossly unsuitable. Now, we intend to fly towards Sydney airport if the air traffic permits, then see what transpires when we attempt to land. But we can't possibly guarantee what year it will be, or anything bizarre like that because we don't even understand how we got here in the first place. We can only hope and trust that this time people will be friendly towards us and sympathise with our plight. Other than that, don't promise our passengers anything that we know can't be verified or sustained. That is: don't sell them false hope.'

Roslyn turned around and told the purser, 'Whatever eventuates Haneed, we'll be attempting to land in less than an hour, then it will all be over – one way or another. We can't do any more than that. But it's been wonderful working with you.' They all shook hands in the last moments of one of history's most bewildering and bizarre flights, then Zaresh, still perplexed and devoid of a satisfactory answer, scratched his head and bade them farewell and good luck.

After a while, Tom leant over between the two hard-working pilots and said, 'Hey Boss, it's time for your big speech to the masses.'

Cardin turned around and half grinned. 'Didn't I tell you not to call me Boss?'

'No Boss. Never heard you say that, Boss.'

'Well, show me what you've written down. And I'm not reading out any rubbish here.' Cardin perused a few lines, made some scribbled corrections, consulted with his First Officer, then picked up the P.A. phone.

'Ding Dong! Hello everyone, this is the world's most unpopular captain Ray Cardin once again, speaking for probably the last time before our landing. I have no more lectures for you this time. Now, as your purser may have already informed you, we are making some quite complicated manoeuvres using old fashioned navigation methods and backup instruments to hopefully fly back into Sydney on a reciprocal flight path to the one on which we flew out. We are hopeful that this unique manoeuvre will alert the controlling authorities and help them to identify who we are and just what are our intentions. Without the usual radio and electronic data signalling to and from the ground this is the only method left to us. Ah, a stewardess has just handed me a note saying that the Purser has advised everyone to . . . ah, watch the cat if all else fails!'

'Ha! It's not quite that bad - let me assure you. Now, a pioneering pilot called Wiley Post became the first person to fly solo around the world in 1931. He battled through rain, hail and snow by using his newly-acquired deduced reckoning skills; the very same skills we have utilised here today. So if Post made it back home one day, there's no reason why we can't do likewise.'

'I say our next party should be held in a month's time at a location to be advised. A happy reunion. Ah, finally, on behalf of the extremely hard-working crew of AA200 we strongly recommend that you take the boat next time . . . Hey, who the hell wrote that? Tom . . . Tom! Get over here!'

The giant plane arrived at its air position named Toxar on the RNC radio navigation chart. This was just an educated guess, of course, there being nothing to identify down below but white horses on a blue ocean. Roslyn Steinhouse turned the great ship of the skies to the right, then followed DR procedures to head directly back to Sydney. Eventually Cardin took over the controls and, aiming for the required final approach path fix, it would soon be battle stations for all hands while everyone eagerly prayed that they now had a fighting chance, at least. What actually lay ahead, however, was still the great unknown but was fervently hoped to be at least an improvement over their last eerie and inhospitable port of call.

285

FLASH! They were all nearly blinded by an incredible flash of pure while light. It illuminated the entire visible sky behind them, even though it was nearly midday. Like millions of strobe lights all going off on at once, the three pilots were stunned and shaken.

'Hell, fire and brimstone!' exclaimed Cardin. 'That looked like a nuclear explosion. Did you two see that?'

'Of course,' said the First Officer. 'It's the second time I've seen that. It was just like the other night when we nearly collided with those mysterious lights.'

Cardin was astonished. 'Well . . . now it's gone. And there's no mushroom cloud or anything like that. But, could this be their crazy wars that those people told us about?'

No-one knew, and the subject was soon overshadowed as Tom, standing between the two pilots and peering forwards, suddenly shouted in triumph: 'Land ahoy!'

And it was too; an absolute elation of victory for all. Greatly heartened, Cardin quickly returned his attention to the task in hand and descended the plane to three thousand feet while Tom monitored their progress and whispered to Roslyn, 'You know that they'll arrest us for stealing a million or so of US currency.'

She glared across at him. 'I don't need that on my mind just now, Tom.'

Cardin heard them and said, 'No, I don't think they will. Let me explain why: the airline will be so overjoyed when we've returned their precious pile of nuts and bolts to them that they'll eagerly pay any fine or imposed penalty for that missing safe. This plane is worth maybe two-hundred million so its return will be a huge saving for them - plus they'll have avoided the inevitable litigation should we never have returned. So I'm guessing that this whole affair might cost one billion dollars if we don't return, as against returning without that relatively insignificant little safe which would be insured anyway.'

'Remember that if they were to suffer a complete hull loss, AA's insurance might not pay up. This is because there would never be any proof either way if the plane was hijacked, sabotaged or otherwise recklessly operated by its crew. So, they'll be dancing a jig of joy when we show up with the damn thing unscratched, and AA will have avoided crippling adverse publicity when the world rejoices that they didn't lose a single passenger after all.'

Tom blew a breath of relief. 'Wow! For a time I could almost see myself breaking rocks on a chain gang for the next fifty years or so. How about you, Ros?'

Roslyn Steinhouse didn't hear him, but was staring fiercely ahead at the wonderful sight of the Sydney coastline approaching on this sparkling sunny day. With the commander in his left-hand seat, they ran through several pre-landing checks obtained from old printed cards, instead of using the usual digital screens that were still not operating.

'Okay troops, now listen up!' demanded Cardin. 'Now is about the time they'll be picking up our primary radar paint. They will panic at first, and then activate national security alarms and procedures, as well as calling us on various frequencies. If they get no replies they'll go straight to stage two which is where they'll call out the military. Fighter jets might be scrambled from Williamtown and Richmond and can race to protect Sydney much faster than we can get there. That's why we are now slowing right down to 180 knots initially so they don't think we are, say, a Russian or Chinese high-speed enemy.'

'When they intercept us, they will easily see our airline's name painted right down each side in letters that I once described so eloquently as the size of freaking barn doors.'

'Anyway,' Cardin continued, 'the interceptors should tell Sydney control that we are headed directly towards them, but in radio silence. It should be blindingly obvious by then that we have somehow returned from wherever we were and now intend to land, and it should not be too difficult for them to reorganise their traffic patterns to allow one extra landing amongst all the other air movements constantly taking place. In fact, they should really designate us as emergency traffic and award us the highest priority. So, while it all sounds fine in theory, we must remain acutely aware that, in reality, we are barging silently in to their primary control zone airspace without any clearances and it will cause no small kerfuffle to all those other planes in the air and especially to the controllers on the ground.'

Roslyn remarked, 'Well, it's really going to be like the old days when we learned to fly in light planes: the control tower was there, but we still had to maintain a vigilant see-and-be-seen lookout for each other.'

Cardin agreed, 'Yes. Now, eyes peeled, everyone. Ah, now we can see Sydney harbour and there's the harbour bridge, so we all know where the airport is now 'cos we can see the damn thing from here! But we still need to be primarily looking out for traffic. Ros, you're in charge of seeing what runway they're using, and Tom, it's your job to spot any traffic conflicts. I'll try to do both those things as a cross check.'

'They're using runway one-six!' cheered Roslyn. 'I see a jet on long finals for one-six. Oh, and there's another one on finals for zero-seven.'

'Fine,' said Cardin. 'So now we know that the wind is probably somewhere between the two runways. If we land on one-six there could be a small crosswind component from our port side. Ha! Who needs an ATIS?'

Roslyn pressed the P.A. button. Ding Dong! 'Attention everyone: Seatbacks upright please, tray tables stowed and seatbelts securely fastened. Cabin crew, all doors to AUTO and crosscheck, then be seated for landing. Our journey is over and we wish everyone the very best for a long and happy future. Thank you.'

From the corner of his eye, Tom Tyson saw another huge flash in the sky to the distant East where they'd just been. It illuminated the entire horizon again. Then, with shock, he saw their pilots' control panels come alive and flash red, then green, then amber. They went dark again, then the whole panel of electronics came back to illuminate the cockpit and stay lit. This sudden interior light show was a massive distraction to the pilots who were frantically looking out their windows for raw and basic flight input! Suddenly swamped with reams of electronic data after being deprived of it for so very long, this may have been the very last mystery that any of them needed just now.

The first screen to load itself was the company's CPDLC. It said: 'URGENT! 637 unread messages!' Then the radios blared back into life, nearly deafening the three pilots because they had been left on full volume. Next came scrolling warning screens with hundreds of checklists and emergency directives to follow. The glass screens indicated that there were several hours of urgent work facing them, but Cardin had no intention of attending to them.

He glanced across at Roslyn who could scarcely believe her eyes, then exclaimed, 'Wow! *Now* they all come back to life just when we don't need them!'

A screen flashed a new warning, accompanied by frightening claxons: 'EMP ALERT!'

Cardin yelped, 'What the hell is that?'

Tom answered, 'Electro-Magnetic pulses, Boss. Massive surges of radiation . . . probably from those flashes just then. Or like the pulses received from a solar flare or a nuclear explosion. Maybe it's a naval war out to sea?'

Cardin wiped his sweating brow then smirked, 'Oh how calming and therapeutic; just what we need right now. But what the hell! Let's forget it boys and girls: it's nothing compared to our little holiday.'

He deftly manoeuvred the 747 to slot in between two incoming jets approaching over the suburb of Hunters Hill, then made a cheeky left turn to commence a final approach as Roslyn prepared to call the control tower while Cardin ordered 'Gear down?'

Ros replied, 'Affirm. Gear down and five greens.'

'Flaps thirty?'

'Roger, flaps thirty. Auto brakes max. Speed brake armed. Runway numbers ah, one-six right - and missed approach is set.'

'Roger.'

Finally, and to everyone's enormous relief, Roslyn made radio contact with the ground! 'Sydney Tower, Australia two-zero-zero. Hope you don't mind but we've been out of contact for a very long time and, ah, we just turned on to finals for runway 16-right behind that twin jet ahead. Request landing clearance.'

A greatly welcomed reply came back, 'Australia two-zero-zero, yes we have you visual and are also receiving your squawks now. But where on earth have you guys been? And where did you land?'

Roslyn, grinning from ear to ear, replied, 'First, how long is it since we departed?'

The answer was patched to speakers throughout the whole aircraft. 'Well, it's been about five days and the whole world was . . . .'

Ray Cardin overrode the air/ground conversation and announced to everyone on board: 'Ladies and gentlemen, boys and girls; that statement was from the horse's mouth: you heard the control tower say it: we've only been missing for about five days, not seventy-three years - and now we're back home! We made it!'

And from the very back of the plane a triumphant little girl's voice yelled: 'See, I told you so!'

As Tom glanced enthusiastically down at Sydney's renowned Harbour Bridge, Roslyn silently and gratefully thanked whomever or whatever had saved them, then decided she would persist with her beloved pilot's job after all.

Swamped in joy, she asked the two men, 'But . . . how did all this happen? What will we tell everyone? And ah, what can we possibly tell the whole world?'

'The truth, the whole truth and nothing but the truth,' Tom Tyson laughed.

'But what really is the truth?' Roslyn beamed.

'Who knows?' Tom grinned.

'And who the bloody hell cares!' snapped the captain.

And now, on short final approach to land, they all heard the tower say, 'Australia two-zero-zero, runway one-six-right, clear to land - and a huge welcome home!'

But before Roslyn could reply, someone - probably mischievous Tom, switched their headsets' reception so that they heard instead this bubbly ditty come over the P.A.

> *Oh, he got us lost, yeah really damn lost,*
> *Out over the deep blue sea.*
> *So we threw a bloody great party . . .*
> *The party of the centur-eee!*
> *Then round and round and round we went*
> *Hoping it was all for free . . .*

And when we landed somewhere
I was a hundred and three-eee!

With his trademark sledgehammer subtlety, Captain Ray Cardin barked, 'Switch that damned noise off!'

Then, just as the eighteen big wheels crunched onto the runway with their customary screech and gushing clouds of blue smoke, the pilots heard four hundred people behind them chant with elation: 'Oi!'

As the thrust reversing buckets on all four of the mighty Rolls Royce RB211 engines slid back into their lock positions, followed by a deafening roar as ninety-percent of full engine thrust rocketed back into them and decelerated 325,000 kilograms of barrelling weight back down to nothing, Second Officer Tom Tyson chirped on the intercom: 'Hey Boss, guess what: I've been making notes of our entire crazy flight, and now I reckon I'm gonna write a book about all this.'

As the great plane came to a halt at last, then slowly exited the runway onto a taxiway called *Charlie four,* a triumphant Captain Ray Cardin turned around to his second officer and beamed, 'In that case Tom, you'd better make sure you designate it fiction - a novel - because no-one in the world will ever believe a single word of such a great load of bull.'

Once again Cardin's glamorous co-pilot disagreed with him. Roslyn Steinhouse – who could have become a school teacher or a fashion model, blew a huge and thankful sigh of relief as she glanced out at the real world from her pilot's window and whispered, 'Well I certainly will . . . '

www.ingramcontent.com/pod-product-compliance
Lightning Source LLC
Chambersburg PA
CBHW071903020726
47502CB00003B/877

* 9 780646 963945 *